ASSASSIN

of

SHADOWS

A Novel

LAWRENCE
GOLDSTONE

PEGASUS CRIME
NEW YORK LONDON

ASSASSIN OF SHADOWS

Pegasus Crime is an imprint of
Pegasus Books Ltd.
148 W. 37th Street, 13th Floor
New York, NY 10018

First Pegasus Books cloth edition June 2019

Interior design by Maria Fernandez

Library of Congress Cataloging-in-Publication Data is available.

ISBN: 978-1-64313-130-6

10 9 8 7 6 5 4 3 2 1

Printed in the United States of America
Distributed by W. W. Norton & Company

ASSASSIN

of

SHADOWS

To Nancy and Lee

ASSASSIN

of

SHADOWS

1

Chicago. Friday, September 6, 1901

A muffled click from outside the front door. Metallic. Four heads swiveled.

Andrei Vytvytsky instantly stopped counting, a twenty dollar bill suspended two inches over the third stack. Tiny, ruddy, and Ukrainian, with a scar that ran from temple to jaw, crossing where his left eye had been, Vytvytsky sat so still he might have been in a Steichen pictorial. After a few seconds, the little man cocked his head toward the far wall, one quick jerk to the side, like a terrier trying to puzzle out human speech. Janos and Imre, two light-skinned, light-haired, light-brained Hungarians, both unshaven, both with thick hands and thick bodies, nodded perfunctorily, then padded across the bare floor to grab shotguns off a rack. They stood opposite the door, paint-faded and chipped, but an inch of oak all the same, with a new Yale six tumbler lock fitted into a reinforced jamb and three oversized steel hinges anchoring the off side.

One-eyed Andrei laid the twenty on the stack, then, with a quick puff of breath, blew out the two candles that gave the room its only light. He pushed his slat-backed, wobbly chair away from the equally unsteady table, lifting the chair from underneath so that it didn't scrape on the floor. The click had not been repeated—the only noise now in the room was the muted rasp of four imperiled men breathing. Andrei made his way to a heavily curtained window next to the front door and grasped the thick gray fabric between thumb and forefinger. The thumb had a piece of raised, gnarled flesh where a fingernail once grew. Carefully, Andrei moved the curtain an inch out and to the side. A glow appeared in the tiny slit. From the moon, certainly; streetlights weren't wasted on this neighborhood. He held the curtain still and angled his good eye to the opening. After a few seconds, he set the curtain back in place.

Andrei noiselessly pirouetted to face his companions and held up five fingers. Each man in the room knew that if five adversaries were visible, at least that number were not. Four men, even heavily armed, might hold off ten for a time, but eventually they would be overwhelmed by superior firepower. And the guns the men outside wielded would be either Winchester Eliminators, the finest repeating rifle made, or Browning Auto-5's, a .20-gauge automatic loading shotgun that could rip out a man's chest with one blast.

Andrei pointed to a rear door. The other three nodded. The Hungarians tipped the table onto its side and positioned themselves behind it. They would hold off the invaders while Andrei and the fourth member of the gang, Walter, a dark, bearded giant, a foot taller and eighty pounds heavier than his boss, emptied the safe in the back room and cleared a path of escape from the back of the frame house. This part of the city was a warren of tiny streets and back alleys and, once away, the gang could vanish into the labyrinth. Unless, of course, the men outside had friends at the rear. But Andrei had assured his compatriots that he had mapped out a foolproof path to safety.

Andrei swept the money on the table into a burlap sack and gestured to Walter the giant to follow him into the back room. Walter nodded almost imperceptibly. The big man spoke rarely and was slavishly loyal. He trailed after Andrei, walking lightly, like a show dancer, feet remaining close to the ground. His upper body barely moved. He had two Colt pistols, army issue, stuck in his belt. No one ever doubted that he would use them—readily and often. Andrei had been around—in prison both in Europe and America—and still he considered Walter one of the scariest men he had ever met.

But scary men were an invaluable asset, as long as they scared one's enemies, so Andrei kept Walter close by his side. The one-eyed Ukrainian knelt by the safe stuck in the corner of the room and bolted to the floor—a Siemans that an intruder would need a stick of dynamite to blow. He quickly turned the dial; left, right, left, right, short left, then right again. The safe sprung open like the door to Ali Baba's cave. Piles of crisp, new greenbacks lay inside, wrapped to the size of bricks. These were quickly swept into the burlap sack as well. Then, instead of returning to the front to signal for Janos and Imre to join them, Andrei made for the far corner of the room. He threw back a faded Navajo rug, removed a pocket knife from his vest, placed the blade between two of the floor boards, and jiggled it from side to side. A piece of wood popped up, revealing a handle in the floor. Andrei pulled the handle and a three foot by three foot section of the floor came up, exposing a set of stairs descending below. The smell of mildew and rodent excreta suddenly filled the room.

"Come on," he whispered to Walter, gesturing toward the stairs for emphasis. "This leads right to the river. I've got a boat."

"What about the alley?" Walter asked.

"Can't get out that way. It'll be crawling with coppers. You didn't believe I made some magic path, did you? That was for them." Andrei cast a contemptuous sneer toward the front room.

"So you're gonna leave them?"

3

"Fuck 'em. They'll cover us. You're the only one worth saving. And two shares is better than four."

Walter considered this for only a moment. "Okay. Let's go."

Andrei nodded and smiled. He made the first two steps without incident but, as he started for the third, his feet were suddenly rising instead of falling. The sleeves of his jackets cut into his armpits as he left the ground, seemingly hooked like a trout on the back of his jacket. Before he could speak, he had been turned about to face Walter, his legs kicking as if on a gallows, which, as Walter knew, would be his ultimate destination.

Andrei only had a second or two of awareness to realize that he was suspended in air, held aloft by Walter's left hand before Walter's right hand smashed into his jaw. From there, only unconsciousness.

Walter laid Andrei down softly, as if he were a swaddled infant. With the Ukrainian dealt with, Walter pulled the pistol from his belt, took one deep breath, then kicked open the door to the front room. Janos and Imre were facing the front door, girded to repel a frontal attack. At the sound of the door flying open, they spun, but before they got halfway round, Walter's Colts had established who was who in the room.

Walter waggled the Colts and the shotguns were laid gently on the floor. Walter nodded to Janos—or was it Imre—to unlock the front door.

The door swung open to reveal a thick-chested, bull-necked man in a skimmer, a long mustache laying walrus-like down to his jaw. His gun was drawn, another Colt, and he was backed by at least twelve other men. All wore badges: gold five-pointed stars with USA debossed in the center. The man in the skimmer, Harry Swayne by name, surveyed the scene—one man crumpled in a heap, two with hands raised—then replaced his weapon in a shoulder holster. Harry put his hands on his hips, pursed his lips, and nodded with only slightly exaggerated admiration.

"Nice work. Got the dough?"

Walter nodded to the sack that lay at the entrance to the back room.

"How much?"

"Fifty thousand, I'd say. Maybe more," Walter replied, seemingly unimpressed by the amount.

Harry Swayne sniffed. "And not a cent of it genuine."

Soon afterward, the back door of the Black Maria was closed and locked, Andrei Vytvytsky deposited on the floor in the back, the two Hungarians sitting on either side. By that time, Janos and Imre had become aware that their supposed comrade-in-arms had intended to abandon them to the law and, the last Harry and Walter saw of them, they were taking turns depositing kicks on Andrei's head and chest.

After the Chicago coppers had hauled the crew away, Harry doffed his skimmer and ran his hand over his plastered hair. The moonlight reflected off the pomade in a single line, as it would have on the surface of a still lake. "You think Vytvytsky will make it to the station before they kill him? I'd hate to have him die before we can swing him."

"He'll make it," Walter said. "And I'm not sure even hanging will kill him."

"They're quite a score," Harry sighed happily, still staring at where the paddy wagon had clattered off over the cobblestones. "Anarchists and counterfeiters in one shot."

Walter shook his head. "Vytvytsky's no anarchist. Just a thief. He thinks being political is splashier."

"Walter, the man claims to be an anarchist and that's enough for me."

"That's because it's splashier to arrest an anarchist."

"So? What's wrong with splash? When the head of the division is a newspaperman, splash gets noticed. Or are you against advancement?"

"Advancement is fine . . ." Walter let the thought trail off. In truth, he didn't know how he felt about it. Promotion was somehow . . . impure. There was always the assumption that something not quite right had been done to achieve it. Staying where one was, however . . . Walter felt the beginnings of grin but suppressed it before it made it to his lips. The purity of low rank. Seemed pretty moronic now that he thought about it.

"I'm glad you think so," Harry said, breaking into Walter's thoughts, "because you're about to get a hefty dose of it." Harry placed a hand on Walter's shoulder. He had to reach up to do it. It was the same motion he had used to pat his horse when they were in the cavalry. "Go home and pack a bag. Our train leaves in ninety minutes."

"Where are we going?"

"Buffalo. McKinley's been shot. There's going to be a big investigation." Harry allowed a slow smile to form. "We're heading it."

2

W e'll change in Cleveland," Harry said as they settled into a first class compartment on the Lake Shore Limited. Harry had started to take the seat facing front, but for some reason thought better of it and gave it to Walter. "But we'd better get some sleep on this leg." When Walter inquired about the luxury—leather seats, head cushions, private toilet—Harry told him that their chief, John E. Wilkie, had insisted. "But Mark Hanna's paying," Harry had added, referring to the millionaire plutocrat, now senator from Ohio, who had almost single-handedly put McKinley in the White House. There was no shortage of whisperings, both in Washington and without, that for all practical purposes, Hanna *was* president. "Well," Harry added, with a respectful sigh, "he's not *really* paying. He pretty much owns the railroad."

On the ride to the station, Harry had filled Walter in about the shooting, or at least as much as he had learned from a series of telegrams and two trunk telephone conversations with Wilkie. The would-be assassin had struck at about four in the afternoon, only six hours earlier. Details were still hazy. After a speech, President McKinley had been on a receiving line at the Temple of Music at the Pan-American Exposition when a man with a bandage wrapped around his right hand got off two shots at close range from an Iver Johnson .32 caliber safety automatic revolver that he had hidden under the wrapping. The first bullet struck the president's breastbone but didn't penetrate; McKinley had apparently later picked it out of his chest himself. The second, however, perforated the president's abdomen. The assassin was wrestled to the ground by a bystander before he could get off any more shots. McKinley was rushed by electric ambulance to the fair's emergency hospital, located right on the grounds. A doctor who had been on the premises saw to the president's wounds and stitched him up.

Just before they boarded the train, Harry had received a final update. The president, it seemed, was recovering remarkably well. Harry had chuckled. "The first thing he asked after he came out of the ether was how his speech went, if you can believe it. A politician rising from the grave would probably ask how his funeral went over."

"Anyone know anything about the assassin?"

"A Polack. Claimed to be an anarchist."

"Like Vytvytsky?"

"This guy was serious. When they asked him why he did it, he said, 'I done my duty.'"

"Done his duty? To who?"

"That is the question, isn't it? The chief's sure there's more to it than the one man. He said it's time to break the anarchists once and for all."

"Very convenient," Walter grunted. "He's wanted to do that for years."

Walter had been partial to Bill Hazen, the previous chief, whom McKinley had sacked. Hazen had supposedly overstepped his authority in the previous administration by unofficially offering Secret Service protection to President and Mrs. Cleveland. In his place, McKinley had appointed Wilkie, a personal friend, a newspaperman of all things, from the *Chicago Daily Tribune*. In fairness, though, Wilkie had supposedly done a bit of spying against the Spanish during the war. As soon as Wilkie got the job, he offered unofficial Secret Service protection to President and Mrs. McKinley. Now Hazen was in New York City, rising to stardom in the detective bureau, and McKinley was lying wounded in Buffalo, his hand-picked chief waiting to dump the mess into Harry and Walter's lap.

"What's wrong with going after anarchists?" Harry growled. He hated the Reds, although his reasons had always remained vague. "You're not going pretend anarchists *don't* pose a threat to the country, are you?" His chin jutted forward. "And the guy *offered up* that he was one of them. *Bragged* about it. I don't think you can lay *that* on the chief."

"He's a reporter," Walter muttered, injecting an extra measure of distaste into the noun. "He always wants the big story."

"*Was* a reporter. He's head of the Secret Service Division now. *Your* superior."

"Yours too." Walter decided to change the subject. Harry would never forego the last word. "What's his name? This assassin who claims to be an anarchist."

"He gave a phony name at first. Called himself Fred C. Nieman. Nieman means 'nobody' in German."

"And *guten tag* to you too."

"Very funny. It was in the report. But we got his real one now." Harry removed a folded piece of the paper from his vest pocket. His fingers were long and thin, like a pianist's with carefully manicured nails. He had kept them that way, even in the army. An odd vanity for a cavalryman.

"C-z-o-l-g-o-s-z," he spelled. "Lord knows he pronounces it."

"*Chōl*-gōsh, most likely," Walter said. "The 'z' is usually like an 'h.'" He thought for minute. "Odd."

"What is?"

Walter shook his head. "Nothing. So why us?"

"Czolgosz was in Chicago before he went to Buffalo. Or so he says. Very talkative fellow I'm told. Went to see Emma Goldman off at a train. Claims to be her devoted follower. Sounds like love. Went to see other people too. Other anarchists. You know Abe Isaak? The Jew who publishes that anarchist scandal sheet, *Free Society*? He's one of them. Chicago dicks are going to pick a bunch of them up." Harry patted Walter on the knee. He loved physical contact; it made Walter cringe. "So Wilkie wants the investigation run out of Chicago. He asked me straight out who should head it and I told him you."

"I thought you said 'us.'"

"I didn't want the other boys getting jealous. They already think you're the glory king of the outfit. I was just looking out for morale."

"Thoughtful of you, Harry. So how's come you didn't tell Wilkie you'd do it?"

"Hell, Walter, if you find out what Wilkie and Hanna expect you to find out it's still my outfit."

"And if I don't . . . it'll still be your outfit."

"Yep. But we both know you will."

"Can I talk to him? Czolgosz?"

"Sure. Why wouldn't you?"

"Locals. I'm sure they're not happy about a bunch of outsiders stealing the biggest case they've ever had."

"Don't worry. The locals are going to stay local. You're going to be able to do anything you want to do."

Walter thought for a moment. "Where were our guys when this happened?"

"George Foster . . . you know him? And Sam Ireland?"

"Met them once in Washington. Good men."

"Not this time. Foster was standing right next to McKinley but turned away to check out some big nigger in the receiving line. Ireland was right there too. They both let a little fellow with the gun hidden in a bandage slip right past them. Funny thing is, the colored guy was the one who tackled Czolgosz afterward. Probably saved McKinley's life. The doc only had the one bullet to deal with instead of four. There were three rounds still in the chambers. We had three other operatives there, but they were all on the far side of the president when it happened. The colored guy got there first. Foster jumped on after and busted him in the mush with a left."

"Pretty lucky. The Negro, I mean. Also pretty lucky to have a doctor just happening by."

"Luckier than you think. He wasn't there as a doctor. The guy raises flowers, if you can believe it. He was exhibiting at the horticultural pavilion. What man would do that? Delphiniums . . . whatever they are."

"Larkspur," Walter said. "Long stems of flowers. Blue or purple usually. They're very pretty, actually."

Harry drew back. "Now how would you know that?"

"Read about 'em."

"Of course. Anything you ain't read about? Anyway this doctor . . . Mann was his name . . . went with McKinley to the emergency hospital and fixed him up."

"He was a surgeon?"

Harry shook his head, a grin playing in the corners of his mouth. "Nope. Gynecologist, if you can believe it."

"I believe it, Harry."

Harry scowled. He hated when Walter mocked him, but had never been able to figure a way to stop it without looking dumb. "Seemed to do a good enough job though. We're lucky he didn't get confused and deliver McKinley's stomach."

"My stomach's not too happy either, Harry. We going to have time to get something to eat in Cleveland?"

"Forty-five minutes."

"Undercooked steak and runny eggs, but it'll have to do. Maybe we should try and get some sleep now."

"I suppose."

Walter leaned down in his seat, letting the bucking of the train take him. Just like a horse, really, except side to side instead of up and down. Was that all modernity was? A change in axis?

"Speaking of food, why don't you come for dinner?" Harry asked, just as he saw Walter's eyes close. "We'll be back in Chicago in a couple of days."

Walter refused to reply, hopeless as the gesture was.

"It's only dinner," Harry went on, with the studied innocence of a bad liar.

"And Lucinda is a fine cook," Walter added before Harry could.

Harry shrugged. "Wasted on me, I'm afraid. But I don't have your sensibilities."

From here, unless Walter acceded, Harry would repeat the litany of how he preferred living alone but he owed it his widowed sister—a war widow, after all—but what she really needed was a place of her own, well, not exactly of her own. He would recite all of this precisely as he had the last time, as if it had just occurred to him. Harry was indefatigable. He could go two days in the saddle and not doze off even once; a train ride to Cleveland was child's play. He wouldn't shut up until they were in the station.

"I'll come for dinner."

"Wonderful. Knew you would."

"It's not really fair, you know. To Lucinda, I mean."

"Oh yes it is."

Walter grunted and turned to watch the Indiana night hurtle past the speeding train. Lucinda's face appeared in the window. She was a beautiful woman, there was no doubting it. Chestnut hair. Big eyes. Full lips with a cupid's bow in the center. Harry managed to appear coarse with almost precisely the same features. But where Harry gave off an air of insouciant ease even with bullets shaving his sideburns, Lucinda evidenced that look of controlled desperation that widows wore. As if they would leap at you and hold on, white-knuckled, if you tried to leave the room. Couldn't blame her, of course. Even beautiful, she was still twenty-seven, and sand was flowing faster and faster through her hourglass.

But why *him*? Why did Harry insist on thrusting Lucinda on *him*? Hadn't he made it more than clear? Was it for her? For him? Or maybe

Harry was doing it for himself. Probably a bit of all three. Lucinda had grit and was loyal. And nobody's fool. She would, in truth, make someone a fine wife. She *had* made someone a fine wife. A husband now dead. A hero of the Philippines. Or perhaps it was important to call everyone who died in a questionable war a hero. It had certainly been that way in *his* war. A war against an out-gunned, out-manned opponent wearing feathers and animal skins, who was all the braver and more honorable for his hopelessness. All the soldiers who died in that war had been heroes too.

"Walter?"

From the tone, Walter knew Lucinda had been filed away. He turned back to Harry without answering.

"There's no middle ground here, Walter. If we figure out who put this Czolgosz fellow up to shooting the president, we can write our own tickets. If we don't, everyone will be happy to blame us."

"Us or me?"

"Both."

"You don't like McKinley, do you?" Walter said suddenly.

Harry shrugged, exaggerated, which was answer enough. Then he glanced about, although they were alone in the car. "I don't like what he did to the division."

Walter didn't reply. He didn't need to. Most of the operatives felt the same way, he supposed, although nobody talked about it. It was never a good idea to complain about your boss, especially when your boss was a chum of the president. If the bullets had done McKinley in, Roosevelt would have taken over the White House and Wilkie would have been shipped back to typesetting. McKinley and TR hated each other. TR had once said that McKinley had less backbone than a chocolate éclair. Amazing that McKinley took him on the ticket, no matter what the New York pols promised him. How could you make someone your vice president after that? Likely, it meant that TR had been right.

Walter emitted a soft sigh. Not a man in the division who wouldn't rather work for TR.

3

Saturday, September 7, 1901

T he Limited pulled into the New York Central Exchange Street Station in Buffalo at eight the next morning. The New York Central had invested a good deal of money in the exposition, but the station was a peeling, dilapidated disgrace. To cover the blight, either the city fathers or the railroad had hung bunting from the walls and ensured that the common areas were heavily patrolled by Buffalo coppers.

Walter wondered what the mood would be, whether a pall had descended in the wake of an assassination attempt on the president. Instead, the station throbbed with energy. Perhaps it was because McKinley had only been wounded and was expected to be fine, but there was an almost celebratory feel, as if Buffalo had bested other cities in a competition. Across the floor, hawkers with official exposition badges accosted the new arrivals, selling tickets that may or may not have been genuine, giving directions that may or may not have been accurate, and

serving as a whispered conduit to whatever sub rosa services an uniniti-
ated visitor to the city might require. Advertising places of lodging was,
for some reason, strictly forbidden, so the hawkers, having accepted
gratuities from inn keepers and rooming house owners, were pleased,
for an additional gratuity from an arrivee, to provide an enthusiastic but
oblique testimonial for a local hostel.

As Walter and Harry stepped out on to the platform, Walter large and
unmistakable, a ruddy, corpulent man in a flat cap pulled down to his
right ear sidled up to them. He moved with the stiff-legged, belly-first
walk of a lifetime copper.

"One of you Swayne?" he asked, as if the answer could be incriminating.

"Me," grunted Harry in return. No local dick was going to back him
down.

"And you're George," the copper noted, as if he had just deduced a
vital piece of evidence. "I'm O'Hara. Assistant chief. Come with me."

O'Hara made no effort to hide that he had been asked to go on an
errand he thought beneath him, and neither Harry nor Walter intended
to give him the satisfaction of asking any questions. Conversation would
allow him to establish sway he didn't deserve.

Outside the station was a police wagon, with a uniform at the wheel.
O'Hara opened the door, hesitated for a second, then, hating himself for
it, got in before Harry could go past him. Harry and Walter followed,
Walter's bulk absorbing whatever small space would have been left sitting three across.

No one spoke during the ride. O'Hara sat tight-lipped, seemingly
content to bounce along the cobblestones. At one point Harry and
Walter glanced at one another. Their looks said the same thing: the
local police were stuck with the blame for what happened. A million-
dollar celebration of their city would only be remembered for one Polack
lunatic shooting the president. The federal detectives would be gone
in a few days, but the Buffalo coppers would wear the tar until the day
they died.

The automobile headed for downtown, the driver blowing his air horn regularly, as much to announce their presence as to clear traffic. About ten minutes later, he pulled to the curb on Eagle Street in front of the portico of an immense, eight-story, French Renaissance building, with "Iroquois" written in gold across a deep green awning. Two dicks muscled the porter out of the way to open the automobile door.

"Best hotel in town," muttered O'Hara, before they got out, unable to help himself. "A thousand rooms. All electric. New Otis elevators. Telegraph and telephone. Whole place is fireproof. Four bucks a night for a room during the fair." Then, realizing he sounded a fool, he added snidely, "Nothing's too good for our friends from Washington."

O'Hara left them at the entrance. An operative neither Harry nor Walter knew directed them across the carpeted floor to a wood paneled, gilt trimmed elevator set apart from the others. The white-haired Negro at the switch pulled the outside door closed, then the inside grate, mumbled something about standing back, and headed to the top floor.

Only three doors faced out on the corridor when Harry and Walter left the elevator. Each was high lacquered mahogany adorned with a brass plate at eye level, buffed and scalloped, with black script. Harry walked to the farthest one. He grabbed the doorknob, an ornate brass affair, but didn't turn it. "Wait a minute," he said, after seeming to give the matter thought. "I'll let Wilkie know we're here."

Walter took Harry by the wrist. "You have to let him know we're here with me outside?"

Harry shook off the hand with one sharp flick of his wrist. "Don't worry, Walter. No one is plotting against you." Harry was toughest man pound-for-pound Walter had ever met and one of the few he could not physically intimidate.

Harry opened the door only halfway and slipped inside so that Walter could not look in the room. About three minutes later, the door opened. Harry had his official face on. He stuck out an arm and waved for Walter to come inside. Harry, it seemed, had set one foot firmly on either side

16

of the crevice. To be fair, Walter couldn't blame him. McKinley might have lived through this, but there were a number of careers that wouldn't.

Walter blew out a breath and entered, girding himself for a heart-to-heart with Chief Wilkie. Instead, seated behind the large rosewood desk in the center of the room, backlit by the morning sun pouring through the half-opened Venetian blinds, was Mark Hanna.

Unlike the caricatures that portrayed an immense, overshadowing figure dressed in suits festooned with dollar signs—power, after all, *must* be large—Marcus Alonzo Hanna was, in fact, a small, balding, rather formless man. His head was dominated by ears that seemed to stretch from crown to jaw and a bulbous nose that, while not quite Morgan-esque, was nonetheless formidable. He was dressed in a gray suit and vest, and under his ample chin was an incongruous green and red plaid bow tie. He wore position with sufficient ease that he could slouch in his chair and turn slightly sideways, seemingly on the verge of throwing his feet to desk top, and still look commanding. The senator, Walter realized, had booked himself the Presidential Suite.

John Elbert Wilkie, chief of the Secret Service Division, stood with military bearing at the side of the desk to Hanna's right, staring out through his pince-nez, trying not to blink. He was a dapper man, hair parted down the center, the tips of his mustache twirled, oiled, and turned upward in perfect symmetry. He wore an ochre linen suit, perfect for early September in Washington, or even Ohio, but a bit flimsy for Buffalo. He stood facing the door, his ostentatious efforts to project authority succeeding only in making him appear more of a retainer. The fingertips of his left hand rested possessively on the polished desk top, as if contact with the rosewood made him an extension of the man in the chair.

"We've got an important job for you," Hanna said without prelimi-naries. His voice was deep and his enunciation casual. He gave off a faint odor of lilac. Or maybe that was Wilkie. Hanna didn't elaborate, but instead sat regarding Walter, waiting. He didn't move, not even to drum his fingers on the desk.

What does he want? Walter wondered. Fealty? An eager reply stating he was honored to be offered such an important job by the president's Svengali? Fuck him, Walter thought, and declined to offer a response.

The standoff lasted about five seconds. Then Hanna gave a short, single nod, as if Walter had passed a test. "You up for it?" he asked.

Walter merely continued to look Hanna in the eye and Hanna knew that was a yes. He was more than a bit surprised to realize that, albeit grudgingly, he liked Mark Hanna. Or at least respected him. Walter respected men you could communicate with without a lot of talk. Men who knew where they stood. Or sat.

Wilkie spoke for the first time. "I have personally recommended you to Senator Hanna." His fingertips remained on the desk top.

Walter glanced to his putative boss and offered a nod of thanks. He had never been in the least surprised that he did not like Wilkie.

"We're going to send you back to Chicago," Hanna said without looking at Wilkie. "That's where this conspiracy was hatched."

"We are certain there was a conspiracy then?" Walter spoke softly.

Hanna considered the question. "It's a fair assumption. Unless you think that this Czolgosz fellow . . ." He pronounced the name correctly. "This Czolgosz fellow just suddenly out of nowhere got it into his head to shoot the president."

"I won't know what's in his head until I speak to him."

"You'll speak to him." Hanna injected just the slightest note of irritation into his voice. It said, "You don't mouth off to me, boy." After he was comfortable that the message had been received, he pushed himself to his feet.

"But first, Mr. McKinley would like to meet you."

4

President McKinley had been brought for his convalescence to the Milburn mansion, the home of the president of the fair. Walter, Wilkie, and Hanna rode in a shiny black brougham with brilliant gold trim pulled by a glistening black horse in gleaming golden harness. The driver wore a top hat that Walter couldn't afford and sat with posture that would have pleased a master sergeant. Harry had been left behind at the hotel, supposedly to get reports from Chicago. Walter sat facing the rear. As the carriage pulled away, he could see Harry through the oval window, standing at the curb. Harry had his hat in his hand and was rubbing his other hand across the top of his glistening head. Walter stifled a grin. Who was left in the hallway now?

The drive took about ten minutes and no one spoke. The streets around Delaware Avenue had been cleared for a block in all directions, a combination of coppers and army men standing silent vigil to the wounded president. The brougham was waved through a crowd of well-wishers and the morbidly curious who stood respectfully outside the line of uniforms. The onlookers were unable even to see the house. Maybe it was enough for some people just to say they were there, although Walter could not imagine why. The allure of passive participation had always eluded him.

When they pulled up at Milburn House, a man in a Stetson who looked no more than twenty was waiting to open the door. He wore a gold star Secret Service badge pinned to his vest, although Walter was mystified at how he could have gotten into the division so young. Hanna alit first, ignoring the boy's proffered hand, followed by Wilkie. Wilkie stopped and whispered something in the boy's ear. The boy nodded, quite serious, and then said, "Don't worry, dad. I'll see to it." Young Wilkie then marched off toward the side of the house, swinging his arms tightly at his sides.

The walkway to the front door was a good forty feet in length, protected by a line of low trimmed boxwoods running along the sidewalk. Dense vines of English ivy covered the front of the house, cut only to prevent them from encroaching on the surface of the eight-foot windows on the first floor and the six-footers on the second. The main entrance was at the center and three other doors were spaced along the width of the house. Walter felt more as if he was entering a university or government administration building than a private home. If this was an example of the housing, even for a Brahmin, Niagara Falls powered electricity had rendered Buffalo a good more deal prosperous than Walter had realized.

Wilkie waited for him at the front door. "You address him as 'Mr. President,'" he stage-whispered. Walter walked past him, pretending not to hear.

In the front hall of the mansion was enough manpower to mount a decent assault on a medieval fortress. Some were in uniform, most in plain clothes. When Hanna entered, a path was cleared to allow him a straight line across to a door at the far side. Hanna was remarkably bow-legged—Walter wondered if he had contracted rickets as a child—but everyone assiduously avoided giving notice to his rolling gait. Wilkie had easily regained his position close at Hanna's heels. Walter didn't rush, but was large enough to clear his own path.

He looked around as he walked through. Wilkie must have expanded the division because Walter didn't know a soul in the place. Foster and Ireland were nowhere to be seen. Presence at the Temple of Music was apparently a disqualifying factor.

With little to do but stare at each other and try to establish territory, the lawmen were milling about or had broken off into small groups, muttering, swaggering, and fingering their weapons. Walter had always been amused at the impressive after-the-fact display of force that could be counted on in the wake of a screw-up. The bigger the screw-up, the more impressive the display. Can't get much bigger than letting a president take two bullets at close range with almost as many Buffalo dicks, division operatives, and uniformed coppers standing around as were in this room now.

Hanna had reached the far side of the hall. Wilkie paused for a moment to whisper to a clean-shaven man in a blue suit whose close cropped hair was running to gray. Walter overheard the name Bull, for William S. Bull, the aptly-named Buffalo chief of police.

The president had been given a sitting room on the second floor that faced out over the Milburn garden at the rear. Mrs. McKinley, whose nerves were known to be quite brittle, occupied a bedroom down the hall, attended by her personal physician. A uniformed Buffalo copper was posted on either side at the foot of the staircase and another was posted at the second floor landing. Two more stood at either side of the door to the president's chamber. All the guards made it a point to stand at attention and ignore their fellows, as though they were the palace guard for Queen Victoria.

Hanna nodded and one of the coppers swung open the door, stretching his arm so as not to place his body in the entrance. Hanna crabbed through, followed by Wilkie, then Walter. As he passed, the copper with his arm out favored Walter with a glare. Walter considered saying thank you, just to rub it in, but bit it back. The door closed softly behind him, the copper not daring to slam it as he would have preferred.

The parlor was a large, dark room, lined with dark wood paneling, furnished with dark plush furniture. The house had been wired for electric lighting, but the lamps were turned down low, giving the interior a feeling of perpetual late evening. A bed had been moved in, placed at the far side opposite the door. There, propped up on four pillows, wearing a white nightshirt open at the neck, was William McKinley, President of the United States.

The bulldog countenance of his photographs was not misleading. With a jaw as square as if it had been fashioned by a draftsman, McKinley might have been pale and wan, but otherwise looked remarkably fit for a man who had been shot twice just the day before.

Three men and two nurses flanked McKinley on either side of the bed. Walter assumed the men were all doctors. He wondered which one was Mann, the horticultural gynecologist. All five took a step back when Mark Hanna entered the room. This Walter took to be not only a testament to Hanna's power, but also to McKinley's progress in overcoming the effects of his wound.

Hanna and Wilkie moved toward the president, but Walter stood in the doorway, waiting for an invitation. McKinley raised his right hand and wiggled his fingers, bidding Walter to approach. Walter walked slowly to large bed, the president's eyes on him for the entire journey. McKinley's gaze was clear, his expression stolid. Walter could not read what he was thinking.

"Mr. Wilkie here tells me you're his best man," the president began. His voice was soft, but strong, unwavering. His speech betrayed a rural twang, but had acquired an overlay of cultured smoothness. A man who believed in self-improvement.

"Mr. Wilkie flatters me, sir," Walter replied, not daring to look to a boss who had never done it before.

"No, I don't believe he does. I'm a good judge of men and I feel quite bully about you being the one in charge of finding the people who set this up. Remember, Mr. George, this is not about me. I'm only one man. This is a crime against the nation we all love."

"Yes, sir."

"But listen to me carefully, Mr. George. There'll be a good deal of panic and more than a little blood lust. I don't want anyone railroaded. If someone was responsible in this affair, they should be brought to justice, but I don't wish to see those innocent of the crime dragged before the bar simply because of their political beliefs."

"Yes, sir. I understand." He answered casually, but was stunned all the same. Had William McKinley of bedrock Ohio, bastion of conservatism, taken an ecumenical view toward his enemies?

"There are some who would use this poor lunatic to sweep with a broader brush. Let me be clear. I'm no more fond of anarchists than any other right-thinking American, but our nation lives by the letter of the law. Do you agree?"

"Of course, sir."

"If ever you believe you are unable to do your duty to your country as you think proper . . . for this is certainly a duty to the United States of America and not one to me personally . . . you need only to inform Mr. Wilkie or Senator Hanna. They will get word to me and we will halt any untoward activities in their tracks."

"Yes, sir."

"I'll be out of here in a week or so, according to these gentlemen . . ." McKinley cocked his head toward the doctor standing at the left of the bed, a bald man with a white, walrus mustache and long, thin face. He ignored the two on the right. "They tell me I'm making a remarkable recovery."

"I'm very pleased to hear that, Mr. President."

"I think that's enough for now, Mr. President," intoned the bald man. "You need rest above all."

"That's McBurney," McKinley went on. "Up from New York City. Best abdominal surgeon in America, right doctor?"

"I would never claim as much, Mr. President," McBurney replied in a manner that made it plain that the president's assessment matched his own.

"He wants me to rest because he knows the vice president is due. Mr. Roosevelt exudes sufficient energy to suck the juices out of a man, and my juices are somewhat diminished at the moment. Isn't that correct, doctor?"

"I am simply trying to ensure a speedy recovery, Mr. President."

"Dr. Mann saved my life but these gentlemen have now taken his place. I'm assured that the danger of peritonitis is now minimal." McKinley grinned. The corners of his eyes crinkled, leaving him to appear almost boyish. "Although I'll spare you the details of how they made such a determination. In any event, I intend to be back in Washington and on the job as soon as possible."

McBurney would brook no more, even from the president. He moved in toward the bed, signaled the nurses to follow and Walter knew the audience had ended. When he reached the door, he turned back toward McKinley, gave a short bow, and said, "The country will rejoice at your rapid recovery, sir. I'm extremely honored to serve you."

Walter heard the last phrase come from his lips as if listening to someone else. He had always thought of McKinley as a stiff-backed, humorless man who cared only for power. And for Walter, authority had always borne an unsavory whiff. Although he knew it was childish, insubordination had always provided him intense satisfaction. But with McKinley, he seemed to have been in the presence of that rarest of species: an honorable man. Perhaps the United States was not in such bad hands with William McKinley at the tiller after all.

On the ride back, Walter once again sat facing Hanna and Wilkie in the rear.

"You seemed surprised by the president," Hanna offered as they pulled away from Millburn House. "What were you expecting?"

"He was very . . . fair." Walter wanted the words back as soon as they were out.

"Were you expecting him to be unfair?" Wilkie asked.

"I'm sure Mr. George meant no such thing," Hanna interjected smoothly. "I'm sure he was simply surprised that the president held so little personal animus for the poor deranged wretch who shot him. That's correct, isn't it, Mr. George?"

Walter nodded, relieved for the reprieve, false though it may have been.

"Yes, the president is a fair man," Hanna continued, gazing out the window. "Fair and decent." He turned back to look at Walter. "Sometimes too fair and decent for his own good. Too forgiving. Too willing to ascribe a cowardly act to one man when it would seem certain to less fair, decent, and forgiving men that others must certainly have been involved." Hanna lifted his left hand and toyed with the folds under his chin. "But you seem like a smart fellow, Mr. George. I feel certain you already figured all that out."

5

They left Mark Hanna at the Iroquois. The senator, having said all he intended to say, climbed out of the carriage without a word, scuttled down the red carpet, and disappeared through the door, his path cleared by a bevy of obsequious officers and hotel employees. Wilkie and Walter watched him go, as if it would be the height of disrespect to resume their journey until the man was out of eyeshot. McKinley might be president, Walter decided, but Mark Hanna was king.

"Police headquarters," Wilkie barked at the driver, the moment the door closed and the spell was broken.

"Wait, driver," Walter said quickly. "What about Harry?"

"Harry has work to do here," Wilkie replied evenly. "Can't you interrogate a prisoner alone? I was told you were quite good at it."

"I will speak to him alone. But I want to see the Exposition grounds before I question Czolgosz."

"Why do you need to see the bloody grounds?" Wilkie asked. He had affected a vaguely British manner of speech since his appointment. "There's no mystery about what happened. I want you to finish here, and get back to Chicago, preferably by tonight. The Chicago police have already made arrests and I want you to interrogate those anarchists before those buffoons can have at them."

"I'll be on the train as soon as I can, Chief," Walter, raising his voice a half octave to convey sincerity. "But I'm going to need a picture in my head to understand what happened."

"A picture in your head? Of what? The Pabst concession."

"Just like a newspaper article paints a picture for the guy reading a story. Like you used to do at the *Tribune*."

Wilkie nodded slowly. "I heard you were a smart mouth, Mr. George. And that you preferred Hazen . . ."

Walter considered a denial, but decided against it.

"I want to remind you that my predecessor presided over the failure to stop the worst counterfeiting ring this nation has ever seen. An entire run of currency had to be recalled, if I remember correctly. His dismissal was hardly political, regardless of whatever whisperings are being passed among his acolytes."

"It wasn't Chief Hazen's doing," Walter interjected before he could stop himself. "He asked for more manpower but was refused by the treasury secretary."

"Who then appointed me when Hazen was gone," Wilkie replied. "Yes, Mr. George, I know the story. The simple truth is that dismissal for failure is the nature of responsibility. No one cares about the excuses. The failure itself is all that matters. I assume you understand how this pertains to you."

Walter stared across the carriage, aware that he was unable to suppress his distaste and not caring a whit. He could have asked Wilkie if the division's failure to protect the president would result *his* dismissal, but what would that achieve?

"The point is, Mr. George," Wilkie went on, flicking the left point of his mustache as if to remove an errant speck of dust, "I could not care less whether or not you loathe me. For the moment, we are in this together. It might surprise you to know that it is my intention to run this bureau to the highest standard of professionalism. Hazen did not. A wonderful man to work for, I'm told, everyone's chum, but most of our operatives are woefully untrained. Do you wish to tell me I'm wrong?"

Walter didn't reply.

"I thought not. For the record, I'm appalled that we had four men within arm's length of Czolgosz, but the one to wrestle him the ground was a Negro bystander. If we can conclude this investigation successfully, Senator Hanna will impose on Congress to mandate Secret Service operatives as *official* guards to the president. The bureau will gain in size and prestige. If you contribute to that eventuality, you will benefit accordingly."

Walter wanted to laugh. Everyone waving carrots in front of him, when their real incentive was the stick.

"All right," he grunted. Wilkie had to at least get points for straight talk. "But I'm going to do this properly. No one is going to look very rosy if we railroad a bunch of people who it turns out can prove they had nothing to do with it."

"As long as you work fast."

"I'll work fast enough. Faster than the Chicago coppers at any rate."

"Very well, Mr. George. We shall play it your way. Go get Mr. Swayne and spend some time at the fair. After all, I wouldn't want to provide you incentive for not getting results. Perhaps you will even have time to ride the miniature railway. Just make sure that before the day is out, you're on the real one. I want you in Chicago before the sun is up tomorrow." Wilkie removed his watch from his vest pocket, an Elgin hunter-case model that appeared to be gold. After he checked the time, he closed the cover, wound the stem a turn or two, then replaced the watch in his pocket. "I won't be able to see you before you leave. As the president

28

noted, Mr. Roosevelt is arriving from Vermont within the hour. It was a bit difficult getting to him. The vice president has a penchant for out of the way locales. But I expect you to keep me posted. I want telegrams. Regularly. And telephone messages where practicable." Wilkie allowed himself a tight grin. "But don't think this means I don't trust you."

"Of course not. We're in this together, after all. For the president."

"Yes. For the president."

6

So, Walter, how was the session with your new friends?"

Walter and Harry had borrowed Hanna's brougham for the trip to the fairgrounds.

"You jealous, Harry? After all the trouble you took to go in to see Hanna alone first?"

"Okay. I guess I can't squawk. I just didn't want to get cut out."

"You think I'd cut you out, Harry?"

"Nah. Not you. Anyway, what did you think of McKinley?"

"I liked him. A lot actually."

Harry arched his eyebrows.

"Yeah, but McKinley doesn't run the show," Walter said. "I'm not sure he ever did. And Wilkie's right in there with Hanna. Harry, this stinks worse than you did after two weeks in the saddle."

"You weren't no rosebud either, Walter."

"This is a conspiracy to find a conspiracy," Walter muttered. He drummed his fingers on the window. The clouds had blown away leaving a brilliant early autumn sky. "I'm supposed to come up with something whether it's there or not. McKinley says no, but Wilkie and Hanna are the nuts and they're just giving me rope. If I disappoint them . . ." Walter just shook his head. "I don't want to pour sand in your beer, but you're coming along with me."

"Okay." Harry was showing remarkable equanimity. "I'll get somebody else."

"What do you mean?"

"Well, if this deal stinks so bad, you should get out of it. Don't fret. I'll find somebody. You can go back to Chicago and be an operative. You won't have to worry about advancement or conspiracies. No one will bother you. You'll have a grand time."

Walter dropped his hands to his knees. "Fuck you, Harry."

"Oh, you don't *want* me to get somebody else. Mind telling me why?"

"You know why."

"Of course I know why. Because you're the best we've got. Right? The deal may stink but it would stink a whole lot worse with someone else doing it. That's it isn't it? Well, Walter?"

"Yeah," Walter growled, wanting to wring Harry's neck. "That's it."

"I thought so. So why not stop being so jiggy about it and just do the job? Why don't we find out if there *is* something before we worry about what's going to happen if there isn't? After all, just because those jokers are determined to find a conspiracy don't mean there isn't one."

"Mebbe. But I'm with the president. I'm going to want to be sure before we start buying rope."

"Very noble of you. And, for your information, I intend to be as careful as you. As far as buying rope, Chicago coppers beat you to it. They already arrested nine anarchists, with more on the way. Emma Goldman's gonna be one of them. Seems to me that with them doing the dirty work, we can just sail along behind and jump in if they screw up."

"Wilkie wants us to sail in front."

"Well, I'm pretty sure we can figure a way to do that too and still keep our skirts starched."

Walter thought for a moment. "All right. Let's talk to that colored fellow. And let's talk to him where it happened. At the Temple of Music . . . Lord, what a silly name."

"Don't you want to go there with our guys? Or the coppers?"

"No, Harry. I especially don't want to see it with our guys or the coppers. I don't figure they're going to be real honest and open after they let some runt lunatic Polack outsmart them. I'd rather hear the story from the guy who did something about it. Now who is he and where can we find him?"

"His name's Parker. He's a waiter. And he works right on the grounds. At the Plaza Restaurant. Boss gave him an hour off work to shake the president's hand. Lucky for McKinley he did."

"Let's go over to the restaurant and find him. Little early for lunch, but the staff'll likely be around. Hope Saturday isn't his day off."

"I doubt it. Seems he's become quite the hero. Everybody wants to shake *his* hand, nigger or no. No way the restaurant manager's not gonna have him there." Harry grinned for a moment. "Walter, I think you're going to find Mr. Parker interesting for a reason you don't expect. Might even change your foul mood."

◆

The Pan-American Exposition of 1901, or "The Pan," as its organizers had dubbed it in an effort to be folksy, was the most stunning, garish, awesome, exhilarating, and stifling monument to capitalist America ever attempted by an outlying American city. Undaunted by the inevitable comparisons to the Columbian Exposition in Chicago eight years earlier, The Pan was set on 432 acres (to Chicago's 600) and boasted over 150 buildings (to Chicago's 200). It contained a mind-boggling variety of exhibitions and pavilions, mundane to exotic: the Acetylene Building;

Beautiful Orient; Nebraska Sod House; House Upside Down; Trip to the Moon; Philippine Village; Miniature Railroad; Infant Incubator. Exhibits were devoted to horticulture, forestry, mining, dairy farming, graphic arts, women, and Indians. Private exhibits and government buildings competed for visitors' attention and dollars.

In the center of the midway rose a 410-foot, forty-stories-tall Tower of Electricity, officially dubbed Propylaea. Elevators were available for an additional fee. On a clear day, Niagara Falls was plainly visible from the viewing tower at the top. Powered through the hydroelectric facility at the Falls to the north, Propylaea was lit every night in a brilliant display visible across the border to what was hoped to be a suitably awed Canada.

The Tower of Electricity always had waiting lines, as did the exposition's most popular venue, the Pabst Pavilion. The fair even had its own official flag, a three-paneled diagonally divided pennant, one outside panel in blue, the other in red and, in the center, a golden eagle crowned by a halo of sunlight clutching a green ribbon in its talons on which was proclaimed "Pax, 1901," a design chosen from 300 submissions for which a Miss Adelaide Thorpe of New York City had been paid $100.

The grounds, as Walter and Harry arrived, had added to the usual odors of dewy wood and stale food, the unmistakable aroma of anticipation. McKinley's shooting might have been a nightmare for the coppers, but it was a boon to the merchants. Even at midmorning, coffers were filling from mobs of the curious, who, because the president had survived, were allowed to appear festive rather than stunned, pleasantly shocked rather than morbid. Fairgoers peered about in breathless expectation, as if the attempt on McKinley's life had been staged, a grand part of the planned entertainment, and today would bring an event of similar scope and surprise. The enthusiasm of the customers stood in stark contrast to the grim, angry coppers. Sour-faced men in uniform lurked everywhere as if Czolgosz's act would spawn dozens of imitators stalking the midway with revolvers secreted in bandages.

Just inside the north entrance a couple of smartly dressed, rouged young women smiled at Harry and Walter through the bright red lip paint that announced them as prostitutes. The day promised a windfall to their particular brand of commerce as well. They followed Walter and Harry for a few steps then, discerning no interest, returned to their posts.

"A little early, don't you think?" Harry mumbled as they walked on.

"You're slipping, Harry. Used to be that any time was good for you. I remember the whorehouse in Bismarck. You and that old Lakota squaw . . . what was she . . . about three-hundred pounds?"

"Ha, ha, ha, Walter. I was drunk. As I remember the chink you ended up with had one-eye and no teeth." Harry turned back. "Those two look pretty nice though. Quite classy."

"Just one of the many attractions of The Pan," Walter replied.

The restaurant was at the far end of the main esplanade, in the shadow of the Tower of Electricity. It was too early for lunch, so only a sprinkling of diners were present at the restaurant. Harry showed his badge and said something to the girl waiting with menus at the entrance. She scurried off, presumably to fetch Parker.

James T. Parker emerged from the kitchen. Harry grinned as he saw Walter's reaction. Parker was at least six-feet-six-inches tall, a good three inches taller than Walter, and at least thirty pounds heavier. He appeared to be in his mid-forties, chocolate-skinned, with a wide nose and full lips. Unlike most excessively tall men, Parker walked erect, not bent slightly forward to make himself appear more normal. He wore a waiter's white shirt and black trousers, although where the restaurant had found a uniform to fit him was anyone's guess.

"Now you know how the rest of us feel when you walk in the room," Harry whispered.

Parker smiled shyly as Harry and Walter approached him, making no effort to hide his discomfort with celebrity. That will serve him well when the celebrity fades, Walter thought. As it inevitably will.

"Mr. Parker," Walter said, stepping forward and extending his hand, "it is an honor to meet you. It isn't every day that a man saves the life of the president of the United States."

Parker grinned dopily, now fully embarrassed. He had a tooth missing on the upper left. "Tell you the truth, sir, it was kind of an accident. I just jumped on the man before I thought about it. By the time I did think about it, I had the gun. He was kind of little. Wasn't that hard. He did try to get off another shot though."

"We'd love to see exactly the way it happened. Why don't we walk over to the Temple of Music and you can show us?"

"I'll be pleased to help you gentlemen as long as I can be back before the luncheon business starts. People work hard enough without having to cover for me."

"Don't worry, Mr. Parker," Harry said, patting the colored man's enormous forearm, "we won't keep you long. Will we, Walter?"

"No. I'd just like you to describe what happened. Just a few minutes."

As the trio strolled the esplanade, passersby glanced Parker's way and whispered to each other as they went. Parker could not have helped but notice, but tried to pretend they were looking at something else. He continued to minimize his heroism. "I was next in line, you understand. It wasn't like I had to run to tackle the bastard."

"Still, you are the bear's claw right now," Harry noted.

"It's true, Mr. Swayne. Newspaperman told me I was the most popular nigger in America. A woman came up to me on the way to work this morning and asked for a lock of my hair." Parker snickered. "I offered her a kink."

Walter congratulated himself on his luck. James Parker, "Big Jim," as he was unsurprisingly called, was going to turn out to be the perfect witness; honest, forthright, and one of those people you met only occasionally who were totally without artifice. Everything he heard from this towering colored man would be absolutely the truth as Parker had experienced it.

As soon as they arrived at the Temple of Music, Walter realized he had been wrong in anticipating incongruity. "Temple" was precisely the right term for this immense, almost impossibly gaudy square monument to the muse. The building stretched 150 feet across on each side, with cylindrical, domed appendages truncating each corner to give the impression of roundness. Predominantly red, with gold and yellow trim, and panels in blue and green, the structure was topped with a dome almost two hundred feet high and festooned with ornate sculptures paying homage to the glory of the Great God Music. To the extreme disappointment of the gaggle of fairgoers loitering outside, a ring of coppers had been placed around building to prevent anyone from visiting the crime scene.

Inside, with seating for more than two thousand, the Temple of Music had the largest capacity of any building in the fair and had thus been the site for President McKinley's speech and his ill-fated hand-shaking session. The vast floor of the hall had been cleared of chairs, save a line from the entrance curving to the far wall and then back to a spot in the center, almost directly under the center of the dome. A small "X" had been lightly painted where the president had greeted his admirers. A row of tall potted plants stood behind, placed there to protect McKinley's rear.

"Is this the way it looked yesterday, Mr. Parker?"

"Yessir, Mr. George. The chairs was lined up that way to keep everybody who wanted to shake Mr. McKinley's hand in one line."

"And where were the police?"

"There was officers all along the line, 'cept near the president. There was about five or six men on either side of him. Lots of other folks too. Politicians. Least they looked like politicians."

Walter walked around the line of chairs. He rested his hands on the back of one and stood for some moments, taking in the scene. A long single file, snaking through the hall, operatives on both sides of the president watching the well-wishers inch closer. McKinley shaking hands, greeting each person and passing a few pleasantries. The lines of sight were perfect. How could Czolgosz have gotten so close? The bandaged hand should have been like red to a bull. So easy to have checked it.

"Mr. Parker, how did Czolgosz carry himself? Did he favor the hand with the bandage? Hold it across his chest, maybe?"

"No, Mr. George. He wasn't holding his arm like it was hurt at all. It was down at his side, like he didn't want no one to see it."

"But you saw it."

"Couldn't miss it. O' course, I was standing right behind him. I'll tell you, Mr. George, it was real odd about that hand. The bandage, I mean. It was twice the size of what his hand woulda been. Then, when he got to Mr. McKinley and raised it up, I remember thinking, how's he gonna shake hands with that? Maybe that's why I jumped on him so quick. Like I smelled something wrong without knowing it. Something else . . ."

"What?"

"It was wrapped over his sleeve, not underneath. Now who waits to bandage a hand hurt enough to be completely covered until after they put on their suit?"

"Who indeed? You have a very good eye for this, Mr. Parker."

"I was a constable in Georgia. I'll tell you, mister, we'd have known what to do with that bastard down there."

"You gave up being a constable in Georgia to come to Buffalo and be a waiter?"

Parker smiled. "You ain't never been a black man in the south, Mr. George. I get a whole lot more respect waiting tables here than I got as a constable there."

"What happened before the president was shot. Show me."

Parker walked to the X. "The president was standing like so . . ." He moved to where the line would be. "I was here, right behind that little bastard . . ."

"So you were all sideways to the president until you reached the front of the line."

"Yeah. But everyone was turned a little bit. You know, to see him better."

"And Czolgosz's right hand would have been on the far side of president until he turned toward him."

"Right. Mr. McKinley had his hand out when the little coward turned. Then, instead of shaking hands, he fired. You could see the bandage kind of explode with the first shot. Then I jumped on him."

"What happened to the president?"

"Mr. McKinley fell backward into the plants. He knocked over two of them but they're back the way they were now. I was wrestling on the floor with the bastard when suddenly someone jumped on both of us and slugged the little bastard in the jaw. Found out later it was Mr. Foster. Then a bunch of other folks jumped on as well. Your folks had to drag them off to keep them from killing the guy."

"Did Foster slug Czolgosz before or after you had gotten the gun away from him?"

"After."

"You certain?"

"Oh yes sir, Mr. George. Definitely after."

"And no one else looked suspiciously at this guy the whole time he was in the line."

"Not that I could see," Parker said. "They all seemed to have turned away . . . 'cept the one looking at me."

"Did you see anyone else? Not just helping Czolgosz, but even just standing around who looked like they didn't belong. Maybe someone off to the side who didn't try and join the receiving line."

"Not that I remember. Everyone like that rushed to help when the president was shot. I figured they was all detectives, like you."

"Thank you, Mr. Parker. You've been a great help."

"Really, Mr. George? I hope so." Parker looked down and shuffled his feet a bit. "Uh, Mr. George, I heard that President McKinley has asked to meet me. To thank me an' all. I'm kind of nervous."

"Don't be, Mr. Parker. I've met him. He's a very fair and decent man."
Walter realized he had used Mark Hanna's phrase.

Parker's feet did not stop their little dance. "It's not just that, Mr.
George. Don't say nothin' please, but I voted for Mr. Bryan."

"You saved President McKinley's life, Mr. Parker. I don't think he'll
hold your vote against you." Walter did not bother to mention he had
voted for Bryan too.

"Thank you, Mr. George. I like you. You're the only one around here
who calls me 'Mr. Parker.'"

"That's your name, isn't it?"

"Not to some."

Walter and Harry walked outside and bid James Parker good day.
They watched him saunter off toward the restaurant. He hadn't gone
fifty feet before a man in a derby and woman in a pink dress had stopped
him and asked to shake his hand.

"Foster and Ireland around?" Walter asked Harry. "Now'd be a good
time to talk to them."

Harry shook his head. "Wilkie sent them back to Washington. Not
hard to figure out why."

"No. Not hard at all." Walter reached under his hat to scratch his hair,
although he realized his scalp didn't itch. "Odd though," he mumbled.

"What's odd?"

"Nothing. Forget it."

"What, Walter? This is the second time you've said something is odd.
Now what is it?"

"Just funny how Foster and Ireland could have been so . . ."

"What? Been so what?"

"Dumb, Harry. How could they not check out a bandage on someone's hand big enough to hide a .32 when some colored waiter could tell
it was suspicious?"

Harry grabbed Walter by the forearm and turned him so they were
face to face. "What are you saying, Walter?"

Walter shook off Harry's hand. "I'm not saying anything."

"Oh yes, you are. You're wondering whether Foster and Ireland might have let that Polack through, then turned away on purpose."

"No, Harry. That's not . . ."

Before Walter saw his hand move, Harry had stuck his manicured finger into the middle Walter's chest. It felt as if someone had jabbed him with a poker. "We're looking for anarchists, Walter. Anarchists. The people who threw the bomb at the Haymarket. The people who kill coppers. Who want to overthrow the government and give it to a bunch of slobs who don't even speak English. We're not looking for our own." Harry raised his finger off Walter's chest, then jabbed it back without being delicate about it. "Whaddaya think, Walter, that Foster, Ireland, and the Polack *knew* each other? Or that Foster and Ireland had taken money to let McKinley get shot? I know you're not saying that either of them did it because they was anarchists themselves."

Walter swatted Harry's finger away. He had often wondered, if the two of them really went at it, who would be left standing at the end. "I'm not saying anything about anything, Harry, so keep your damned finger to yourself. I said it was odd. And it is odd. That's it."

Harry pulled the offending digit back. "Walter, you asked if Foster and Ireland could be so dumb. Well, I've learned from eight years in the army and four on this job *never* to be surprised at how dumb people can be. Why don't we just leave it at that?"

"Okay, Harry. Anything you say."

7

When Walter and Harry arrived at Buffalo police headquarters, a squat, rectangular building, two stories high, the air in the lobby chilled noticeably even before they announced themselves to the sergeant at the front desk. They were obviously expected. The sergeant, a ruddy-faced fellow whose bovine neck bulged over his uniform collar, made to look through papers before acknowledging their right to speak to the prisoner. After a few minutes, Harry cleared his throat, but the sergeant merely raised a fat finger and returned to his shuffling. Finally, he must have tired of the theatrics because he dropped the papers back on his desk, looked down at Harry and Walter like they were insects, and flicked his left index finger toward a far door. A uniformed copper stood guard. When Walter and Harry turned his way, he crossed his arms, and moved his feet slightly apart.

"Harry, why don't you sound out the coppers while I'm talking to Czolgosz?" Walter said softly.

"Sound them out for what, Walter?" Harry glared around the room. "They don't want to talk to us, wouldn't you say? You trying to get rid of me?"

"They'll talk to you, Harry," Walter whispered. "Everybody talks to you. It's your animal magnetism."

"Fuck you, Walter."

"I'm serious, Harry. Not about the animal magnetism. But if there really was a plot, there must have been someone else in on it here in Buffalo. Do you think Emma Goldman, or anyone else for that matter, would send some kid to kill the president and not send along someone to make sure he didn't screw it up? We need to find out how much the coppers know about Czolgosz since he got here, and how well they checked his comings and goings."

Harry considered the reasoning. "While you question Chol . . . the prisoner . . . by yourself. Shit, Walter, why do they all have those jaw busting names?"

"Part of the plot. You know it's better for one person to talk to him. You want to do it? I'll talk to the coppers. But it might be tough, though, if you can't even pronounce his name."

Harry mulled it over. "No. You go ahead and talk to him. You're better."

"Don't worry, Harry. I'll tell you what he says."

"Sure."

"Does he know McKinley is still alive?"

"Probably."

Walter walked past the uniformed copper through the door towards the cells, neither man offering pleasantries. The area was pretty clean as lock-ups go, but the smell of stale urine still hung over the place like a calling card. There were eight cells in the room, set in one long row. They were generally used as holding facilities until a suspect could be carted to one of the larger jails. For Czolgosz, though, the other seven had been cleared. A sergeant sat just inside the door, making certain that the prisoner didn't chew through the bars or vanish into thin air. In one of the center cells, on his cot, back against the wall, feet up, was Leon F. Czolgosz.

The would-be murderer of William McKinley could not have been more unlikely looking. He was tiny, less than five-foot eight and not one-hundred-fifty pounds, with a smooth, open, boyish face, light blue eyes, and sandy hair. He did not appear to need to shave more than once every three days. A bandage was stuck on his right cheekbone, where Foster had delivered his left. Czolgosz glanced toward the door as Walter walked through, showed a bit of surprise at Walter's size, but otherwise he seemed unimpressed. With all the attention he had been getting, one more lawman was not going to be much of a difference.

The sergeant stood up as Walter entered and strode to the entrance of the cell. He grasped one the bars above the keyhole with his right hand, as if to say, "This is my prisoner, buster." Then he stood, looking Walter in the eye, challenging the federal man to ask him to leave.

Which is exactly what Walter did.

The sergeant responded to the request with a tight smile and a shake of the head. He was shorter than Walter, but wide. His stubby fingers looked like sausages on the bars. Walter glanced past the sergeant, watching Czolgosz. The boy remained on his bunk, taking in the scene between the two lawmen. His eyes were alert but without fear or hatred. He might be crazy, Walter decided instantly, but he was certainly not stupid.

You have only seconds to decide how to interrogate a prisoner, whether to be friendly or official, whether to flatter or intimidate. You must decide from that first eye contact, that first sizing up of a prisoner's posture, his intelligence, his fear, his stubbornness. Did he want to talk or to remain silent? Once the choice of approach was made, there would be no opportunity to change tacks. Any attempt at alteration would alert the prisoner that he was witnessing a charade.

Walter decided to use the sergeant to help him establish himself with the prisoner. Instead of taking the man aside and reasoning with him before pulling rank, Walter simply said, "If you're not out of this room in ten seconds, I'm going to get your chief to throw you out. And if that doesn't work,

I'm going to get the president to send a message. I'm here on his express order and he wants me to speak to this man alone. So shake your ass, friend."

Czolgosz leaned forward, pulled up his knees, and grasped them with his hands. The sergeant had tightened his grip on the bar until his fingers were white, wishing it was Walter's throat. Walter put his hands on his hips and stared the copper down. The corners of Czolgosz's mouth had turned up slightly. The sergeant started to say something, then bit it off. He didn't have the horses and they both knew it. With a flick of his left hand he hurled the ring with the cell keys at the middle of Walter's chest, where Harry had jabbed him less than an hour before. But a Buffalo police sergeant was no Harry Swayne and Walter caught the key ring easily.

Both Walter and Czolgosz watched the sergeant stalk from the room.

Czolgosz didn't change his position when Walter unlocked the door and entered the cell, except to move his head to follow Walter as he grabbed a rickety wooden chair by the back and placed it near the bunk. Czolgosz didn't wrinkle his brow as Walter lowered himself down, the chair creaking at the weight. He seemed calm, at peace, prepared for what was to come. Up close, Czolgosz looked even more like a boy, although Walter had been told he was twenty-eight.

Walter by this time was certain of one thing. Here was someone who wanted to talk. Wanted to prove he was important. He just put two bullets in the president, but he needed to prove he was important.

"Well, Leon . . . ," Walter began, pronouncing the name with Slavic stress.

"Leon," the boy retorted, saying his name in Americanized form. "I ain't no immigrant. I was born here."

"Where?"

"Detroit."

"I don't know Detroit too well," Walter lied. "What was it like?"

Czolgosz tilted his head sideways, drumming the fingers of his left hand once quickly on his knees, rat-a-tat. "Dunno. We moved when I was a kid."

"Where?"

The boy's eyes narrowed and he emitted a quick snort. "Whaddaya wanna do, write my life story?"

"Nope." Walter shifted mood. "Just trying to figure out why someone would want to shoot the leader of his country."

"He ain't *my* leader. I done my duty."

Walter nodded slowly, as if to digest the same answer the boy had given everyone who asked him. "Your duty to who?" he asked finally.

"To all them who go hungry whilst others make millions."

"You think you're going to change that by shooting the president?"

"I done my duty."

"Any regrets? Still feel good about it?"

"Sure. Why not?"

"Well, didn't you hear? The president is going to recover. Not much of a gun you used. One of the bullets didn't even go through. He picked it out of his chest in the ambulance."

Czolgosz scowled. "Live. Dead. Makes no difference. I done my duty."

But it did make a difference.

"You did your duty even if the president survives?" Walter paused, rocking a bit in his chair. "Very well."

"He don't matter," Czolgosz insisted. "It just matters that someone *did* something."

Walter nodded. "I see. Yes. You mean matters to the people you did your duty to."

Czolgosz blew out a breath, exasperated at trying to make a point to this dunce. "Yeah, whaddaya think I meant?"

"And to others in your movement as well, I suppose."

Czolgosz jerked back. His fingers tightened on his knees. "Whaddaya mean? Who are you anyway? You ain't no Buffalo dick."

"Anarchists," Walter replied, ignoring the questions. "You said when you were arrested you were an anarchist. I just figured it would matter to them too." Walter shrugged. "But you don't have to talk about what you believe in if you don't want to."

"What about you?" Czolgosz asked suddenly. "You come from a rich family and you're doing the plutes' work for them?"

"I was raised in an orphanage. I ran away when I was fourteen."

"No bull?"

"No bull."

"Why'd you run?"

"To get away from the priest." Why did he admit that? But he neglected to add that he had smashed a bottle against the side of Father Timothy's head as a parting gift.

Czolgosz eyed Walter for a moment, deciding whether to pursue the matter.

"So how come you decided to work for the rich?"

"The president isn't rich, Leon. He never made much money."

"Yeah, but them's around him are plenty rich."

"How do you know that?"

"I read. Whaddaya think, I can't? I probably read more n' you."

"Probably. Read a lot of anarchist stuff?"

"Sure. How'd you think I learned what I learned?"

Walter changed direction suddenly. "So who did you meet when you got here? To Buffalo, I mean."

Czolgosz's hands tightened on his knees. Not much and just for a second, but he saw that Walter noticed. "Nobody. And I'm done now."

Walter nodded. "All right. Can I get you anything?"

"Whaddaya mean?" Czolgosz eyed Walter with suspicion.

Walter let his hands drop between his legs. "I don't approve of what you did, Leon," he said softly. "I won't pretend that I do. But you're going to the penitentiary for a long time. Maybe twenty years. Maybe forever. I don't expect things will go too well for you in there. I don't see the harm in you being a little more comfortable in the meantime."

Czolgosz pressed his lips together. Walter could hear his breathing coming in shallow bursts. For the first time, the boy looked afraid.

He had figured to kill McKinley and die for it; a hero to the cause. Prison obviously scared him more than hanging. Probably should too.

"Could you get me a book?" Czolgosz asked after a few moments. "From my room?"

"Sure. "Which book.""

"*Looking Backward*."

"Edward Bellamy."

Czolgosz nodded. "Yeah. I read it eight times already. Great book. You read it yet?"

"Sure. Hasn't everyone?"

"Whaddaya think?"

"I liked it. I hope the future is like he said." Actually, Walter thought the book was a load of tripe—all that nonsense about people living together in harmony. People fought for what they wanted. Always had, always will.

"So you'll get it for me?"

"I said I would. Tell me where to find it."

"It's in the top drawer of the bureau in my room. If the coppers didn't take it." Czolgosz gave Walter the address of his rooming house.

"I don't think you have to worry about any of those guys . . ." Walter flicked a thumb toward the door he came in. "I can't figure any of them stealing a book."

Czolgosz smiled tightly. "Yeah. You're right."

Walter nodded and pushed himself to his feet. He started to the cell door, then turned back. "Is that what made you do this, Leon? The book?"

Czolgosz shook his head. "Course not. No book's gonna make someone do his duty."

"Other people might."

Czolgosz started to respond but thought better of it.

As he passed out of the cell block, Walter tossed the key ring back to the sergeant who glared at him with undisguised hatred.

8

Walter looked to collect Harry for the trip to Czolgosz's room, but Harry was nowhere to be seen. Walter checked the bathroom, a vile stinking affair that, only after he emerged, he discovered was for visitors. The desk sergeant happily admitted that the coppers had their own on the second floor. Walter checked that one as well, but no Harry. He returned to the desk. The desk sergeant repeated his paper-shuffling charade, refusing to acknowledge Walter's presence.

"I'm looking for the guy I came in with," Walter said finally.

"I'm sure I don't know who you mean . . . sir," the sergeant replied in a monotone, with exaggerated slowness. "Do you wish to fill a missing persons report?"

Walter wanted to reach up and grab the wisenheimer and drag him over his desk, but he held his temper. "Look, pal, we're all just trying to do a job here. So tell me what I want to know, or I'll have Mark Hanna ask for me."

"I believe the gentleman said he was off to check on something. Although I suspect he slipped around the corner for a pint."

"Did he happen to mention where he was going afterward?"

The sergeant finally looked up. "No. But he ain't real welcome here. Like you."

Harry, in truth, would not have favored these clowns with details. Thinking unpleasant thoughts about the Buffalo police, Walter headed alone to McCraig's rooming house. Czolgosz had told the police who arrested him that he had arrived in Buffalo five days before. He seemed to have walked in a random direction from the railroad terminal and chosen the first rooming house he could find with a vacancy. The exposition was drawing large crowds, so he was fortunate to arrive at Mrs. McCraig's just as one of her boarders was leaving to return home on a family emergency. The widow found the slight, well-mannered, soft-spoken young man at her door to be an ideal replacement and had rented him a room on the spot for the Exposition rate of $1 per week, only twice her usual charge. During his stay, Czolgosz had come and gone at regular hours, had no visitors, and, other than the fair, she had been unaware of any unusual destination on the young man's agenda.

Walter found the copy of *Looking Backward* precisely where Czolgosz had said it would be. From the looks of the room, the police had created quite a mess during their search, but, no surprise, they had not been especially thorough. Walter proceeded to look through Czolgosz's possessions with care. Czolgosz had a change of collar, underwear, and socks, but otherwise was wearing all he brought with him in the small burlap satchel with a faded wooden handle that had been thrown in the corner. The coppers had not impounded any cartridges, nor were there any in the room. Czolgosz had therefore come with one revolver and five rounds. Other than *Looking Backward*, the only other reading material was a *Buffalo Evening News* from two days previous and two brochures extolling the thrills of the Exposition. No other indication of how Czolgosz spent his five days was to be found, not even a matchbox.

49

Walter stopped to speak with Mrs. McCraig on the way out. She was a widow of about sixty, a small, thin, sparrow-like woman with white hair pulled back in a severe bun. Her eyes were brown and crisp behind wire-framed glasses, and her jaw line was as sharp and chiseled as a woman's half her age. She stood very straight. Walter wondered if he was looking at a precursor of Lucinda. Or at least of Lucinda if Harry did not succeed in marrying her off.

"Did he ever ask you for anything?" Walter inquired, more solicitous than he normally would be and realizing it was guilt. "He was new in town, after all. Directions maybe? To a tavern? Even on how to get to the fair?"

"No, only the library."

"He asked you about the library?"

"He was a studious young man. Like I told the other detectives. He couldn't spend *all* his time at the fair."

"I see. Were the other detectives interested? Did they go to the library, do you know?"

"I doubt it. Not after the way they laughed when I told them." She lowered her voice to a growl. "'We ain't interested in what he read, ma'am.'"

Walter laughed. "That's quite good, Mrs. McCraig. I hope you won't imitate me that well."

The old woman giggled and suddenly Walter saw her thirty years younger. "Oh no, Mr. George. I would never. And besides, you don't sound like that at all."

Walter felt himself begin to go red. "Thank you." He cleared his throat. "So which library did Czolgosz go to? Could you give *me* directions?"

The walk to the library was less than ten minutes, but ten minutes was apparently too much of an imposition for the Buffalo dicks.

Walter paused inside the door. He remembered when he was on his own—after St. Margaret's—the library was the one place he could spend an entire day. Miss Stefano had spotted him right away; tall, skinny, and haunted. She sat him at a table, recommended books, and even gave him food to eat. She was warm and round and miserably childless. Walter had often wondered in those days if his real mother—the one he could not remember no matter how hard he tried—was anything like this. Whether she ached for having been forced by crushing poverty or illness or some other justifiable reason to give up her son. Did she cry herself to sleep each night? Had she secretly inquired of the sisters of his progress and well-being? Would she, at some point in his life, magically reappear and beg his forgiveness?

Eventually, Walter began to spend a good part of every day at the library, the scruffy, gangly urchin with a pile of books in front of him. Miss Stefano had offered more than once to take him in, or at least to let him sleep at her apartment in the tenement on Rivington Street, but he always refused. Trust would simply not extend that far.

The Buffalo library looked a lot like the one on Hester Street. Or at least it conjured up the same feelings of familiarity. Walter wondered how many of the operatives in the service could go into a library and find out anything? Not many, other than Wilkie. To most of them, reading anything other than official reports was considered an affectation. Even Harry, and Harry was one of the slickest men in the division.

Walter sized up the staff behind the desk and knew at once whom to approach—the severe looking woman with the regal bearing, dressed in a gray, high-necked frock with black trim. She was reed-thin, did not seem to have a figure at all; her hair, like Mrs. McCraig's, was pulled back in a bun, and she wore a wedding ring. Not every librarian was a spinster. But mostly, she exuded superiority. She would pride herself on knowing more than anyone else and, with the right kind of prodding and a bit of misdirection, be happy to flaunt that knowledge. The trick was to know in advance which approach would prime the pump. Walter needed to establish whether the woman was sympathetic to Czolgosz or antipathetic to know how to pose his questions.

When he got to the desk, he placed the copy of *Looking Backward* on the counter top and smiled shyly. The woman with the bun walked over, making it a point to turn her attention to the book to demonstrate she was impervious to Walter's charm.

"Not ours," she said after a glance, gesturing with a flick of her index finger and turning to leave.

"Yes, ma'am, I know," Walter said. "This is mine. I was looking for something else. Do you have the work of writers who aren't American?"

"You mean like Shakespeare?" the librarian asked in a tone that implied she was talking to an unschooled dolt.

"Actually, I was looking for a copy of Proudhon's *What is Property?* Translated, of course. I don't read French."

"Proudhon? The anarchist?" The librarian's eyes narrowed like a gunfighter's. Word that the president's assailant was an anarchist was, by this time, common knowledge. Walter had his answer.

"Do you have it?"

"I can't help you," the woman said coldly and turned on her heel to leave.

"Just a minute, ma'am," Walter called after her, shifting to his official tone.

The woman turned back, still glaring, until Walter said softly. "I'm with the United States Secret Service Division. I'm investigating the shooting of the president."

The librarian drew back her head, like she was trying to avoid a jab. "So what do you want with Proudhon? You can prove what you say, can't you?"

Walter withdrew his badge from his vest pocket and let the woman examine it. She ran her fingers over the embossed image of the star and the eagle before handing it back to Walter.

"So you were testing me?"

"I'm sorry, Mrs. . . . . but I had to be certain of your . . . point of view before I asked."

"Mrs. Haverstraw. Now that you are certain, ask."

"The man who shot the president . . ."

"Czolgosz." She also pronounced the name correctly.

"He was in here. Probably more than once."

The woman could not have been more mortified if Walter had asked for a Japanese pillow book. "In here? In my . . . in a library? Why would he do that?" Then she coughed softly and turned to the side where a boy of about twelve was waiting patiently at the desk. "Do you mind?"

"Not at all," Walter replied, dropping his voice to a whisper. The boy was small and fair, dressed in shabby shirt and knickers that, while not new, showed no obvious signs of age or mending. He looked nothing and everything like Walter had at that age.

The boy asked a question and the woman patiently shook her head. "I'm sorry. *Richard Carvel* is out. If you write your name on a piece of paper, I'll hold it for you when it comes back." Mrs. Haverstraw turned back to Walter. "All the boys want to read Winston Churchill. All that derring-do. I wish they would read books with a little more substance, but how can one compete with adventure? *Richard Carvel* has sold two million copies." Mrs. Haverstraw heaved a sigh at the injustice of popular fiction. "You know," she went on, "there is a young writer in Great Britain named Winston Churchill. It must be terrible to be burdened with same name as a genuine literary icon. It will probably haunt the poor fellow for his rest of his life."

"Probably so," Walter said. "But we were talking about Czolgosz."

"Yes. I know. I asked you why he would come here. A killer."

"He liked to read. And a library is a good place to pass time when you've got no place else to go."

Mrs. Haverstraw tilted her head to the side. Traces of a smile flickered in the corners of her mouth. "You know this for a fact, Mr. . . . ?"

"George. Walter George, ma'am."

"Walter George what?" the librarian asked and Walter started. The tables were turning fast and Walter didn't like it one bit. His own past had nothing to do with any of this.

"Never mind," the librarian said quickly. "Why don't you tell me what this man looked li—" She emitted a small gasp and looked down at the book. "That was his copy, wasn't it? Not yours."

Walter nodded.

"Yes. He was in here. Every day for almost a week. Until two days ago. The first day he brought the book. I thought it odd that someone should bring a book into a library. I thought the same thing when you did it, but I didn't make the connection. I suppose I wasn't thinking."

"You say he only brought it on the first day?"

"Yes."

"What did he do while he was here? Both the first day and the others."

"He read mostly. Sat at a table over there. She pointed to the far corner of the room, under a big window. Kept to himself. Only seemed to talk to Esther."

"Esther?"

"Esther Kolodkin. One of our librarians. She's not here today."

"Day off?"

The librarian shook her head. "No. Her sister is coming from Chicago to see the Exposition. Esther took a couple of days off to show her around."

"So she wasn't here yesterday either."

"No, but I see nothing nefarious in that." She paused and eyed him. "But you do, Mr. George. Indeed you do. So, before you ask, I will tell you that I have never seen any evidence that Miss Kolodkin held views contrary to American values. She seems a perfectly respectable young woman. She has been with us almost six months, ever since she came here . . ."

"From Chicago?"

"Yes. But I should tell you that I came here from Chicago as well."

"But you were not seen speaking repeatedly with a man who attempted to assassinate the president."

"As I was saying, Mr. George, in my experience Miss Kolodkin has always comported herself with decency and good values. The fact that she may have been kind to a young man who was a stranger in town paints her neither as an anarchist nor a conspirator."

"Thank you, Mrs. Haverstraw. I'm certain you are correct. I have no doubt that after I speak with her for five minutes, the truth of what you say will be apparent."

"Are you mocking me, young man?"

"Not at all. By the way, did Miss Kolodkin happen to mention what part of Chicago she came from?"

"Oh yes. Evergreen Park on the near South Side. I'm from Hyde Park. We spoke often."

"She missed Chicago, did she?"

"You obviously know nothing of Chicago, young man. Once one has lived there, one always misses it. I would not have left except for Mr. Haverstraw. He's an engineer. When he got an offer to work at the pumping station from the Falls, we packed up and left. A woman must follow her husband, after all."

"But Miss Kolodkin had no husband."

"I do not pry into people's private lives."

"No. Of course not."

Mrs. Haverstraw's mouth tightened. If she was ever of a mind to make Mr. Haverstraw pay for forcing her to leave Chicago, Walter had no doubt whatsoever that she could exact a steep price indeed.

"But I've taken far too much of your time," he said quickly, suddenly desperate to be free of this woman's company. "As I said, I'm certain that I can put to rest any thought that she and Czolgosz had spoken in any way but coincidental to tragic events of yesterday. But in order for me to speak with her, I'll need to know where she lives . . ."

9

I'm looking for Esther Kolodkin."

The landlord looked Walter up and down, letting a sneer play on his lips. He was of indeterminate age, short, bald, and unshaven, with stubby gnarled fingers and a torso once thick and muscular, now gone to fat. A laborer who had saved enough money, Lord knew how, to buy this fleabag of a rooming house.

The building, two stories of peeling wood and cracked windows, was in the southeast part of the city, a tumble-down neighborhood of immigrants and laborers; of families squeezed into tiny apartments; of the mixed smells of cooking fat, spices, and unwashed humanity; where English was rarely spoken and commerce was conducted by raised fingers in barter; where no matter how hard one worked, or for how long, or how many members of the family participated, the best they could hope for was not to grow poorer. Similar neighborhoods in cities all across

America grew potential radicals like so many stalks of wheat, just waiting for the Emma Goldmans to happen along with a scythe.

The landlord sniffed in deeply. Walter thought he might spit, but whatever he had loosened, he swallowed. "Copper?" The man's political views were apparent in the one word.

"Don't matter what I am," Walter replied. "Is Esther Kolodkin here or isn't she?"

"Ain't."

"Since when?"

"I don't own no watch." The accent was vestigially Eastern European. Walter surmised the landlord had been in America for some time. Gave him a leg up on more recent arrivals.

"Do you know where she went?"

The old man tilted his head sideways. "Thought you was a copper. Why don't you tell me?"

Walter smiled and nodded. "You're a very funny fellow." Then he took a step forward and grabbed the old man by either panel of his vest. Grime was sufficiently prominent that the serge felt slimy to the touch. Walter tightened his grip on the fabric and pulled up until the old landlord was barely on tiptoe.

"Listen, my humorous friend," Walter said, so softly that the landlord turned his head slightly to better hear. Walter figured he was deaf in one ear. "I'm going to be asking the questions and you're going to be giving the answers. And if I think your answers aren't up to snuff, I'm going to haul you up to the second floor of this rat trap and toss you through one of your own windows. You understand me, don't you?"

The man glared. He'd experienced the ministrations of police before. But Walter had learned to combine size with manner to achieve what more bullying coppers couldn't. He held the man, not moving, keeping his gaze fixed on the landlord's rheumy eyes. Finally, the man nodded, grudging, filled with loathing.

"Good," Walter said soothingly. But he did not release the man. "Now where is Esther Kolodkin?"

"Left yesterday morning," the landlord snarled. "Ain't been back."

"Left for where?"

"Dunno. Work I figured."

"Was she meeting anyone?"

A shake of the head. "Not that she said."

"Did she ever talk about any relatives? A brother maybe? Or an aunt? Or a sister?"

Another shake of the head. "Nobody."

"Think she left town?"

"How would I know?"

"She paid up on her rent?"

The old man shook his head. "Owes a week. Six bits."

"Don't you get paid in advance?"

"Usually. But she was a librarian an' all. Quiet. Kept to herself. I figured she was good for it."

"She have any politics?"

The old man shook his head again, but they both knew he was lying.

"Do *you* have politics?" Before the landlord could deny it, Walter said, "Better tell me the truth, old man, or you'll be talking to a cell full of angry coppers downtown."

"Socialist." The word came out in prideful hiss.

"Was she a socialist?"

"Anarchist."

"Is that why she stayed in this dump? Because she knew you wouldn't give her trouble?"

The old man nodded.

"She ever have any visitors? Men?"

The old man shook his head.

"Friends who dropped by?"

"Nobody."

He was lying but there was no way for Walter get the truth. The old man might be willing to talk about the dead, but he wasn't going to give up the living. He let the man down. "See how easy it was to have a polite conversation. Now show me her room."

The landlord stood in the doorway for a moment, reluctant to allow a copper defile his sanctum. But, after a moment, he turned and headed for the staircase. Walter hoped the rotting wood would support his weight.

When the door to Esther Kolodkin's second floor room opened, Walter thought he was looking through a portal to another world. The walls had been recently washed, flowered chintz curtains hung on the windows, a patchwork counterpane adorned the single bed, and a rope rug lay on the floor. The room was furnished sparsely but was scrupulously tidy.

Near the bed was a bookcase, just knocked together pine boards. Back issues of *Freiheit*, "*Forward*," Johann Most's rag, and other subversive periodicals, occupied one shelf. A variety of anarchist books filled the other. Walter was amused to see the Proudhon, in translation, of course. Not surprising. *What is Property?* was as common to anarchist bookshelves as the Bible was to preachers'. Walter leafed through the books and magazines, looking for papers or letters from the fabled sister from Chicago or anything else to provide a clue to Esther Kolodkin's life outside of work or home. There was nothing.

An ancient armoire stood opposite the bed. The doors hung at haphazard angles and had ceased to have clasps, so were tied shut with lengths of ribbon. Walter undid the bow and checked the contents. Three dresses, all cleaned and pressed, hung inside, as well as a gray wool coat and hat, each at least six or seven years old. Walter held up one of the dresses, a dark green frock. Esther Kolodkin seemed to be of medium height and weight. The garment would be appropriate for a woman of Mrs. Haverstraw's age, although Esther Kolodkin was much younger.

He opened the top drawer, needing to jiggle it to overcome the warping. The drawer was filled with slips, stockings, and personal undergarments. Esther Kolodkin seemed, as Mrs. Haverstraw had described, to be a solid working woman with good values and both feet firmly on the floor. And an anarchist. But, despite what the scandal sheets would have one believe, neither personality nor personal hygiene was defined by politics.

Other than the clothing and the reading material, no hint of the woman's character could be found. But the very absence of such a hint was revealing in itself. No one lives that anonymously except by choice and effort. She had either maintained the room in such a fashion on an ongoing basis, or cleared it of material before she left. In either case, Walter was convinced that Esther Kolodkin had left this room for good.

She had, in all likelihood, run. The question was, had she done so for fear of persecution or because she had reason? The answer was critical, and Walter would need to find it out without the help of the Buffalo coppers. That cord had been permanently cut.

10

Walter and Harry had worked together for so long that they didn't need speech to communicate. They'd left their valises at the Iroquois, so Walter headed back there. When he arrived, Harry was waiting for him in the lobby. Walter motioned with a quick jerk of his thumb toward a far corner.

"There may be something to this after all," he said softly, but still at conversational levels. Nothing attracts eavesdropping like whispering. Walter told Harry briefly about Esther Kolodkin speaking with Czolgosz in the library and the subsequent visit to her room. "It might be nothing, but I don't think so. Even if she's not directly involved, I'm sure he talked to her, or at least hinted at what he was planning to do. She'll make this go a lot faster. She's either somewhere in Buffalo or she skipped town, probably to Chicago. Back to Evergreen Park. We need to find her."

"I found her," Harry said. "And she's not in Chicago."

"You found her? Where is she? And why were you even looking for her?"

"I wasn't looking for her. I was trawling. Trying to get the dope on the resident anarchists here. The coppers were actually quite helpful. Especially when I told them how pushy you were, bossing everyone around, and how I hated working for you. They got real sympathetic after that."

"So where is she?"

"That's the problem. She's in the morgue."

"She's dead?"

"Well, she doesn't work there, Walter. Of course she's dead. Seems to have been a robbery. She was stabbed. Three times. No purse on the body."

"Three times? When?"

"Last night. Probably a couple of hours after McKinley. Ordinarily would have been big news . . . young, pretty girl knifed on the street. Not yesterday though."

"Where was she found?"

"The waterfront. Up near the narrows. No one knows what she was doing there, since she lived on the other side of town. But there's lots of anarchists on the boats. All a bunch of foreigners anyway. Maybe she went down there to meet some friends."

"Maybe. You said 'seems.' Why 'seems'?"

"What are you talking about?"

"You said, 'It seems to have been a robbery.'"

"Ah. Well, I wasn't there, was I?"

"No other reason?"

"No, Walter. What are you driving at?"

"She left her rooming house two days ago. Wasn't at work. That leaves a day and a half unaccounted for. I don't think she was just walking along the lakefront all that time."

"You think she was with Czolgosz?" Harry had gotten a little closer to the correct pronunciation. "You think she was that involved?"

"I don't know, Harry. But she was *somewhere*. Nobody knows where Czolgosz was the day before, do they?"

"He wouldn't talk about it."

"So maybe they were together. She came here six months ago. Unless he just happened to run into a fellow anarchist at the library, that would go a long way to proving Wilkie's theory."

"Walter, no one would have been planning to kill McKinley in Buffalo six months ago. No one even knew he would be here."

Walter waved his hand impatiently. Sometimes Harry couldn't follow a trail unless it had flags in it. "No, no, Harry, that's not . . ." He thought for a moment. "Did Czolgosz say he had the gun when he came here?"

"He didn't say. Everyone just assumed he did."

"What if he didn't? Safer to travel unarmed. In case he was stopped."

"You think he got the gun from this librarian?"

"Maybe. Or maybe she just did some scouting for him. Or maybe they just sat and read Bakunin together."

"Who?"

"Doesn't matter. But she took off from work, lied about the reason, left her rooming house without saying why, and turned up dead right after Czolgosz botched killing McKinley. I'd say that's a kind of odd string of coincidences."

"Okay. So it's odd. Your favorite word. So what now?"

"I want to talk to Czolgosz again. Give him his book. Then let's take a look at the body."

◆

The watch had changed from Walter's last visit. Inside the cell block sat an ordinary young copper, pale, pimpled, and eager. Czolgosz was in precisely the same position as he had been when Walter had arrived earlier, knees up, one hand clasping his other wrist. The copper left without a fuss. Walter handed the book to Czolgosz without making him get up to get it, then pulled up the same rickety chair to sit opposite.

Czolgosz played with the book, running his fingertips over the cover like he was caressing a woman. He was going to need Bellamy's syrupy vision of the future where he was going.

"Thanks for this. You're not bad . . . for the law."

Czolgosz for the first time seemed genuinely human. Just a dumb kid who truly believed he was striking a blow for humanity. Let's see, Walter thought, if that sentiment could be carried through.

"Esther Kolodkin is dead," he said curtly.

Czolgosz continued to fondle the book, except for the briefest hesitation, which he attempted to hide by going back to the same spot on the cover a few seconds later. "Who's that?" he asked finally. Walter wondered if Czolgosz knew how bad a liar he was.

"A librarian. I thought you knew her."

Czolgosz lifted his hand. "Yeah. I did know a librarian. Esther? Was that her name? I never found out. She was just someone to talk to."

"Ah. So I guess it doesn't matter then."

"Well, sure it matters. Young girl gets killed."

"I didn't say she got killed. I just said she was dead."

"Well, how else? Young, healthy woman. I just figured she musta got killed. 'Specially with you bringing it up. How was it? Traffic accident or something?"

"She was stabbed. A robbery."

Czolgosz placed the book next to him on the cot, as if to protect his precious object from the news.

"A robbery, huh? Poor people is driven to crime by the oppression of the capitalist class."

"Very lofty sentiments, Leon. Get that from Emma Goldman, did you?"

"Hey! Emma Goldman is a great woman. If your friends cared more about the working man like she does . . ."

"You wouldn't have needed to do your duty?"

"You can make jokes, but it's true. If you really came from an orphanage, you'd know."

Walter had no intention of discussing himself again. "I hear Emma Goldman believes in free love. That what got you to like her so much?"

"Fuck you." Czolgosz took a breath, looked down at the book, and nodded slowly, a smirk playing on his face. "Pretty fair, copper. They got who done it?"

"I'm no copper. Done what?"

"Killed the librarian. What else would I be talking about?"

"Nah. Probably never will. You know what these street robberies are like. Could have been anyone."

"Yeah," Czolgosz replied somberly. "I guess it coulda."

Walter pushed himself to his feet. "Except we both know it wasn't just anyone. We both know that you didn't meet her by accident. That you brought that book to library the first day to let her know who you were." Walter started for the cell door. "I thought you'd feel a little worse that she's dead . . . seeing that it was most likely your fault."

"Whadaya mean, 'my fault'?" Czolgosz had sprung to his feet. Only Walter's size kept him from rushing across the cell.

"You botched it, Leon. The president is fine. I saw him. He's healthy as can be. You hardly scratched him. He'll be back in Washington by next week. Whoever's idea this was is just cleaning up the loose ends. Like Esther Kolodkin. Lucky you're in here. You're about as loose an end as there is." Walter paused, as if considering an idea that had just popped into his head. Outside, the clock rang the hour. "Unless, of course, you want to talk to me."

"Fuck you, copper. I ain't talking to you or nobody else." With a stiff right index finger, the same one that had pulled the trigger, Czolgosz poked himself in the chest. "I done my duty and I'm proud of it."

Walter heaved a sigh. "Okay, Leon, if that's the way you want it." He walked through the door and closed the cell door, making sure it clanged loudly. "Well, I've got to go now. Things seem pretty wrapped up here. See you in twenty years." Then he turned his back and made for the door.

"Hey, copper."

Walter turned back, but only from the waist up. His feet still pointed to the exit. "Yeah?"

"Do you think if I . . ." Czolgosz lifted his hand and rubbed across the bandage on his cheek.

"What?"

Czolgosz shook his head. "Never mind."

"What, Leon? Do I think if you what?"

"Nothin'."

11

The Erie County Morgue was two blocks away from police headquarters. The bodies themselves were in the basement, while the first and second floors held offices of the county coroner, the health department, and the water commissioner. The morgue area had not been part of the original building but, with the commercial development of liquid-air refrigeration, a cooling plant had been installed in the rear of the building to facilitate temporary storage of the city's dead.

The morgue attendant was an immense, impossibly affable man named Childers. He was an inch shorter than Walter, but twice as wide, all in the waist. "Call me Chill," he said, breaking into a broad, welcoming grin at the sight of Harry's badge. "Everybody else does. 'Cause of the temperature down here. Get it?"

Harry assured the man the joke was not too deep for them, then asked to see Esther Kolodkin.

Childers heaved a sigh. "She was a pretty young thing." He attempted, without total success, to sound appropriately solemn when discussing a deceased. "And a librarian to boot. Terrible to die like that when she could have been home raising a family."

He led them down the stairs and through a corridor to a set of double metal doors. "Gonna be cold. You boys want some coats?"

Walter shook his head. "Not going to be here long enough."

Childers shrugged, looking like a mountain of gelatin in an earthquake. "Okay by me." He grabbed a large fur coat off a rack against the far wall. "I gotta. Been working in the cold so long, I can't feel my feet anymore."

"Can't see 'em either," Harry whispered to Walter.

As soon as the doors swung open, Walter cursed himself. A blast of cold like January in the Dakotas slammed him the face. But he refused to give Childers the satisfaction of grabbing a coat, so he followed the man inside, an equally stoical Harry next to him.

The room was twenty by thirty, each wall lined with a series of large drawers, three high and eight deep. Childers stopped at the first row on the left and pulled out the center drawer.

Esther Kolodkin, chalk white and naked, stared at the ceiling of the morgue. She was the height and weight Walter expected, with dark hair, eyes slightly almond-shaped, and a full lower lip. She would have been attractive without being beautiful. Her legs were long and thin, her waist tapered, and her breasts full. Walter and Harry looked from her face to her feet without letting their eyes linger anywhere.

They then both turned their attention to the three puncture wounds, each within inches of the other two, just below the rib cage. The wounds had been cleaned and only a small crust of mottled blood surrounded each one.

"Always feel a little funny undressing the girls, especially the nice looking ones," Childers said suddenly. "They don't mind, o' course, but I've taken a good bit o' sass from my wife. She don't say nothin' about the hags though."

Walter glanced to Harry and, when he was certain Harry had seen the same things as he had, they nodded to Childers to push the drawer closed.

"Got her clothes?" Harry asked.

"Outside."

Thank God, thought Walter.

The burst of warmth that hit Walter and Harry entering the hall was of equal intensity as the burst of cold going in. The effects of the dead were kept in labeled burlap sacks in a large storeroom. Childers stood beside them as they checked over Esther Kolodkin's clothing and the scant possessions—a cheap bracelet and phony garnet ring—found with the body. After a minute or so, Harry handed the bag back to the attendant.

"Find what you wanted?" Childers asked, leaning forward to catch any chance bit of salacious gossip.

"Yeah," Harry grunted. "Just like it seemed. Poor kid. Wrong place, wrong time."

"That's all?" asked a clearly disappointed Childers.

"Yeah," Harry grunted. "What'd you think there'd be?"

"I'll never complain about August heat again," Harry muttered once they were back on the street. "'We don't neeeed no coats.' Walter, sometimes you're an idiot."

"I suppose. What do you think about the girl?"

"Wasn't like no robbery I ever seen."

"Me either."

"It was two guys, not one."

"One grabbed her from behind. By both arms. The other did the work."

"Her arms were pulled back. Stretched the dress so it tore ragged when the knife went in."

"And they stabbed her first. Only took the purse later."

"Yeah, no struggle. She was killed before she knew what was happening. No need to do that with a woman. Just grab the purse and go. If she made a beef, then mebbe you kill her to keep her from being heard. But no one is going to do it first, especially when there's two."

Harry nodded. "Unless you were trying to make it look like a robbery when what you really wanted to do was to kill her. Then you take the purse to cover the killing instead of killing her to cover the robbery."

"Wonder if she's really got a sister in Chicago. Would help if she did."

"She does. One of the coppers had her name and address as next of kin."

"You're joking. A Buffalo copper? How in hell did he even know to check?"

Harry shrugged. "Dunno. Someone on the force must be smarter than they look."

"That wouldn't be hard."

"So, Walter, an interesting day's work, wouldn't you say? Wilkie and Hanna don't seem so crazy after all."

"People can be right by accident, Harry."

"You'd know, Walter."

"Maybe. But I'm still not positive."

"C'mon, Walter. *Something* went on here."

"Something is not the same thing as *the* thing. Maybe Czolgosz did just meet the girl after he got to town and they were drawn together by a mutual desire to overthrow the government."

"And the knife wounds?"

"We're guessing. And I can't see why you're so anxious for Wilkie to be right . . ."

"I'm not anxious," Harry protested. But they each knew what it meant if Wilkie and Hanna had been correct. If Czolgosz was simply some lunatic acting alone, Ireland and Foster's failure to spot the gunman could be dismissed as bad luck, or even incompetence. But the more it seemed like Czolgosz was part of something bigger, the more it seemed that Ireland and Foster might have part of something bigger as well.

"Doesn't matter anyway, Harry. We've got a trail to follow in any case. Let's give Wilkie his wish and hustle on back to Chicago. There's an express leaves at six. We can just make it."

"You don't want to stay here and try to find who killed the librarian? Might be a helpful piece of information. You're going to leave this to the coppers?"

"I'll bet you that dinner you want me to come to that we have a better chance finding whoever killed that girl in Chicago than in Buffalo."

"You're on. But not for the dinner. It's tomorrow night. And you'll be there."

Harry headed to the Iroquois to collect their bags. They didn't say much on the walk, but each knew what the other was thinking. Had one or more operatives, men in their outfit, turned traitor?

As they neared the hotel, Walter heard something. Actually, he didn't really hear it; more like he sensed it. As they turned the corner on Eagle Street, Walter suddenly grabbed Harry by the wrist and pulled him into a doorway. He didn't have to put a finger to his lips. Harry already knew to shut up.

They waited for a few seconds, then Walter took off his hat and carefully peeked out from the doorway. Then he moved quickly back onto the street, retracing their steps, Harry a half-step behind. As they neared the corner, a clack of boot heels echoed from the pavement. They turned on to Washington Street just in time to see a man in a black coat jump into a coach facing back the other way. It was black with no markings. The coach tore away from the curb and took off over the cobblestones. At the next corner, it careened around to the right and disappeared.

Harry took off his skimmer and rubbed his hand across his pate. "Well, we sure got someone's attention."

"Look like a copper to you?"

"Nope. You?"

Walter shook his head. "Might be Hanna keeping tabs on us."

"Mebbe," Harry admitted. "Can you figure out why he'd feel the need to do that?"

"No."

"Me either."

"Who else then?" Walter asked.

Harry glanced at him but didn't answer.

12

Sunday, September 8, 1901

Walter and Harry arrived at the Grand Passenger Station on Canal Street at seven the next morning. They had taken the overnight from Cleveland and Harry had decided to book sleeping berths and charge them to the bureau. After all, he had observed with shrug, with the way Wilkie and Hanna were throwing orders and money around, it seemed only right to arrive fresh for a day's work.

But Walter never slept well on trains. In truth, he never slept well at all. For as long as he could remember, there had always been one or another reason for vigilance. The sisters had always assured Walter he was safe with them, but he had learned that safety was something you created for yourself, not counted on others to provide. Even now, the slightest noise—the click of a shutter, a rustle of a curtain—could wake him.

Walter played through the threads of the problem for most of the night, Harry's rhythmic breathing and occasional snorts his only distraction. He must have dozed on and off, but had no awareness of it. The puzzle dominated his thoughts. The puzzle. That was all that mattered. Imposing his skill and his brains on an adversary. Harry did know him well. No matter how stacked the deck, Walter would always choose to sit in rather than leave the game.

So, sleep or no, Walter felt refreshed as he stepped from the train to the platform, eager to play out the drama. When they reached the immense waiting room, the din became a physical force. The Grand Passenger Station was one of the myriad buildings Chicago had thrown up since the fire that trumpeted the city's rebirth and prosperity. Red brick and sandstone, almost one hundred yards long, three floors high, with a mansard roof and clock tower in the center, the building had cost $250,000 to erect. The terminal could accommodate thirty trains, sending passengers to and from such exotic destinations as Denver, Seattle, and San Francisco. Mrs. Haverstraw, the librarian, had been correct. Once in Chicago, no place else could measure up. Buffalo could erect forty-story electrical towers, but could never match the genuine grandeur of this urgent, throbbing metropolis.

The press of humanity was stifling. Travelers, baggage handlers, vendors of food, drink, and wares, hawkers, pickpockets, prostitutes, and coppers both in uniform and plain clothes, loitered or scurried about, frenetic, seemingly aimless, an explosion of raw energy. The perfect arena to observe without being observed. As familiar as they were with the techniques of surveillance, neither Harry nor Walter had any chance of determining whether or not they were being watched in a place like this.

Outside the station, the scene only gained in intensity. Harry made to stretch.

"Why don't we head home first?" he suggested, unsuccessfully attempting to do a mask of innocence. "Just drop off our valises and change clothes."

Walter laughed. "Let's just go, Harry. Hannigan's going to be mad enough having to show his face on a Sunday. No need to stick a second burr on his saddle."

Harry sighed and nodded grudgingly. "All right. Can't be enough burrs on that mick's ass though."

They made for Adams Street, which would take them to La Salle and then north to City Hall. People, horses, carriages, and pushcarts were everywhere. Italians in derbies with long, drooping mustaches mixed with thick, fair-haired Slavs in grimy overalls, and Jews with enormous beards and dressed in black. Women in long dresses with shawls pulled tightly about them moved watchfully up and down the street. The smell of pushcart food was everywhere and everyone seemed to speak at once. Three decades after the fire, buildings were still under construction in every available niche. Children darted in and out of the foot traffic. Two street arabs began to make a grab for Walter's valise, but were dissuaded by one quick glare from the huge man in the bowler.

City Hall was part of a massive, five-story, H-shaped complex with the look of a Muscovy fortress. The building also held the Cook County Court House and offices for top brass of the police department. One wag had noted that the senior cops wanted to be in a place where they didn't have to walk too far to collect their payoffs.

Mark Hanna had called ahead to both Illinois's Governor Richard Yates and Chicago's Mayor Carter Harrison to ensure the full cooperation of the coppers. That meant Captain of Detectives Michael Hannigan would have been summoned from his day of rest to await them. As a rule, Chicago coppers in general and Hannigan in particular conducted themselves like a separate branch of government. But, although Hannigan might be a thug, he was no dunce. If Mark Hanna wanted him on Sunday, Hannigan would be there.

Inside the Dearborn Avenue entrance, Harry walked ahead of Walter and told the police sergeant manning the desk who they were and whom they had come to see.

"Captain Hannigan's on the second floor," the sergeant replied, in flat, oblivious cadence. "Second door on the left."

"Let me do the talking, Walter," Harry said softly as they mounted the stairs.

"Sure, Harry. You've been waiting for this moment for years."

Just after Harry had joined the bureau, a counterfeiting case had gone bad when the ring was tipped off that Secret Service detectives were planning a raid. Harry could never prove anything, but Hannigan, one of the three Chicago dicks who knew about the plan, had started showing up with new, tailor-made suits, and rich man's shoes. Being a crooked copper was hardly a sin in Chicago, so Harry didn't have any choice but to keep his mouth shut and bide his time. Until now.

One step inside Hannigan's door was all it took to see how far he had come up in the world from his days as just another grafter. His outer office was manned by a secretary, a petite brunette no more than twenty, with round cheeks, long eyelashes, full lips, an even fuller bosom, and a pleasant, vacant expression. She showed no sign of resentment to be toiling on the Sabbath. Harry and Walter did not need to glance at each other to know that they each knew that as soon as they were out the door, Hannigan would have her go from this job to her real one.

Harry told the girl who they were, as if anyone else would be showing up, and she asked them to wait in a tinkling-bell voice. She raised herself up, managing to jiggle a good deal of succulent flesh on the lift, then opened the door and mumbled something that neither Walter nor Harry could make out. She turned back with a becoming smile and told them that Captain Hannigan would be with them shortly.

Shortly turned out to be a five minute wait that everyone knew was for show. The secretary did not lift her eyes from her desk for the duration. Finally, the door to the inner office opened and Captain Mike Hannigan filled the frame. The chief of Chicago's detectives had white hair cut short, a thick neck, chest, and arms, and a midriff worthy of Grover Cleveland. He sported a TR-style pince-nez, which made his eyes goggle and left him appearing like an outsized snapping turtle. These features would have appeared almost comical on someone else, but on Hannigan they came off as menacing. He raised a hand perfunctorily to bid Harry and Walter enter. His hands were slabs, veterans of many a sucker punch to anyone who he decided had crossed him.

The inner office was large and opulent, dominated by a huge desk in the far corner. On one wall was a giant map of the city, broken into police districts, and on the other a series of photographs featuring Hannigan and a string of luminaries, everyone from both Mayor Harrisons, father and son, to Frank Chance, the young right fielder of the Chicago Orphans.

Two leather armchairs faced the desk. Harry and Walter settled in without being asked. Harry leaned back crossed one leg over the other. He might have been relaxing at the ball yard, watching the White Sox make hay with the Brewers. Harry and Hannigan couldn't even root for the same baseball club.

"Talked to your prisoners yet?"

Hannigan lifted a letter opener off his desk and made to remove an errant particle of dirt from under his fingernail. "Sure," he grunted after an appropriate delay.

"How many you got so far?"

"Twelve. Gonna be thirteen. The Goldman tramp's on her way back from St. Louis."

"A baker's dozen's a pretty big haul, Mike. How come you brought in so many? Just being thorough?"

Hannigan shrugged.

"Says in the paper you did it because the Secret Service Division asked you to. But Chief Wilkie only asked you to pick up old man Isaak. You got his son, his wife, and his friends. Probably would have pulled in his dog if had one."

"They only had a cat. I like cats. You stickin' up for 'em, Harry?"

"Course not. Looks good on the page though." Harry traced an index finger in the air, like he was moving it across a headline and dropped his voice an octave. "'Chicago Police Net Closes Anarchist Conspiracy.'"

"Yeah, that does sound good. You must have been taking lessons from your boss."

"Charge them yet?"

"Yeah. Conspiracy to kill the president. They'll be arraigned as soon as we have Goldman."

Harry snorted out a guffaw. "Got any proof?"

"We'll get proof."

Harry and Walter knew what *that* meant. "You'll never make it stick," Harry grunted.

"Don't be so sure."

"But maybe you won't have to," Harry said, as if an idea had just come to him. "Maybe just raising the stink is enough to . . ." He let the thought trail off.

"Enough to what?" Hannigan never had been quite smart enough not to take the bait.

"Enough to take the heat off you. There's a rumor going around that you're going to bounced for evidence tampering. Might even be brought up on charges, if Bobby Burke decides to throw you to the wolves." Robert Burke was titularly Sanitation Commissioner, although his real job was running the local Democratic machine. "Chief O'Neill hasn't been so happy since his daughter had twins." The chief had aligned himself with reformist Mayor Harrison, and he and Hannigan would have shot each other on sight if either could have gotten away with it. Maybe even if they couldn't.

But Hannigan merely shrugged. "Like you said, just a rumor."

Harry leaned back a bit farther, but Walter could read his disappointment. He had fired his big gun, but Hannigan hadn't blinked. "So what'd they say?"

"Isaak and his crew? They denied everything. Did you think they was gonna admit to it?"

"I don't know, Hannigan. You're such a good interrogator . . ."

Hannigan grinned. "Okay, Harry. Isaak said he met the Polack twice. First time was at the train when he was seeing Goldman off to someplace. The Polack was hanging around Goldman like she was a goddess." Hannigan blew out a sigh. "I can't figure it. Ugly little hound like her. All these guys swooning over her. Must have something that don't show in daylight." He shrugged. "After she left, Czolgosz . . ." Hannigan pronounced the name properly. At Harry's surprise, Hannigan grinned. His teeth were yellow, but appeared as thick and indestructible as the rest of him. "Didn't think I knew it, did you, Harry? So after the train was gone, Czolgosz sounded out Isaak about joining up . . . this is Isaak's story . . . but Isaak didn't tell him nothing because he thought the little rat was a police spy. Even says he put it in his rag last week, but we gotta check that out."

Harry nodded. "Good work, Mike."

"Got your standards to live up to."

"Got a list of your suspects?"

"Sure." Hannigan retrieved a piece of paper from a drawer and slid it across the desktop. While Harry read the names, Hannigan turned to Walter. "Ain't got nothing to say, George? Not like you. I figured you'd quote me some Greek philosopher."

Walter looked Hannigan in the eye for a moment but didn't reply. Then Harry slid the paper over and Walter read the twelve names without changing expression.

"So?" Hannigan asked. "You want to talk to them? Governor, mayor, and the chief said I gotta let you. And I do what I'm told, dedicated public servant as I am."

"Nah," Harry replied. "Not yet anyway. You found everything we would've. Maybe after you get Goldman."

Hannigan shrugged. "Suit yourself." He pushed himself to his feet. "Sorry you fellows can't stay longer . . ."

"Yeah, us too," Harry grunted. "By the way, very pretty little secretary you got out there."

Hannigan removed his pince-nez. His saucer eyes had narrowed into slits.

Harry stopped at the door. "She met your wife yet?" As they passed through the outer office, Harry made a point of thanking the secretary for coming to work on a Sunday. She looked up and smiled, unsure of whether to say "You're welcome."

Walter and Harry didn't speak until they were back out on the street. Then Walter said, "She wasn't on the list."

"No."

"No sense following his leads."

"True enough. That's like getting the second shift at a whorehouse."

"Very poetic, Harry."

"Yeah, well . . . so you want to do it? I'll drop your valise at your place."

"Where you going?"

"I've got some ideas I want to check out. We'll meet up for dinner. I'm sure you remember my invitation." Walter's mouth opened, but Harry was too fast. "Be there at six."

Walter started to leave, but Harry cleared his throat.

"You saw, right?"

Walter nodded and continued on his way. The same man in the black coat who had jumped into the carriage outside the Iroquois in Buffalo had walked through to the far end of the lobby as they passed through.

13

He wasn't sure how, but Walter knew it was her as soon as she turned the corner on to West 88th Place. He took off his hat as she approached. His hair felt prickly, so he quickly licked the tips of his fingers and tried to pat it down.

As she got closer, Walter saw the resemblance. Although she was blonde and not dark, she had the same almond eyes, robin's-egg blue. She was dressed in a black dress and dark bonnet. Mourning clothes. Walter realized that she was likely coming from church. She wore no coat although an autumn chill had blown in off the lake and begun to permeate the air. She saw the huge man waiting hat in hand and knew he was waiting for her. Her eyes fixed on him, her face tightening.

"Miss Kolodkin? Natasha Kolodkin?" Esther Kolodkin's naked body flashed into Walter's mind. He fought the urge to stare.

She stopped opposite, but kept her distance. Like her sister, she was not classically pretty—her cheekbones were too prominent and her nose too short. Her mouth was not as full as Esther's, but she had a Cupid's bow in the center of her top lip that lent her a sensuous air that her sister had seemed to lack. Of course, it wasn't entirely fair to compare a living woman with a corpse.

"My name is Walter George," he said in his stiff, official voice. "I was wondering if we might speak. It's about your sister's death. I'm very sorry."

"Are you from the police?" Her voice was slightly husky, with careful pronunciation that proclaimed her as educated. She did not seem impressed with his solicitude.

"Not precisely."

She tilted her head a bit to the side, studying him. "Could you explain what 'not precisely' means?"

"I'm with the United States Secret Service Division." He hadn't meant to tell her, but officiousness somehow now felt foolish.

"I've heard of your department. Why would people who arrest counterfeiters be interested in the murder of my sister?"

"We also guard the president."

Natasha Kolodkin placed her hands on her hips. She dropped her chin and peered at him from the tops of her eyes. "You are implying, Mr. George, that poor Esther's death has something to do with President McKinley's shooting?" Her tone was that of a mother questioning a claim that the cookie jar fell off the shelf on its own. Walter heard the sound of her boot tapping on the pavement. He felt his feet shift.

"You're not by some chance a school teacher, are you?" he asked.

She stiffened, her face suddenly growing quite red. Her hands dropped to her sides. "Yes. As a matter of fact, I am."

Walter ventured a small smile. "No one has made me this nervous since the sisters."

Natasha Kolodkin didn't smile in return, but her expression softened which, for Walter, was just as good. "I certainly would not want to make you nervous, Mr. George. I suppose I do treat everyone as if they were eight years old. But *are* you implying that Esther's murder had something to do with the president?"

"I'm not certain."

Natasha Kolodkin shook her head, as if she couldn't decide which of them was unhinged. "But how? My sister was a librarian. She was killed in a robbery."

"I'm not certain of that either."

Natasha Kolodkin sucked in a breath, forcing her breasts out against her dress. Walter tried not to let his eyes move down.

"You truly believe her death was not random?" she asked, now more curious than skeptical.

"It's too soon to say. There are aspects of . . . the incident . . . that merit further investigation."

"The incident?" she repeated, and Walter felt ridiculous.

"Her murder. Could you answer one question for me?"

"Yes, I believe I can manage that."

"Had you been to Buffalo to see your sister recently? Or were you planning a trip?"

"That is two questions, Mr. George. And the answer to each of them is no."

"Thank you, Miss Kolodkin." There were at least a dozen other questions to which Walter wanted answers, but suddenly he could not remember any of them. He was about to slink off when Natasha Kolodkin gestured to the door of the building on her left.

"There are some things I would like ask you, if you don't mind. Would you care to come in? We can sit in Mrs. Freundlich's parlor."

"Certainly." He began to add, "I'd like that very much," but bit it off.

There were four steps leading to the front door and Walter noticed she walked the stairs with excellent posture and deportment. It occurred to him that she had likely been to school with the sisters as well.

The rooming house was tidy, clean, and well kept. A good deal of bric-a-brac was scattered throughout, making it slightly dangerous for someone of Walter's size to move about without knocking something over. A slight smell of ammonia permeated the hall. Mrs. Freundlich herself was a round, jolly widow of about sixty with apple-red cheeks and a thick German accent. She made a show of clucking at the sight of a man in her establishment, but could not suppress her pleasure that Miss Kolodkin had a gentleman caller.

Mrs. Freundlich offered them tea. Walter accepted although he loathed the stuff. The landlady scurried off to prepare it as Walter and Natasha Koldokin sat in chairs that flanked a low table. On the wall of the parlor were framed prints protected by glass, pastoral scenes mostly, some of boats on a broad river. The legends indicated that all were of Germany. The wallpaper was brown stripe. On Walter's left, a large window looked out on the street. The drapes were pulled back, letting the late morning light stream in.

"Might you tell me the source of your suspicions, Mr. George?"

"I and a colleague examined your sister's . . . your sister," Walter offered.

"You mean you saw Esther's body after she had died."

"Yes. The wounds . . . are you certain you wish to hear this?"

"Yes, Mr. George. I'm not squeamish."

Walter spoke in a careful monotone, more for his sake than for hers. "The wounds did not appear to have been inflicted in a struggle, as those in a robbery almost certainly would have been."

"You are saying then that you believe whoever killed my sister tried to make it appear as a robbery although it wasn't."

"That is possible, yes."

"In that case, the killing would have been planned in advance."

Walter wasn't certain how he came to be on the wrong side of the interrogation. "Yes, it might have been."

"Did she suffer? Can you tell?"

"No. I shouldn't think so. I expect it was over quickly." There was no way to know, of course, but also no reason to say so.

"I'm grateful for that anyway." Walter noticed that she didn't say, "Thank God," as most people would have.

"I'm sorry to have disturbed you coming from church, Miss Kolodkin. Especially under such circumstances."

"I wasn't coming from church, Mr. George. I was at the mortician's. Esther's body is being returned by railroad. I'm meeting the train tomorrow."

"Your politics are as your sister's were then?"

Natasha Kolodkin scowled. "I don't believe my personal beliefs are germane. But I would wish to know why you believe that Esther was connected with President McKinley's shooting."

"I'm not at liberty to discuss that, Miss Kolodkin." Walter felt the air go out of him. Why were these people always so thin-skinned about their politics? Did they think they could change the world by getting high horse at everyone who asked a simple question?

They sat uncomfortably until Mrs. Freundlich returned with a pot of tea. She looked from one to the other of them with disappointment. She poured two cups and quickly left the room. Walter heard her sigh as she headed back to the kitchen. He put two teaspoons of sugar into his cup and then stirred the tea too energetically. Natasha Kolodkin placed a small wedge of lemon in hers. They remained silent for a few moments sipping from their cups. The tea was strong and bitter, even with sugar. Walter wondered how Natasha Kolodkin could stand the taste of it.

"They spoke," Walter said finally. "Czolgosz and your sister."

"I don't see where that . . ."

"They spoke often. Czolgosz appears to have gone out of his way to contact her."

Natasha Kolodkin shook her head. "That isn't possible. Esther couldn't have . . ."

Suddenly, she stopped speaking. At the same moment Walter turned his head. Afterward, he couldn't be certain if he had done so because of the sound or an instant before. But whichever it was, the next thing he was aware of was window glass flying into the room. He dove across at Natasha as the first shot ripped through a lamp, sending chunks of ceramic across the room. Two more bullets landed in the wall and another dislodged a print of a barge making its way up the Rhine. The remains of the lamp tipped over and kerosene spread across the carpet.

The shooting stopped as quickly as it began. Walter looked down at the woman underneath him, feeling her breasts and her hips against him. Her eyes were like saucers. Walter could see white at top and bottom. But she didn't seem hit. He pulled her away from the kerosene, but made certain that her head remained below the level of the window sill.

"Are you all right?"

She nodded. Two short, terrified jerks of her head.

Walter crawled on all fours to the window ledge. There had been an automobile. He was certain. Black or dark brown. He had taken it in without realizing. He pulled the Colt, then raised his head carefully. Nothing. The street was empty.

Walter dashed for the door. Natasha had begun to get up. No blood anywhere. She definitely hadn't been hit. "I'll be right back," he barked. "Stay away from the window." As he burst into the hall, the landlady was standing outside, cringing under a framed photograph of her dead husband.

The street was empty. A horse and cart was at one end, its owner emerging from underneath. Up and down the block, men and women were beginning to poke their heads out of windows and doorways.

The man under the cart would have had the best view, so Walter began with him. His name was Tomassini, and he sported hair more slicked than Harry's and a handlebar mustache at least six inches on either side. Walter saw from the honing wheel on the inside of the cart that Tomassini was the local grinder.

The Italian brushed himself off with exaggerated dignity, then claimed haughtily to have seen nothing. His head, he assured Walter, was buried in the cobblestones as the men were shooting. When

Walter asked how Tomassini knew it was "men" and not "man" if he wasn't looking, the grinder experienced a sudden failure to understand English. One grasp at the man's vest, however, restored both Tomassini's language skills and his memory.

There had been two plus a driver. One used a pistol, the other a long gun. The automobile—Tomassini couldn't tell one from another—had rumbled down the street and come to a stop outside Mrs. Freundlich's rooming house. And no, they hadn't paused anywhere else on the street. The man with the pistol wore a derby, the other a flat cap. They both had mustaches. Actually, maybe one had a beard.

After talking to other residents, all that Walter could determine was that both men were clean shaven and there were four men firing, perhaps five, three with shotguns. When he returned to Mrs. Freundlich's, Natasha was seated in the kitchen, sipping something from her cup. She was holding the cup with both hands while lifting it to her lips, but her hands weren't shaking and she seemed to have recovered her color. Walter excused himself for a moment to check the parlor. He couldn't tell from the bullet holes in the wall whether the shells had come from a rifle or pistol, but there was certainly no sign of a shotgun. He decided to go with Tomassini's version.

When he once more entered the kitchen, Natasha was better yet.

"Schnapps," asserted Mrs. Freundlich. "Makes ze tea better. One for you?"

"Danke."

"You're welcome. I'm an American, young man."

"Sorry. I'd love one. Thank you. I don't need any more tea."

Walter pulled up a chair opposite Natasha. "Were they shooting at me or you?" she asked immediately.

"I can't tell," he replied softly, although the correct answer, he knew, might well have been "both."

Walter didn't want to answer any more questions right away, so he was grateful when he heard a commotion coming from the street. The coppers had arrived. He stood up from the table just as Mrs. Freundlich was entering the room. He took the glass, threw down the brandy, and headed for the front door. The burn in his throat was invigorating.

About ten coppers were milling about outside, six in uniform, the rest dicks. Walter knew one of the detectives from a counterfeiting investigation, a sergeant named Flaherty, basically a good egg.

"Who you got taking shots at you this time, Walter?" Flaherty asked after Walter walked up to him. "I'd say it was our guys, but you'd think I meant it."

It might well have been your guys, Walter thought. "Dunno, Pat. You never know who's gonna be sore from an old beef." Walter had reverted to copper vernacular. The better you spoke in this crowd, the less cooperation you got.

"So you think they were after you, do you?" Flaherty's smiled had dropped a bit.

"Who else? You think somebody has it in for school teachers?"

"So what were you doing here, then?"

"Woman inside. Her sister was murdered in Buffalo. Since I knew I was coming back here, I told the Buffalo police I'd look in on her. Make sure she doesn't need any help getting her sister's body back."

"That her in the window?"

Walter turned. Natasha was standing in the parlor, looking out.

"Kinda sweet," Flaherty observed. "Good of you to volunteer. But you always was gallant like that."

Walter shrugged.

"So what's the deal about McKinley? I know you're working on it. It's the anarchists, right? They been spoiling for something like this since we stretched their pals after the Haymarket."

Walter nodded. "Sure looks that way. Hannigan grabbed everybody up. He'll probably just shake the bunch until a guilty one falls out."

"Don't be so hard on old Mikey, Walter. He's got a lot of heat under him right now."

"Oh c'mon, Pat. You really think a couple of plaster saints are gonna change anything around here? Harrison's got as much chance of cleaning up this force as me flapping my wings and flying to Moline."

"Dunno, Walter. Harrison's got some big money behind him. Lotta people are sick of Billy Burke running the city. Hannigan might be the price Billy pays to keep his spot. Unless Hannigan uncovers them that conspired to murder our beloved president, of course. Then Mikey'll probably get made chief."

"You don't like McKinley?"

"Just another plute. I voted for Bryan." Flaherty cocked his head toward the window. "*She* doesn't have anything to do with any of this, right Walter?"

"No, Pat. It's like I said. Errand of mercy."

Flaherty considered Walter's tale for a bit, then patted Walter on the shoulder. "Well, Walter, if you find yourself too busy, give me a call. Maybe I can help out. I'm good at mercy."

"No chance, Pat. I was here first."

Flaherty sighed. "Oh well. So how do you want to handle this? Revenge attempt on the life of a Secret Service operative? You're investigating your own? Keep us out of it?"

"That's how I'm going to report it."

"You gonna mention McKinley?"

"You ain't got to worry about that, Pat."

"Good enough for me. I sure don't need the extra work. Been like Deadwood around here the last few weeks. Mikey's not done. He got the word out to grab up every anarchist who spits on the sidewalk."

"Well, Pat, you said it. Best way to get your head out of the noose is to put someone else's in."

"Okay, Walter." Flaherty placed a hand on Walter's forearm. "But if there's anything that comes up . . . more, I mean . . . you tell me first."

"If there's a bust, you get it."

Flaherty spread the word and the Chicago coppers packed up and left. After they were gone, Walter returned to Mrs. Freundlich's kitchen. He asked the landlady to leave them. After a brief protest and Walter's promise that a glazier would be there before nightfall to repair the window, she withdrew.

"All right, Miss Kolodkin. I think it's time you told me the whole truth. If you don't, you're going to be caught between the police and whoever took the shots."

Natasha Kolodkin had more than recovered. The cup sat empty on the table and her expression fell somewhere between neutral and suspicious. "Unless it was the police who took the shots."

"Why would the police have shot at you?"

"Because the police believe that they decide who is free in their country and who isn't. Because they've used the excuse of the shooting in Buffalo to settle old scores, back from the Haymarket."

"Why would that have anything to do with you?"

"Because I believe as my sister believed . . . to answer your earlier question. As Abe Isaak believes. We are not the ones who advocate violence, Mr. George. We believe in peaceful change, if possible. I cannot say as much for the police."

"Your movement can hardly be described as peaceful, Miss Kolodkin. But even if I accept your assertion, it does not explain why the Chicago police would want to murder you in particular. Unless, of course you are a bigger fish than you pretend."

"I am not a fish at all, Mr. George. I am school teacher who exercises her rights as an American to believe as I wish."

"Then why? Or perhaps it was not the police at all. Perhaps it was the same people who silenced your sister . . ."

"Why? I don't see . . . ."

But Walter saw that she did. He decided not to press, but rather allow the uncertainty to play on her. He stood to leave. "But I've got to get back now and report this to my superiors."

Natasha Kolodkin stood as well, but continued looking at him, trying to decide whether to trust someone she would generally have considered an enemy. A leap of faith by the faithless.

"I was at her rooms six months ago when two men came to see her," she said, before Walter could move for the door. "She knew them. They had obviously been to see her before. She told me later they were members of the movement, but they didn't look like any socialists I'd ever seen. Big men in long coats and Stetsons with trimmed mustaches. But Esther told me I was being silly. That of course they were genuine. When she first met them, they showed her letters from people in New York. I asked to see them, but she said they were private. I was surprised because Esther and I usually had no secrets from each other. She got very reclusive after that. A week later, she quit her job at the library here and told me she was moving to Buffalo."

"And who did you think they were?"

"To me, they looked more like police agents than our people."

"And you told your sister this?"

She nodded. "Esther told me she had checked them out and they were exactly who they said they were."

"Checked them out how?"

"She wouldn't say." She paused for a moment. "All right, Mr. George. I suppose that since I've decided to trust you, I might as well do so completely. Esther was a romantic. She read a great deal about silly women who spent their lives pursuing nothing but wealth and social acceptance. Mrs. Humphrey Ward stories. Henry James. Then she read *Looking Backward* . . ."

"It's Czolgosz's favorite book. He brought a copy to the library in Buffalo to identify himself to your sister."

"Really? Poor Esther. In any event, after she finished the book, she decided she wanted to do something important . . ."

"Her duty?"

"If you like."

"Thank you, Miss Kolodkin."

"There was something else. One of the men . . . the taller of the two, although he was not nearly your size, Mr. George . . . was much friendlier than the other."

"Friendlier to Esther you mean?"

"You know precisely what I mean. And if he had romanced her, I would suspect that he knew in advance with whom he was dealing. Esther, it pains me to say, would be quite capable of acting . . . rashly . . . if a beau had asked her to."

"Unlike her sister?" The words were out before Walter could stop them.

Natasha Kolodkin's expression turned stony. Walter felt sorry for any student who misbehaved in her classroom. "Most certainly unlike her sister," she said evenly.

Walter stifled a cough. "You've helped a great deal."

"About finding out if there was a conspiracy to murder McKinley."

"President McKinley. Your sister as well."

"Do you mean that?"

"Yes. I wouldn't say it if I didn't."

"So you think it was those same two men."

"Not necessarily."

"But possibly. From what you've told me, that's what I'd think. What will you do now?"

Walter suddenly felt his clothes prickle at him. He realized he hadn't changed them in two days. He must look like a saddle tramp. Smell like one too. He got quickly to his feet. "I've got to go now, Miss Koldokin. I'm going to ask my boss to assign an operative to watch you."

"No thank you, Mr. George. A policeman is the last thing I need in my life."

"We're not pol . . . aren't you afraid that whoever did this will try again?"

"When you believe as I do, Mr. George, you are afraid all the time. Don't worry. I'll take care."

"Very well." There was no use arguing with her.

He turned to leave, but she stopped him. "Mr. George?"

"Yes?"

"If you wished to come by occasionally . . . to check on my welfare . . . I suppose that would be all right."

14

Pork tenderloins, buttered beets, and mashed potatoes. Thank you, Lucinda. This is glorious."

"Thank Harry, Walter. I was going make an omelet."

"She's joshing you," Harry growled, hurling an angry glance at his sister. "Lucinda insisted on cooking something you liked."

"An omelet would have been fine," Walter asserted without cracking a smile. "Maybe better, in fact."

"See, Harry?" Lucinda replied, turning for the kitchen to fetch the rolls.

"Aw, to hell with both of you." Harry sawed at his pork as if he wanted to cut through the plate as well.

"Serves you right," Walter said softly. The meat, in fact, hardly needed a knife at all. Lucinda cooked well enough for the Palmer House.

"You're lucky to be here," Harry grumbled through half-chewed pork.

Walter didn't reply, but Harry was right. He probably was.

When Walter returned to his rooms, he had immediately taken a bath and sat soaking for almost an hour. Generally, he could not wait to wash and get out, but this time he found the feel of the water luxurious, even long after it had turned cold. Twice, Andrew Swenson from down the hall had pounded on the door. The first time, Walter ignored him; the second, Walter growled at him to beat it. Swenson, a pinched little man, a high-pressure sales clerk at Marshall Field's who sold eggbeaters and such to Chicago housewives, had slunk on back to his room. He had not dared disturb Walter again.

Eventually, Walter emerged from the tub and folded himself into his bathrobe, blowing out a contented sigh as he patted himself dry. On the way back down the hall, he had wrapped on Swenson's door. For some reason, the gesture amused him and he was chuckling as he walked through his door. His valise was waiting for him but everything in there would have to go to the chink's. And fast too. He only had one clean suit of clothes left. Walter dressed carefully, more carefully than he would have if he had not met Natasha Kolodkin. He liked Lucinda. He truly did.

❖

Lucinda backed through the swinging door to the kitchen with the basket of rolls covered with a white cloth. Wisps of steam seeped through the linen into the air. After she placed the basket on a trivet, she pivoted smartly and disappeared to fetch the butter. Once that was on the table, she poured wine for herself and Walter from a cut glass carafe that had been a gift from her husband's parents, and a beer for Harry. Then she sat down.

"Lucinda," Walter sighed in genuine admiration, "I've seen close order drill that can't measure up to you."

"Army brother, army husband, army father." She swept an errant lock of hair from her forehead. Walter realized, as he always did after not seeing her for a time, just how beautiful she really was. "Daddy was never quite able to hide his disappointment that he had a girl."

"I wouldn't have been disappointed." The words were out of Walter's mouth before he could stop them.

Lucinda turned to him and smiled. Her posture, of course, was perfect, and her teeth straight and white. She always seemed to have a soft blush to her skin. "Why, Walter George, I do believe that's the nicest thing you've ever said to me." Harry speared a beet, trying to remain quiet and inconspicuous. But the grin showed through from under his mustache all the same.

"I'm sure I've paid you compliments before," Walter protested lamely.

"Oh yes. But all of those were quite formal. This one sounds like you actually meant it."

"I did. I meant the others too."

Harry sensed the conversation was about to get awkward, so he jumped in. "Walter got shot at today. Amazing they missed . . . big as he is. I wouldn't have."

Lucinda blanched. She wasn't *that* much of an army wife. "Are you all right, Walter?"

"I'm fine." He told her of the incident, trying to avoid dwelling on his presence in Natasha Kolodkin's parlor. Harry noted the evasion with satisfaction.

"Maybe you might think about not going around alone for a while," he suggested, before Lucinda thought to press the matter.

"No. I think I'm safe enough."

"How can you say that, Walter?" Lucinda leaned toward Walter, caught herself, then pulled back. "Whoever shot at you will likely try again."

"I don't think so, Lucinda. Whichever of us was the target . . . me or the murdered woman's sister . . . was a lot easier target on the street. The sister . . ." He avoided the name, glancing to see if Lucinda noticed. "The sister is a school teacher. An easy mark anytime. And me . . ." Walter chuckled. "Well, I'm pretty hard to miss."

"So what was going on then?"

96

"A message maybe. Someone's way of suggesting I stop nosing around."

"Then you *are* in danger. You'll never stop nosing around."

"So, did you get a line on the murdered woman?" Harry interrupted.

"Maybe." He told Harry of the visit Esther Kolodkin had received from the two men and her subsequent emigration to Buffalo. He left out the part about one of them romancing the murdered woman.

"Six months? You think whoever set this up sent the girl to Buffalo six months ago? That's quite a bit of anticipation. Doesn't make sense."

"Oh, I don't know, Harry," Lucinda interjected. "President McKinley was certain to be at the fair at some point." She glanced at Walter for affirmation.

"That's true, Harry," Walter agreed.

"You've sure changed your tune, Walter," Harry grumbled. "First you're all het up that you're being forced to chase a phony conspiracy and now you're saying not only was there a plot but that it was months in the planning."

"At least Walter knows enough to change his mind when the facts warrant," Lucinda muttered.

"As opposed to me, you mean?"

"Take that any way you like, Harry," she said.

Harry turned back to Walter. Lucinda always made mincemeat of him. "But Czolgosz only met Emma Goldman for the first time a few weeks ago."

"So he says."

"Well, I'd hate to have Hannigan be right, but if the Goldman woman's in on it, then the rest the crew probably is too."

"Whoa, Harry. I didn't say Goldman or old man Isaak or anyone else was in on anything. I'm just following clues and the clues say that there may be a link between Czolgosz, the murdered Kolodkin girl, and some peculiar visitors she had half a year ago."

"Have it your way, Walter," Harry said. He stuffed some potatoes in his mouth and swallowed them instantly. Harry had never gotten over eating in the saddle. "I spoke with Wilkie," he added, the moment the potatoes had passed his windpipe. "McKinley sat up in bed today. Asked for eggs and bacon, but the doctors said not yet. Tough bird, no matter what TR says. McBurney's gonna head back to New York."

"How wonderful," Lucinda said.

"You said it," Harry agreed. "Couple of inches either way and he's a former president. TR's gonna leave too."

"Bet he can't wait."

"True enough. Wilkie said that publicly TR is all full of vinegar about how we have to deal with these foreigners who don't respect our values. Privately though . . ."

"Yeah?"

"Well, Wilkie said TR seems, well, a little disappointed."

Walter grinned.

"Disappointed in what?" Lucinda asked.

"Whaddaya think he's disappointed in, sis? He got there from Vermont and jumped out of the car looking like he was ready to lead a charge. Then he found out that McKinley was going to be fine. Wilkie said TR nodded, took off his glasses, polished them, then asked if the docs were sure. When Wilkie said they seemed sure, TR said how happy he was. I'll bet."

"That's a terrible thing to imply, Harry," Lucinda snapped. "No one wants the President to die."

"Czolgosz did."

"You know what I mean."

"Wilkie might be seeing ghosts," Walter said. "He doesn't like TR anyway." He agreed with Harry, but wasn't going to admit it to Lucinda.

"The feeling is mutual," Harry noted. "Wilkie told me that the McKinley people are closing ranks. Agriculture secretary told reporters 'disaster would have followed' if McKinley had died. TR was in the next room when he said it."

98

"You don't wish a man dead because his friends insulted you," Lucinda insisted, getting angrier and angrier. Walter couldn't figure out why Harry was baiting her.

"Maybe not, sis. But TR is pretty ambitious. Nice move from nobody to the White House."

"Harry, you're an idiot." Lucinda pushed herself up from the table, made to clear some dishes, and marched back to the kitchen.

"See, Walter," Harry offered. "She's got spunk."

"Good judgment too."

"Very funny." Harry craned his neck to make sure Lucinda wasn't coming right back. "But what are you going to do, Walter?"

"About the shots? And all the interest in our movements? Nothing. Somebody's gone to a lot of trouble, Harry. Let's wait for a bit and see what they're up to next."

"That's a ticklish game, Walter. What if you're wrong and they actually did miss by accident?"

"I don't intend to fold my tent because someone murdered a cheap lamp and a German river scene. Besides, you got a better idea? The fastest way to flush out whoever's behind this is to give them their heads. Let them flush themselves out."

Harry downed his beer. "I'll be sure to say nice things at your funeral."

"And I think it's time to find out if Czolgosz had any visitors about six months ago."

"Easy enough. Just hop back on the Lake Shore. He was living at home. Cleveland coppers already talked to the family. They're terrified they're gonna be run out of town because of what the kid did."

"I don't blame them. Want to come, Harry? We can catch the express in the morning. Be back late tomorrow, early Tuesday at the latest."

"Nah. You're better with people than I am, Walter. I'll give you the address."

Walter had originally planned to check in on Natasha Kolodkin. Just to see if she was all right. But Cleveland was a must.

The door to the kitchen swung open and Lucinda returned. She flashed Harry a glare, but he pretended not to notice. Instead, he stretched and got up. "Think I'll mosey on downstairs and have a cigar." Without ever looking her way, he made for the door. Lucinda went from angry to embarrassed as soon as the latch had clicked behind him. She began fussing with the dishes. Walter stood up as well. That was what Harry's baiting her was about—an excuse to leave the two of them alone and allow Walter be the soothing influence to Harry's loudmouthed jerk.

Walter started to reach out to help with the dishes, but instead let his hands drop to his sides. His collar suddenly itched terribly.

Lucinda stopped clearing. "I'm sorry about this, Walter. I know you didn't want to come."

"Nonsense, Lucinda. I always enjoy seeing you."

She smiled. "I hope you're a better liar in your work."

"No. I mean it. I do always enjoy seeing you. It's just that . . ."

"You prefer to be alone."

"It's safer."

"No, Walter, it isn't. Not really."

"Is Harry right, then? Do you . . ." Walter could not figure out how to say it.

"Would I be happy if you wanted me?" She reached out and touched his cheek. Her fingertips felt whispery and warm. "Of course I would, Walter. You know that." She sighed and removed her hand. "I hardly knew Arthur. We were only married six months when he was killed, and for five of those he was across the ocean. He was a decent enough man, I suppose." She looked up at him. "But I know you far better."

Walter did not know what to say. Part of him wanted to tell her that he wanted her too, to sweep her into his arms. But the other part screamed for him not to.

"It's all right, Walter," Lucinda said after a few moments. "It just seems silly to me sometimes . . . two lonely people like us, each of whom could give the other comfort. But both have to feel that way. Perhaps one day you'll decide that it isn't such a bad thing. If you do, I'll be here."

"There's no need for that," Walter offered weakly. "You're a beautiful, wonderful woman. You've no need to wait for a fool like me."

She laughed softly. "Oh, don't I now?" She took him by the elbow. "I think we'd better go and fetch Harry. Otherwise he'll be downstairs, puffing on his stogie, making plans for the wedding."

Walter stopped her. "Lucinda, I . . . I want you to know . . ."

"Yes, Walter?"

He shook his head. "Nothing. Another time."

15

Monday, September 9, 1901

Walter was on the express at six and pulled into the Wheeling and Lake Erie railroad station just before noon. According to the paper Harry had given him, the Czolgosz family lived on Fleet Avenue, about two miles south. Although a line of hansoms waited outside the entrance, Walter decided to walk. He could cover the distance in half an hour, the sky was crisp and blue, and the walk would clear his head. He asked directions from a copper loitering near the entrance to discourage pickpockets. The copper was about to tell Walter he'd better take a coach, but then his eyes swept over Walter's bulk and he merely shrugged.

Walter was unmolested on his walk. In fact, the streets showed no sign whatever of being unsafe. Just different, which was usually enough for coppers. Men with broad mustaches and women with shawls went about their business, Slavic-looking children darted about, and just about every ware and product imaginable was purveyed from pushcarts and in storefronts. The section was called North Broadway, but the street signs were the only indication that Walter was still in America. Residents spoke a polyglot of central and eastern European languages, mostly German; newspaper stands sold primarily German language periodicals; pushcarts and storefronts featured legends written in German; and even the local copper of whom Walter asked directions to Fleet Avenue responded in English heavily German accented. The instant the copper heard to whom Walter was headed, his official face was gone.

"Vhy you vant zem? Ve don' vant trouble here, mister."

"No trouble, officer." Walter was prepared to show his badge but hoped he wouldn't have to.

But the copper had, as Czolgosz would have said, done his duty, and didn't press. As Walter turned to leave, however, the copper did suggest hiring an interpreter before making his visit.

An interpreter? Walter thought. In the United States? No wonder these people are outcasts.

Walter thanked the man, but pushed on alone. He refused to believe that he would encounter a household in which not a single person could communicate in the language of his adopted country.

The Czolgosz family lived a tiny, two-story frame house, which lacked any amenities but was nonetheless clean and in good repair. In a better part of town, the house would have had a copper in front, but not here. No need. These people minded their own business. Although the street in front of the house was devoid of gawkers, there was a steady stream of traffic, both on foot and in carts. Everyone who passed the house glanced at it, and then, if they were walking with someone, whispered once they had gone a few steps down the street. One woman crossed herself.

Although it was mid-morning, the inside shutters were closed and, unless Walter missed his guess, bolted as well. He climbed the three wooden steps, knocked at the door, and waited. After about thirty seconds, he knocked again, this time harder and more insistently. In the window to the left of the door, the shutter opened a crack. Walter couldn't see who was peeking through because the inside was dark. He took out his badge and held it up to the opening. A few moments later, he heard the bolt on the door sliding.

The front door opened to reveal a small man of about fifty-five, dressed in a dark suit. He had hollow cheeks, an immense mustache, and gave the impression of a man every inch of whose body had received abuse or injury in pursuit of an inadequate wage. He held himself with extreme dignity.

"*Guten tag, Herr Czolgosz.*"

Czolgosz was unimpressed with Walter's solicitude. "Vat you vant? Coppers already been here."

"*Ich habe Ihren Sohn gesehen.*" I have seen your son.

"Vhy you speak in German? We in America." Czolgosz made no effort to hide his umbrage at Walter's insult.

"I am German," Walter parried.

Czolgosz stiffened. "Vhat your name?"

"Walter George . . . Pforzmann."

"Ain't you sure?"

"Pforzmann's my real name. I haven't used it since . . . I ran away from the orphanage." This was twice he had mentioned the orphanage to a member of the Czolgosz family. Why did he feel the need to justify himself to them? And even Harry didn't know his real name.

Czolgosz stood rigid, his pale blue eyes boring into Walter. But eventually he relented. Without altering expression, the gnarled immigrant moved to the side, allowing the new copper, the German, the orphan, the new tormentor, to pass on through.

The interior of the Czolgosz home was as the exterior; spare and proud. Czolgosz, whose Christian name was Paul, ushered Walter into a combination dining room and parlor. A plain wooden table covered with a chintz tablecloth was surrounded by six chairs squeezed close together.

Czolgosz gestured with a leathered open hand for Walter to sit. The chair creaked as Walter lightly settled in. Czolgosz called in Polish for his wife to make tea. Walter told him it wasn't necessary, but his German was so rusty that he must have said something else, because Czolgosz looked at him strangely. Then Czolgosz turned and called for Jakob.

Jakob Czolgosz appeared a few seconds later. He was a tiny fellow, older than Leon, with the same pale blue eyes and light hair, already aging prematurely from hard work, bad food, and a hopeless future. He was dressed in workingman's overalls and a faded but clean woolen shirt. He frowned when he saw the intruder sitting at the family's table.

"*Sie sprechen für mich*," father said to son. You speak for me.

Walter briefly filled Jakob in on Leon's status; that he was safe, healthy, and unmolested in the Buffalo jail. But, even though the president was going to be fine, things would go very badly for Leon unless he helped in finding the higher-ups who had initiated the plan for the shooting.

"What plan?" Jakob asked. Only slightest trace of central Europe accented his speech.

Walter told him about the arrests in Chicago and the possibility that Leon had been put up to his act, manipulated, by others. He avoided mentioning Esther Kolodkin or two dark men in long coats. Paul Czolgosz seemed to be following what was said, but he was so stolid that to know for certain was impossible.

"Leon was . . . quiet," Jakob began, as if the trait was a mark of strangeness. "He think a lot."

"He was lazy. Didn' wanna work. Thought he was too good for the rest of us."

A young woman had entered the room, bearing a tray with three cups. She was small, but striking; blonde like the others, her eyes cornflower blue. She had long graceful neck and a full, high bosom.

"*Nicht sprechen!*" Paul Czolgosz thundered.

The girl stood her ground. "But it's true, papa, and you know it is. Leon with his grand ideas has ruined it for the rest of us."

"*Nien!*"

"Leave us to talk, Victoria," Jakob said, far more gently than his father.

Victoria's lip began to quiver and her face flushed. She started to say something to Walter, but instead, after a moment, spun on her heel and stormed from the room. Paul Czolgosz stared after her for a moment, then abruptly stood and stalked out after her.

"She's seventeen," Jakob said by way of explanation.

"Seems to be more than that."

Jakob Czolgosz sighed. "Got her engagement broke yesterday. Carpenter's apprentice. Gonna make good money. His father won't have no Czolgosz in the family."

Walter nodded. There will be a lot of lives changed by what Leon did. Some for the better, including Walter's maybe; most for the worse. Walter spoke with Jakob for about five minutes more. Paul Czolgosz did not return to the room. The tea, barely darker than plain water, sat untouched on the table. Jakob spoke openly, but said nothing. To hear him tell it, Leon lived invisibly, confiding in no one, revealing nothing of himself, and existing without friends or acquaintances. He certainly had no visitors. Walter knew it was eyewash, but there was no means to get at the truth. The family was terrified, convinced that if some plot was discovered, they would be accused of being part of it.

Walter left the Czolgosz home to begin the slog back to Chicago, a day wasted, all the worse for preventing his return visit to East 88th Avenue. He had gone about two blocks when, from around the corner ahead of him, an out of breath Victoria Czolgosz suddenly appeared.

"Papa is not a bad man," she said quickly. "He loves America. He loves Leon too. He think we talk to you, we make it worse."

"And you, Victoria? What do you think?"

"I think if we don't talk to you, we make it worse. I think we got to make everyone believe we love America or we going to be run out of here. Maybe killed."

"*Do* you love America?"

"As much as you do."

Walter nodded. This girl was the brains of the family. Maybe the guts too. "So what do you have to tell me?"

"You was right. Leon was put up to this. He didn' think of it on his own. Leon couldn' think of nothing on his own."

"Do you know or are guessing?"

"I know. People come talk to him."

"What people?"

Victoria gave the same description of the two men as had Natasha Kolodkin. "On the way out they told Leon that when he made up his mind, they was staying at the Stillman."

"Thank you, Victoria. If there's anything you need when this is done . . . any help . . . get in touch with me in Chicago. United States Secret Service office. Just ask for Walter George."

"Not Pforzmann?" She looked up at him with a wry smile. That carpenter's apprentice was a fool, no matter what his father said.

"No, Victoria. Just George."

16

The Stillman was an eight story hotel on Euclid Avenue at Erie Street, less than twenty years old, far more grand than one would ordinarily associate with anarchists. The desk clerk was an ancient fellow, stopped over, with about ten wispy white hairs on a bald head, and a hooked nose as large as a land mass. Walter flashed his badge and clerk raised himself, placing his hands on the surface of the desk, seemingly to prevent his collapsing back downward.

"Do you keep back guest ledgers?"

"Some. How far you thinkin' about?"

"Six months. Maybe a little more."

The man nodded. Everything he did was slow, but seemed thorough. "Got those. They're in the office. Why don't you step around and I'll set you up."

A heavyset matron in a maroon dress and ostrich feather hat had approached the desk with two bellboys dragging four large valises in her wake. She issued a harrumph at the clerk's impending departure.

"Be right back, lady," the clerk said in his monotone. "Hotel'll still be standing five minutes from now."

It took the clerk almost five minutes just to show Walter where the ledgers were kept, on the top shelf of a book case in the office. He asked Walter if he needed help, but Walter assured the man he could manage on his own. Gratefully, the clerk nodded and shambled out the door to deal with the matron. Walter ran his finger along the spines, grabbed the ledgers for the dates in which he was interested and sat at a desk to browse.

As he started leafing through the pages, it occurred to Walter that he had no way of knowing what to look for. Guests signing in didn't write "anarchist plotter" next their names. But perhaps one of the entries would stand out—an anarchist name with which he was familiar. Perhaps just a name that sounded properly foreign. Anything for a starting point.

Walter turned page after page, tedium soon replacing whatever anticipation he might have had at the beginning of the chore. He considered asking the clerk if he remembered two dark men in long coats who had registered about six months ago, but the man didn't seem capable of remembering what he had eaten for breakfast that morning.

He was about the give up the exercise as hopeless when he noticed. One page ended with registrations for February 23 and the next began with February 25. Walter was forced to spread the binding and look deep into the well to see where the page that had been removed had been cut. It was clean, as if done with a razor. No casual perusal would have revealed the gap.

So, sometime between February 23 and 25, well within the period that Victoria Czolgosz had mentioned, the two men had registered in this hotel. But why would someone remove the page? The men could easily have used phony names when they registered. No one could possibly have known. Unless, of course, there had been a blunder; something in the entry that gave away more than was intended. Otherwise, removing the page was just a signpost for anyone trying to trace the men's movements. Only if someone had gotten far enough to try to trace their movements at the Stillman, of course.

After looking through the remainder of the pages to make certain nothing else jumped out him, Walter replaced the ledger and returned to the front desk. The matron had apparently been dispatched to her room. The clerk was attending to a man of about forty in a spiffy checked suit and low topper perched at an angle on his head. Salesman, Walter thought. Walter thanked the clerk and told the old man he was finished with the books. The old man nodded.

"By the way," Walter said, after excusing himself to the man in the suit, "I know you might not remember, but were you working any of the days between February twenty-third and twenty-fifth?"

The clerk put up his hand to the suited man, reached under the counter top and withdrew a calendar from a shelf. It was one of those flip affairs, divided by month, each month with a different scene of Lake Erie on the top. He leafed back to February.

"Yep. That was a Friday to Sunday. Wednesday's my day off."

"Do you mind doing this after I check in?"

A salesman, for sure, Walter thought. He reached into his vest and shoved his badge under the man's nose. "Why don't you just go stand by that pillar and shut up?"

The man stiffened, eyes wide, then nodded stiffly and slunk away. When he was gone Walter asked the clerk if, by some chance, he remembered two large men in long coats and a glowering manner who had checked in about then.

The clerk reached up with a crooked finger and scratched the top of his head. "Two men, you say? Dark? Hmm, give me some time."

I'll die of old age, thought Walter. "While you're thinking, why don't you help the gentleman who's waiting and I'll talk to the bell captain."

Walter walked to the stand at the far side of the lobby, where a red-haired man with steel posture, dressed in a gray uniform, was standing. The bell captain looked as if he belonged in a uniform, although not necessarily one of a hotel employee.

"Army?" Walter asked.

"Navy. I was an ensign aboard the *Olympia*."

"Admiral Dewey's flagship. Congratulations. You at Manila Bay?"

The man shook his head. "Mustered out in '96. Missed all the fun. What about you?"

"Army. Six years. Ate a lot of dust in the Dakotas."

"Got to kill some Indians at least."

"Yeah. I did. You working here six months ago?"

The man nodded. "Past two years."

Walter started to remove his badge, but the man shook his head. "I saw. Secret Service, huh? Pretty nice duty. You guys hiring?"

Walter shrugged. "All that's done out of Washington. I'm just a flunky." He leaned in closer. False intimacy had jogged many a memory. "I'm trying to get the lowdown on two hombres who stayed here between February twenty-third and the twenty-fifth." Walter issued the description.

The bell captain laughed. "Them. Sure, I remember. Smith and Jones." He sniffed. "Think they could have announced any louder that the names were phonies."

"Did anyone ask?"

"Course not. Lots of people don't give their right names at hotels. You should know that more than me. Besides, they paid up front. Twenty dollar gold piece. Told Alfred there they'd be here about a week, maybe more. If they left early, Alfred could keep the change."

"Alfred didn't seem to remember them."

"Alfred remembers the shoes he was wearing in '56. He probably figured you were after the gold piece. He didn't exactly share the information with the manager."

"How come you know?"

"I suggested he share it with me."

"I see. Thanks." Walter started back across the lobby.

"Hey, mister."

Walter turned back.

"They really hire out of Washington or were you just putting me off?"

Walter turned and walked back to the desk.

"I want to know about Smith and Jones, Alfred."

The clerk shot a daggered glare toward the bell captain. He suddenly looked remarkably younger. Then he turned back toward Walter, again the old man. "You know, my memory ain't what it was . . ." He threw a glance toward Walter's pocket.

Walter reached in and extracted two bits. Alfred refused to look up. Walter turned toward the bell captain, who wiped the grin off his face instantly. Walter withdrew another two bits.

"They was loud," Alfred noted after sweeping the coins off the counter top and depositing them in his pants pocket. "Drank a lot. One day they tried to lock the maid in their room with them. Nigger woman. Fifty years old with five kids. Manager was just about to throw them out when they upped and left on their own. Middle of the night. Snuck out the back. Didn't matter much though. They had five dollars left from the double eagle."

"And the register. Any chance they removed the page before they went?"

Alfred shook his head. "None. Had to be done later. Most likely after the register book was full and we'd switched to a new one."

"And they never came back."

"Nope."

"So these two register under phony names, make enough of a fuss that everyone can't help but notice them, then sneak out even though their bill is more than paid, get someone to carefully razor out the record of their stay, even though the register page wouldn't have helped track them down." Walter had a thought. "Do you remember if they put down where they came from in the register?"

The old man laughed. "Yeah. They wrote 'Mexico.'"

"Why's that funny?"

"Mister, those two weren't no Mexicans."

"They might have come from there."

"Don't think so. I think they came from Washington."

"State or D.C."

"D.C."

"Why?"

"Cause they sent a telegram. Got a couple too."

"Were they delivered here?"

The old man shook his head. "Fifth Street telegraph office. They left instructions there to hold any incomings. But when they didn't show for three days, the boy brought it here."

"Why would he do that?"

"Dunno. Must have thought they wanted him to."

"How did Smith and Jones take it when they found out?"

"Got all tight lipped, but didn't say nothin'."

Walter blew out a breath. "They did everything but use a megaphone."

"Weren't too inconspicuous, that's for sure. I'll tell you what, mister. I think they was supposed to be quiet about their visit, but when whoever sent them found out how much a spectacle they made of themselves, they sent some other folks to try and cover the tracks. Worked too. Until now."

"Yeah," Walter mused. "Until now."

Walter left the Stillman to head for the telegraph office. Something stunk. Two things, actually. First off, while it seemed that Wilkie had been right about Czolgosz not working alone, the notion that a bunch of skulking anarchists had set this up didn't make any sense. But if not them, who? Second, no matter what anyone said, the trail was pretty damn easy to follow. Oh sure, if the Czolgosz girl hadn't run after him, he wouldn't have know about the Stillman, but six months should have left the smell a lot colder than it was. Of course, it was possible that the hombres in the coats hadn't felt the need to be subtle, knowing it'd be months before anyone starting looking for them and by that time the trail would have been covered by a lot of dead bodies.

Walter had an idea. On instinct, he spun on his heel and headed back to the hotel. As he turned the corner, he ran smack into the salesman in the checked suit. The man jumped, a shocked look on his face. "You again?" he croaked. "What'd I do this time?"

"Nothing," Walter replied. He was about to let the man pass, but instead took him by the lapel. "I thought you wanted to get to your room?"

"I did. I was just going out to get something to eat." The man spoke quickly. But he was, after all, a salesman.

"Where's good?"

"Place called Emilio's two blocks down. I-talian fellow. Makes them noodles in hot sauce."

"Maybe I'll try it."

"I can recommend it highly, mister. Love that I-talian grub." An ephemeral smile popped on his face.

"You come to Cleveland often?"

The man puffed up. "Every other week. Sell linen, right from Ireland. Best quality there is. Tablecloths, drapes, suits . . . just ask for Tony Torrence in any dry goods store in Ohio."

Tony Torrence. Dry goods. Walter studied the man's face. Fleshy, clean shaven, brown eyes, brown hair with flecks of gray at the temples, long straight nose with nostrils that looked like triangles.

Walter let him go. Tony Torrence strolled down the street as Walter watched. He turned back for a second, flashing a salesman's come-on smile. "Remember, mister. Emilio's."

Sorry, Tony, Walter thought. I'm not going to have time for Emilio's.

17

H arry, this just doesn't make sense."

Harry took a pull on his lager. O'Brian's was his favorite tavern in Chicago because they poured cold, clear beer in iced mugs and didn't make him pay.

"It is odd, Walter." Harry seemed in fine spirits. Much as he liked Walter, it didn't bother him much to see his balloon popped every once in while.

"Fuck you, Harry."

Harry chuckled, then got serious. "Okay, but actually it is. Are these guys professionals or amateurs? They seem a little of each."

"Right. That's what I'm saying. They clearly had a role in setting this all up, picked Czolgosz who would 'do his duty' and keep his mouth shut, and then were slick enough to get rid of Esther Kolodkin in a way not easy to trace. Then they leave a trail a mile wide until the telegraph office, when all of a sudden it goes dead. All the records for February were gone. Which is just like at the hotel. Somebody must have done it afterwards."

"Which means this is bigger than what we're seeing."

"Bigger and stranger. I walked into that telegraph office like they meant me to find it. The big fuss at the hotel. The twenty dollar gold piece. Then making such a stink about the telegrams at the front desk. Even making sure the clerk knew they were from Washington. Then no records, no one remembers anything, no way to trace them."

"Maybe they were just having some fun. Maybe they didn't care about the trail they left because they knew it ended in a blind alley."

"Does that sound right to you?"

"No."

"I didn't think so."

"But it could mean that whoever was watching us in Buffalo is connected to Smith and Jones."

"Yeah. And that leads to the question of connected how?" Walter grunted and tossed down his Pabst. "Doesn't seem like any anarchists I've ever heard of."

"Yeah, but maybe there are anarchists out there that we haven't heard of. A bunch that's smart enough not to leave calling cards wherever they go."

"Maybe," Walter agreed. "But let's do it your way. Say they weren't going to let anyone outside their movement find them so easily. After all, if Czolgosz did what he was supposed to, they'd hang for sure, and they picked someone who they didn't think would talk first. But why were they so secretive with their own? They *never* do that."

"We don't know they were secretive with their own."

"Certainly seems that way. And the way they looked and talked? No accents? Long coats? Phony names? Have you ever seen anarchists behave like that before? They always want to make sure *everybody* knows what they did."

"Yeah, but there's a first time for everything, Walter. Maybe this was a big enough deal that they used some brains instead of a megaphone.

Maybe this was one time when they *didn't* want to announce what they was up to."

"Maybe," Walter muttered. "But to me, they sound more like a couple of Pinkertons than some Russian or German fanatics."

"Whoa, Walter, you're not going back to that, are you? If it was Pinkertons, it could just as easily been our guys."

"Not necessarily."

"Don't treat me like I'm dumb, Walter. Once it ain't anarchists, then it could be anyone . . . and I know you're still on Foster and Ireland in your head."

"Well, you may hate to admit it, Harry, but until we either figure out why they messed up so bad, or we find someone else to hang it on, they've got to stay in the mix."

Harry knew it was true, but wasn't going to make it more true by admitting Walter was right. Instead, he changed the subject. "By the way, what did you say to Lucinda when I went down to smoke the cigar?"

Walter's head snapped up. "Lucinda? Nothing, Harry. I swear. Why? Was she mad at me?"

Harry shook his head. "Just the reverse." His eyes narrowed. "I know she can be a pain, Walter, but she's still my little sister."

"I know, Harry. I'd never do anything . . . what'd she say?"

Harry shook his head. "Forget it. Probably just making stuff up in her head."

"Making *what* up?"

"I said forget it, Walter."

"Hey, wait a minute, Harry. What are you complaining about? This was your idea. Weren't you the one who threw her at me?"

Harry's gaze darkened. "Watch yourself, Walter."

Walter heaved a sigh. "Harry, I'll tell you for the last time. If I was thinking about getting involved, Lucinda would be at the top of my list. But I'm not. And she knows I'm not."

"Planning on questioning the dead girl's sister again?"

Walter turned to order another beer, although the one in front of him was not quite empty.

"That's what I thought," Harry muttered.

"It's nothing, Harry," Walter protested lamely.

"As long as it stays nothing."

Now Walter needed the change of subject. "Didn't Hannigan say that Isaak thought Czolgosz was a police agent?" He glanced to Harry to see if it took. Harry was staring down at the bar and, from the glower on his face, he was not thinking good thoughts.

"Maybe I'll go chat with him," Walter continued.

"Can't hurt."

"You set it up with Hannigan?"

Harry lifted his head. "You don't need me, Walter. Just use your charm."

18

Tuesday, September 10, 1901

A be Isaak was being held at the Central Police Station downtown, along with the others that Hannigan had swept up in a raid on the Isaak home on Carroll Avenue. As Hannigan promised, twelve anarchists were now in custody, with a city-wide hunt out for Emma Goldman, who was known to be in Chicago but had managed to stay underground.

The captain had an office at the Central Station as well, although he spent little time there. It lacked both the opulence and the secretary of the office at City Hall. But, with reporters from across the United States parked there, clamoring for information on the anarchist plot to assassinate the president, Hannigan was certain not to be anywhere else. The previous day he had given an exclusive to Wilkie's old paper, the *Chicago Daily Tribune*, which extolled his efforts in bringing the conspirators to justice. The captain had been quoted as saying that "when Czolgosz went

119

to Buffalo on his murderous mission, he was the agent of this group of Chicago conspirators."

With his name in print as a protector of the nation, Hannigan was quite chipper when Walter was shown into his office, a small cubicle at the far end of the second floor. Instead of the pert, young brunette, opening the door for Walter was a white-haired, bulbous-nosed patrolman ready for his pension.

"Hello, George," Hannigan enthused. He always looked unnatural when he smiled, as if his facial muscles were being asked to perform a task for which they had not been trained. "Anyone take a shot at you on the way over here?"

Walter shook his head. "Sorry to disappoint."

"Not disappointed at all, George. We in the Chicago police department understand the value of having our very own contingent from the Secret Service Division to help us in our labors. What can I do for you this morning? Found a phony greenback in your pay envelope?"

"I want to talk to Isaak."

"Which one? We got four of them. Daughter ain't half bad to look at. And seeing how they believe in free love and all . . ."

"The father."

Hannigan spread his hands wide, palms up. He looked like he was waiting for someone to drop coins into them. "If that's what you want. Sure you wouldn't rather have the daughter? I'll get you a private room."

"The father."

Hannigan made to sigh. "If you insist. But he ain't gonna talk to you. These maniacs are tough nuts, I'll say that for them. If I didn't find out anything, you ain't gonna."

"No, probably not. But what if I take a shot anyway?"

Hannigan hauled himself out of the chair. "I'll take you to his cell myself."

"How about I use an interrogation room. And it might be best if you weren't around."

Hannigan was pleased to avoid leaving his office, particularly since Walter had passed a writer for the *North American Review* in the lobby who had just arrived to speak with Chicago's famous captain of detectives.

Walter was escorted to a room in the basement by another Chicago copper who didn't bother to acknowledge his presence. "Interview room" was often a euphemism for where coppers gave prisoners the third degree, but it would have to do. Walter didn't want to speak with Isaak in a cell.

The Isaak family was new in Chicago, having arrived just a year before from Portland, Oregon, where Abe, Sr. had published his rag, then called the *Firebrand*. Like most anarchist publications, it advocated a combination of provocative politics and loose morals. Word around town was that Isaak had relocated east to seek a larger audience for his venom, but Walter had also heard, albeit from the coppers, that he had been asked to leave, and none too politely, by the Portland brass. Isaak was generally referred to as "the old man" to differentiate him from his son, Abe, Jr., who Hannigan had also hauled in but who was being held separately. Walter was therefore expecting a grizzled, white-haired, wild-eyed revolutionary. What he got was a small, well-dressed man in his forties with a trim mustache and hair combed in a pompadour.

Isaak seemed to be like many short men who had cultivated excellent posture in order to wring every possible inch out of their limited stature. But he entered the room bent slightly forward and to the left. Hannigan's work. Ham-fisted blows to the stomach and kidneys. Nothing that would show, and all of which could be denied if the victim chose to make a stink to the newspapers. Even bent over, however, Isaak had ceded none of his dignity to his surroundings. A man accustomed to harsh treatment by the authorities. Isaak lowered himself into his chair, making contact delicately with the hard wooden bottom. Apparently Hannigan had used his boot as well.

Walter would learn nothing unless he separated himself from those whom Isaak would think his colleagues. He slouched into the chair across the table, keeping as far back as he could to minimize the size difference.

"I'm sorry, Mr. Isaak," he began in a soft voice. "The Chicago police are unfortunately prone to unprofessionalism."

A small, mirthless smile formed in the corners of Isaak's mouth. "On the contrary. I found Captain Hannigan exceedingly professional. Do I take it that you are not from the Chicago police?" Only a trace of an accent was present in his speech. But not German. Farther east.

"You're Russian?" Walter asked.

"Very good. Yes, although I've lived in this country for twenty years."

"Did you leave because of political reasons or religious ones?"

Isaak cocked his head to one side. "Are you considering writing a monograph on persecution?"

"No. I simply wish to understand you. It will help me to determine if I believe you had no part in this."

"Why should I care what you believe?"

"I might be able to help you."

"Oh, yes. I'm certain of that. But you didn't answer my question. You are not of the Chicago police?"

"No. I'm with the United States Secret Service Division."

"And your name?"

"Walter George."

"Ah yes. I read about you. The counterfeiting case. This seems to be out of your bailiwick."

"We protect the president as well."

"Not too effectively, judging from recent events."

"I don't believe you're in the position to be flip, Mr. Isaak."

"Why? Do you think my manner will have any effect on whether or not I am railroaded into prison or to the gallows?"

"Perhaps not. But your candor might."

"My candor? You certainly make every effort to separate yourself from others in your profession, Mr. . . . . George, was it not?"

"Yes. And you didn't answer my question. Why did you leave Europe? I've read how difficult it is for Jewish people in Russia. Was that the reason?"

"It is indeed difficult for Jews in Russia, although that had nothing to do with me."

"You've renounced your faith?"

"Judaism? You assumed I'm a Jew? Like that damn Jew whore Goldman? That's how it's generally expressed."

"With a name like Abraham Isaak, it seemed a reasonable assumption."

"Reasonable, perhaps, but totally incorrect. As it happens, I was born an Anabaptist. A Mennonite. I don't suppose you know what a Mennonite is though . . . we're like the . . ."

"The Amish."

"Not entirely, but close enough. Both Mennonites and the Amish are pacifists is what I believe you are saying."

"Yes. Then you *have* given up your faith."

"Altered it to fit the circumstances in which I find myself. As you are doing with me now." Isaak shifted in his chair. The movement made him wince but he seemed angry with himself for showing pain. "And I must say, your performance has been excellent. I cannot remember being questioned by someone so articulate. You seem misplaced in your profession."

"I don't think so."

"Don't you? Very well. But perhaps we could get to cases."

Walter nodded. "All right. You told Hannigan that you thought Leon Czolgosz was a police agent. You said you published it in *Free Society* the week before the president was shot. I looked through the issue. There is only a general warning that your movement has been infiltrated by spies. If you thought Czolgosz was one of them, why not say so?"

"Because we merely had suspicion. Unlike you, we do not accuse people simply on the possibility that they might be an enemy."

"What was the foundation of your suspicion? If you don't mind telling me."

"Not at all. I find it refreshing to talk to a policeman who is not trying to beat the answers out of me."

"Thank you."

Isaak blinked. "We suspected Czolgosz was a police agent because of his eagerness."

"Aren't all your converts eager?"

"We are not a religion. We don't have 'converts.' But to answer your question, Czolgosz displayed an eagerness well beyond what a normal man would. We assumed that he was either insane or acting for someone else. The latter seemed the more likely prospect."

"That's all?"

"No. Subsequently we received . . . information that Czolgosz was not the least bit insane."

"Information from whom?"

"'Whom?' Bravo, Mr. George. We have a wide circle of friends. Wider than I think you would expect. Many supposedly 'patriotic' Americans are disgusted at the way this country represses workers, women, Negroes, and even Jews and Mennonites."

"And your information said that Czolgosz was a put-up. Who was he supposedly working for?"

Isaak shrugged. "I can't do all your work for you. But someone important."

"Or perhaps you're simply trying to deflect suspicion from yourself and your followers. Perhaps you know that, even though the president survived, you're all probably going to spend the next twenty years in the penitentiary."

"Prison does not frighten me. Prison is, in fact, quite a fertile landscape. I can work for the betterment of society there as well as anywhere else."

"Easy to say from out here."

"No. It isn't. But ask yourself this, Mr. George. What have we to gain by having one boy, whom most will dismiss as a lunatic, execute a man even as odious as McKinley? The answer is, we gain nothing unless we let the world know that we are the strong right arm of the people and have struck the blow. When Alexander Berkman attacked that pig Henry Frick, no one denied the gesture. Quite the contrary."

"You didn't admit the Haymarket."

"No. For the simple reason that we had nothing to do with it. The Haymarket was a frame-up. As is this."

"If you are so clever, then, perhaps you might suggest a substitute."

Isaak gave an exaggerated shrug. "Maybe it was Roosevelt."

Before he realized what he was doing, Walter had reached across the table and landed a backhanded slap on Isaak's cheek. Isaak went sailing from his chair.

Walter froze. His fingers suddenly felt thick, inflexible. He could not stop staring, wide-eyed, at the man crumpled on the floor. He had never hit a prisoner before. Never. He wanted to rush and help Isaak up, but he couldn't move. These were people who wanted to destroy America, he tried to tell himself. Who murdered their enemies. Set bombs to kill the innocent.

But Isaak didn't need Walter's help. He pushed himself to his feet lifted the chair off the floor and sat down, again facing Walter across the table. A speck of blood was at the corner of his mouth. Without taking his eyes from his adversary, Isaak removed a small handkerchief from the pocket of his waistcoat. The square of white cloth had several brown blemishes that Walter knew to be dried blood. Isaak slowly and deliberately blotted the corner of his mouth and then, after a brief glance at the newest stain, returned the handkerchief to his pocket.

"Well, Mr. George," he said evenly, but with a note of triumph, "it seems as if you are not so different from the others after all."

19

Roosevelt? Ridiculous. There wasn't a man in America who was more admired. To Walter, and to millions of others, TR *was* America—brave, resourceful, honorable, willing to achieve great things over enormous odds.

Yes, it might be true that TR and McKinley didn't like each other very much, but Chester Arthur and James Garfield didn't much like each other either—and Arthur had been forced on Garfield just like TR had been forced on McKinley—but no one had said after Garfield was shot that Arthur had been behind it. And you don't have to like someone to work well with them. He had been lucky with Harry, but he when he served in the Dakotas, he couldn't stand Colonel Ashcroft but they worked together just fine.

TR. Fuck you, Isaak.

Impossible.

Unless it wasn't.

It had been there from the first, of course, not as a serious hypothesis, but as a logical possibility, the sort of thing that just rattles around for a little while before being dismissed. If McKinley had been a private citizen, running a business, say, and his second in command wanted the job, when he was shot, the first person everyone would have looked at was the guy with the most to gain. And no man stood more to gain from McKinley's death than Theodore Roosevelt.

Walter strode away from the Central Station, the permutations playing in his head despite his attempts to banish them. But, as Walter knew all too well, for him, there would be no banishment of a plausible theory until it had been disproved. His mind was simply not made that way. The question would remain. Could the vice president of the United States have truly been responsible for an attempt on the life of the president?

If TR *had* been behind the plot, the two men who approached Czolgosz and Esther Kolodkin would therefore have been in his employ, or at least in the employ of his agent. And what about Foster and Ireland? Their behavior at the Temple of Music had seemed inexplicable. Harry may not have wanted to hear it, but the pair could not have been more incompetent in their duty than if they had been *trying* to get McKinley killed. And it didn't sound like the two men who approached Esther Kolodkin were Foster and Ireland. The descriptions didn't match—Ireland was fair-skinned with freckles. That meant a wider conspiracy, which fit what they knew. In any case, the aim was clear—to blame the anarchists.

Could Hannigan have been in on the frame-up? Unlikely. No one would trust him with a secret of that magnitude, or of any magnitude actually. But Hannigan would be the perfect dupe. He would cruise around Chicago grabbing up every anarchist that he could find. He would say the right things to the newspapers. There was no need to take someone like that into your confidence. TR's men—if they were TR's men—could move about secure in the knowledge that Hannigan, and other Hannigans throughout the nation, would sweep America's enemies and deposit them in front of judges and juries who would find them guilty if they had been so much as taking a deep breath on September 6. No sane law enforcement official would dare place himself in the path of such a hurtling locomotive.

Almost none, at any rate.

To test the theory, Walter would have to work backward from Smith and Jones, although there would certainly be intermediaries between them and whoever employed them. No one in power—certainly not TR—would have been dumb enough to hire those guys personally.

The swagger the two had demonstrated in Cleveland, almost daring someone to guess who they were, and then cutting off the trail at the telegraph office, certainly sounded like lawmen or Pinkertons. Military? Maybe. Since the Philippines, a lot of army guys had developed swagger. And, of course, TR . . .

Then, of course, there was Wilkie. TR and Wilkie seemed to dislike each other, but in Washington, alliances and allegiances shifted like so many leaves in a breeze. The president didn't want a witch-hunt, but Wilkie, and Mark Hanna for that matter, expressed no such reservations. But those questions could wait. This was a problem that would need to be solved from the bottom up, not the top down.

And finally, what to do about Harry? Walter could hardly share any of this with him. Harry would think it subversive, to say nothing of half-witted. And Walter wasn't certain Harry wouldn't be right. Hell, he wanted Harry to be right. But not to tell Harry was to expose his friend to great risk. A lot more was at stake than their jobs. Yet for the moment, it seemed, Harry would have to proceed in blissful ignorance. Walter wasn't about to allow Harry to be dragged down with him.

Every scenario has its serendipity, however. In this case, it seemed that the best place for Walter to begin tracing the two provocateurs was with the only person in Chicago known to have seen them. Harry would be furious, of course, but that wasn't such a bad thing. His possessiveness of Lucinda would prevent him from even beginning to guess the reason for the visit. Or at least one of the reasons.

◆

Walter learned from a cooing Mrs. Freundlich that Natasha taught four blocks away. He wasn't keen on bursting into a primary school and certainly didn't fancy interrupting her classes—poor children should get every minute of schooling they could—but an inquiry into the attempted assassination of a president definitely was sufficient cause. As he closed the distance between her rooms and the school, he felt his palms grow sweaty and his breath came in big gulps.

He turned the corner. The school was just up the street. Walter could see a set of double iron doors on his side. But when he arrived at those doors and read the sign over them, he froze. Natasha Kolodkin did not teach in a school. She taught at the St. Catherine of Siena orphanage.

Walter stood, staring at the entrance, unable to will himself to push open the door. He could wait to see Natasha, he decided, until evening, or the next day, or anytime that didn't require him to set foot inside that building. He tried to turn and leave, but he couldn't look away from the sign. He began taking small steps backward when the door opened. A nun emerged. She was young, no more than twenty-five, with olive skin, brown eyes, and the air of placidity that comes when one is certain one serves God.

Her first reaction at seeing the immense, gawking, bearded stranger was to draw back as well. She remained in the entryway, unwilling to venture out even a step. After a moment, Walter realized that if he didn't say something, the sister would duck back into the building and call the police. Then it would all come tumbling down then. Hannigan would probably haul in Natasha, and Harry would be furious for him two-timing Lucinda. Walter forced out some words.

"I'm with the United States Secret Service, ma'am." His voice sounded scratchy, artificial. "I need to speak with one of your teachers. Lay teachers."

The nun nodded but her suspicions were not allayed. "You have identification, officer?"

Walter nodded stiffly. He fumbled into his coat and brought out his badge. The sister leaned forward a bit, as to examine it, although from the distance at which she stood, she would have been unable to tell a real badge from a phony.

"Very well," she said finally, her mouth pinched, "but you'll need to speak with Mother Superior."

Walter moved toward the entrance, stiff, his knees hardly bending, but he was unable to lubricate his joints. A few moments later, without being completely aware of how he got there, he found himself standing in the Mother Superior's outer office. A secretary sat entering information into a large journal, refusing to look up. The inner door opened and another nun walked out.

The Mother Superior was tiny, old, with skin that glowed, almost translucent. She appeared to move within an aura of her own. Walter stared for a moment at the network of greenish-blue veins that ran just under the skin at her temples. When he finally looked to her eyes, he saw they were green, placid, without fear. Sister Ernestine, Mother Superior at St. Marguerite's, had appeared much the same. She was likely dead by now. Had she taken her guilt to grave?

Walter was jarred when the Mother Superior spoke. "You wish to speak with one of our teachers, officer?" she asked. Her voice barely cleared a whisper, but could have been heard across a room.

"Yes, ma'am. Natasha Kolodkin."

At the mention of the name, a small beneficent smile passed across the Mother Superior's face. Small crinkles appeared in the corners of her mouth. "Natasha, yes. She is one of our most treasured possessions. A gift from God. And please call me, Sister Helena, officer."

A gift from God who doesn't believe in Him, Walter thought. "Please call me . . . Walter," he said to the nun.

"This is important, Walter? Enough to interrupt school?"

"Yes, ma'am. It shouldn't take more than a few minutes." Walter's voice sounded to him somehow higher in pitch, a boy's voice.

Sister Helena nodded slowly. "Very well. I will take you myself."

She led him out the door, a tiny nun with the massive man slightly in her wake. Walter, twelve, being led to . . .

A chill permeated the halls, even in early September, but still Walter felt himself perspiring. It began under his arms and around his collar, but he soon felt himself drenched. His heart began to pound sufficiently that he felt the throb in his ears. He could not keep his gaze in one place. He began glancing about furtively. Was there a priest? He took in the location of each staircase and door, in case he was forced to flee. He tapped his forearm against the Colt to make certain it was still there. After a moment, the hall began to sway before him, as if he were looking at it through liquid. The nuns walking the halls glanced at the huge intruder behaving so erratically, but they were too well trained to gape, especially since he was with the Mother Superior.

Finally, they reached a room at the far end of the building. Walter saw a classroom filled with happy-looking urchins, all about eight or ten, who had been scrubbed and dressed to the limits of St. Catherine's limited resources. As Sister Helena entered the room, he scoured the student population looking for . . . what? Himself?

A moment later, Natasha Kolodkin emerged. The Mother Superior had remained in the room to tend to the children. Natasha was dressed simply, in a blue frock buttoned to the neck. She wore no bonnet or scarf. She stiffened when she saw Walter.

"Is something wrong, Mr. George?"

He shook his head stiffly. "No. But I need to speak with you."

"Are you ill then?"

Walter shook his head again. "But could we speak outside? The air in here . . ."

She nodded. "Of course." To Walter's relief she turned the other way from whence he had come, toward a door at the end of the hall, just a few feet away. The door led to a side street. Once they were outside, Walter began to draw in deep breaths.

"You're certain you're feeling well, Mr. George?"

"Yes. It was nothing."

"It was hardly nothing."

Walter's breathing returned to normal and once again, he realized how beautiful Natasha Kolodkin was. Far more so than he had thought when he had first seen her. "Do the sisters know of your . . ." He searched for a way to complete the sentence.

"My political beliefs? My lack of, shall we say, piety? Yes, they know. But Sister Helena cares only for the children. She told me that as long as I do well by them, I am welcome in St. Catherine's."

"Very ecumenical of her."

"You don't think much of the sisters? Is that why . . ."

"I grew up in one of those places."

"I see."

"I ran away."

"Were the sisters mean to you?"

"No." Then, before she could ask another question, "Miss Kolodkin, I need a more exact description of the two men who visited your sister."

"I don't understand."

"The color of their eyes. Their hair. How they moved. Was there anything unusual about either of them? Any scars? Odd habits."

"No scars. But one of the men . . . not the one who played up to Esther . . . had a habit of twirling his key chain on his finger . . . you know, let it swing around until it was wound up one way, then swinging it back."

"That's good. What I meant. Was there anything else? Any detail will help."

"You think you know who they are?"

"No. But if I can get a more precise description, I may know where to look for them."

"You don't think they were our people, do you? Who then?"

"I'm not certain what to think. I'm trying to find out."

"I don't understand something, Mr. George."

"What?"

"Why would you go to all this trouble to prove Abe Isaak innocent? That's what you would be doing, after all. Even more than that, it doesn't take a genius to figure out that if the two men were merely posing as anarchists, they would likely be our enemies."

"I would simply like to know the truth."

"Wherever it leads?"

"Yes."

"All right, Mr. George. Would a picture of the men help?"

"Of course. But where will you get a picture?"

"I'll draw you one. I teach the children art as well."

20

W here you been?" Walter had left Harry word that he would meet him at their office on La Salle, but had not given any other information.

"I was checking something out." Walter stood just inside the door of the tiny private office Harry rated as head of the bureau. The other six members of the squad shared the slightly larger office out front. Since Wilkie came in, only the head office in Washington spent more than six bits a year on accoutrements.

Harry leaned his chair back, balancing perfectly on the back legs. He tapped the fingers of his right hand on his thigh. "'Checking something out?' Kind of vague, isn't it, Walter?"

"I don't want to talk about it yet. Give me a day or two."

"I don't want to pull rank on you, Walter, but last time I looked, you worked for me."

"Don't crowd me, Harry. I'll tell you when I'm able."

"All right, Walter. But you'd better be able soon." Harry stood and grabbed his skimmer from the hat rack. "Now come with me."

"Where are we going?"

"To where we don't belong."

A landau was waiting at the curb when Walter and Harry emerged, gleaming black with gold trim, much the same as Mark Hanna's coach in Buffalo. The driver didn't budge from his perch, but Harry gestured for them to get in.

"You have a good a night at poker?" Walter asked.

"It isn't mine."

"Thanks, Harry. I would never have figured that out. Whose is it?'

"Our host's."

"And our host is meeting us where?"

"You'll see when we get there. Didn't you just tell *me* not to crowd *you*?"

The coach turned on 16th Street toward the lake and suddenly Walter knew their destination. "Prairie Avenue?"

"Yeah. We've been summoned."

Prairie Avenue was the wealthiest street in Chicago, rivaling New York's Fifth Avenue for sheer ostentation. After the Great Fire had devoured many of the city's stateliest homes, many of Chicago's Brahmins had moved to the near South Side to rebuild, settling near the lakefront. A six-block stretch of the avenue south of 16th Street was now Chicago's millionaire's row.

As soon as they turned toward the lake from Wabash, Harry played tour guide. "See that one. That's Amour, the meat packer. And there's Marshall Field's. That one across the street is Pullman."

Walter kept his mouth shut and let Harry have his fun, although he had been down this street before. One Sunday about three years ago, he had rented a hansom just to see where Chicago's richest had dropped their roots. Amour, Pullman, Field, Kimball. The next day, Walter had gone to the library and looked them up. Each had been in his late twenties when the Civil War broke out, but not one of them had served a day in the army. They stayed home and amassed millions from war commerce while other, less enlightened Americans went off to places like Antietam and Chancellorsville and did the dying. Now Marshall Field lived in a mansion as big as his store and Phillip Pullman in one as long as one of his trains. Maybe the Reds had a point, after all.

"We're going to that one there," Harry said, pointing to a massive, three-story brick building with a mansard roof, set back from the road and serviced by a hundred-foot circular driveway. "It's Hawkesworth's."

"The banker." Anthony Hawkesworth, another of America's tycoons born in the 1830s who avoided the army, was chairman of the board of the Merchants' Bank of Chicago. He had his finger in almost as many pies as Morgan in New York, and had personally paid for an army of Pinkertons to break a potential strike at the stockyards three years before. William McKinley had paid a call of fealty to Hawkesworth before each of his campaigns for the presidency.

The coach pulled up at the top of the circle and a Negro in black and gold livery opened the door. "You are expected, gentlemen," he said standing aside, with an accent that was distinctly British.

The front door was opened by another Negro servant and Walter and Harry were ushered into the most opulent hall Walter had ever seen. The ceiling was fifteen feet high. A crystal chandelier at least seven feet across hung from a recess in the center. The floor was tiled in white marble with veins of blue and green. Side tables of exotic wood set along the walls shone of highly polished lacquer, and the wallpaper was rich green silk. A tapestry depicting a medieval pastoral scene hung from a side wall.

Walter felt foolish in his three-dollar work suit and dollar-fifty boots, but Harry seemed unconcerned at the contrast of his appearance with that of the room in which they stood. He looked around and grinned, his pomaded pate reflecting the light. "Walter," he whispered, "if we worked until we was eighty, I don't think we could afford a single thing we see here."

From the far door, another retainer entered the room, this man white and dressed in a tailed suit. "Mr. Hawkesworth will see you in the library," he said in a voice smooth as cream.

The library was a thirty-foot walk from a door at the far left. Hawkesworth's home made Milburn House, where the president was recovering, seem like a hovel. Here was true wealth, ruling-the-nation wealth.

Anthony Hawkesworth was seated behind a desk when Harry and Walter were ushered in. The desk was an immense rosewood affair, large enough for Harry to sleep on, but seemed antlike inside the cavernous library. Shelves, floor to twelve-foot ceiling, lined three walls and yet not a single space seemed unoccupied. Blue, green, and red leather spines shone as if they had been just individually polished. Walter felt himself gawk. All these books, all this learning, available to the owner at the flick of a fingertip. He wanted desperately to walk along the shelves, read some of the titles, even to remove a volume or two and feel it in his hands. A sense of immense injustice flooded through him. Why should a rapacious plutocrat like Anthony Hawkesworth possess treasure that he almost certainly appreciated only for its resale value, while others, more worthy . . .

"I don't have a good deal of time, gentlemen." It was Hawkesworth himself, rising from his chair. He was a small man, pale-skinned, white-haired, and bald, with a perfectly pointed goatee and tightly trimmed mustache. His hands were pink and he exuded flaccidity. Everything about Hawkesworth seemed effete except his eyes. Cold, dark eyes. Killer's eyes. He didn't stare and he didn't look away. But he held those at whom he looked in a grip that was almost physical.

Hawkesworth walked from the behind the desk in small steps. He stopped at the side and directed Harry and Walter to a pair of red leather wing chairs opposite. When they were seated, he returned without pleasantries to his own chair behind the desk. He asked if they cared for refreshments, but in a tone that implied they should refuse, which even Harry knew enough to do.

"I've been asked to personally solicit a report on your progress, Mr. George." Hawkesworth's voice had surprising timbre, as if he had practiced extensively to remove all traces of origin from his speech. He gave the distinct impression that he had grudgingly given up more important affairs to inquire about an attempted assassination of the president.

Walter glanced over Hawkesworth's shoulder at the books, taking time to respond as a counter to the banker's impatience. "From whom, if I may ask, Mr. Hawkesworth?" Walter could feel Harry stiffen next to him, but Hawkesworth seemed amused, as if his pet spaniel had performed an amusing trick.

"Senator Hanna and I are quite good friends."

Walter nodded, once then again. "Since I assume you've been in touch with Senator Hanna, may I first inquire about the president's health?"

Hawkesworth raised an eyebrow. He appeared for an instant to almost smile. "Of course. President McKinley continues his remarkable recovery. In fact, he will convene a bedside cabinet meeting on Friday at three P.M. His progress has been so extraordinary that Senator Hanna has departed Buffalo. Mrs. McKinley has taken a carriage ride. The president will likely return to Washington in two to three weeks. As the senator said upon his departure, 'All Americans should throw up their hats and cheer.'" Hawkesworth paused, his eyes not moving from Walter's. "Does that answer your question satisfactorily, Mr. George?"

"Yes. Thank you."

"Now, if you will answer mine . . ."

Not such an easy task, Walter thought. How much to say? Half-truth was best. "I don't believe Czolgosz was acting on his own . . ."

"That is hardly an original hypothesis."

Walter ignored Hawkesworth and continued. He was just like Hanna. The more a man was accustomed to intimidating others, the more he respected strength.

"Two men came to see him in Cleveland about six months ago. The same two, it seems, who visited a girl in Chicago at about the same time. She was also an anarchist, a librarian."

"An anarchist librarian?" Hawkesworth seemed amused. "Do you find that an odd combination, Mr. George?"

"Not at all." Certainly not as odd as the question, Walter thought. "Just afterward, she moved to Buffalo. She and Czolgosz had frequent contact after he got to the city on the first. On the day of the shooting, the girl was found dead in what the Buffalo police considered a robbery."

"And you don't?"

"Mr. Swayne and I consider it unlikely."

"So it appears that the two men who visited this librarian and Czolgosz would be a link to whoever launched the conspiracy. Have you made any progress in locating them?"

"Other than learning about their movements in Cleveland, no."

"The girl's got a sister in Chicago," Harry piped up. "Walter here has talked to her too."

"Any help there?"

"Nothing definite. Just a general description."

"Have you checked the usual anarchist haunts? That would seem to be where to start."

"Walter isn't sure the two men were anarchists," Harry blurted. Walter wanted to backhand him, but the cat was out of the bag. They would be lucky from here not to be pulled off the case.

But Hawkesworth did not register indignation or demonstrate shock at the revelation. He simply pursed his lips, and tugged for a moment at the point of his beard. "Do you mind telling me why not?" Hawkesworth made it clear by his gaze that Walter was to speak for himself.

Walter recited his reasons—appearance, demeanor, atypical modus operandi—but omitted any mention of Pinkertons, other Secret Service operatives, and particularly anyone who might have been behind the plot.

"Do you agree with this assessment, Mr. Swayne?" Hawkesworth asked when Walter had finished.

"I agree that others were involved, but I still think the anarchists are likely the ones. Maybe Walter here is right, but I figure it's just one group of anarchists setting up another one. They do fight each other, you know."

Hawkesworth was silent for a few moments, considering the implications. Walter doubted the banker ever did anything in haste.

"We must protect the president at all costs, Mr. George," Hawkesworth intoned finally. "That I do not need to tell you. Whoever is behind this dastardly attempt must be apprehended quickly. They might well not be dissuaded by failure and make another attempt. It is thus vital that you uncover the source of this plot. You must, therefore, locate the two men you described with the utmost haste.

"But as to whether or not they were anarchists, I heartily second the president's sentiments. This investigation cannot and must not descend into a witch hunt. If that Jew Isaak, or Goldman, or any other anarchists are indeed to blame, the full force of the law should be brought down on them. But if not, we must not allow petty vengeance to distract us from unearthing the real conspirators. Not only would we miscarry justice, but we would leave at large those who might make a second attempt."

Walter was stunned. Grateful for the reprieve of course, but Anthony Hawkesworth was the last man he would have suspected to voice such noble sentiments.

"I assured President McKinley that I would adhere to his wishes, Mr. Hawkesworth," he said. "I am happy to reiterate those assurances to you."

Hawkesworth closed his eyes for a moment, tugging once again on his beard. "Do you like President McKinley, Mr. George?"

"Yes. I did. I found him to be a fair and decent man."

Hawkesworth nodded, the half-smile making another ephemeral appearance. Did Hawkesworth know Walter had used that very phrase with Mark Hanna? "You are certain you don't prefer the vice president?"

Walter's hands tightened on the armrests of his chair. He removed them and placed them in his lap. "In my position, one doesn't think in terms of preference."

"Good family, the Roosevelts," Hawkesworth mused. "The vice president is rather kinetic, however. Part of his charm, is it not?" Walter knew not to a venture an opinion. "But Mr. McKinley will steer us a steady course. Don't you agree, Mr. George?"

"The nation is in good hands with President McKinley at the helm," Walter replied. No reason not to match nautical metaphors. "But if the outcome had not been so fortunate, we would be lucky to get a man of Vice President Roosevelt's abilities to step in."

Hawkesworth reached up with a pink index finger to dab the corner of his mouth. "Yes, fortunate indeed. He would certainly not feel over-matched in the position." He stood. "Now I must attend to other affairs. I would like to be kept abreast of your progress."

Harry and Walter rose as well. "To pass on to Senator Hanna or for your own interest?" Walter asked, towering over the little banker.

Hawkesworth looked up to Walter's face. The height difference did not bother him one whit. Ten million dollars added quite a bit to a man's stature. "I cannot see how that is in the slightest bit germane, Mr. George." With that, he turned on his heel and exited the room through a door at the side of his desk built into the bookshelves. The door through which Walter and Harry had entered opened a second later. The retainer stood just outside, waiting to escort them out.

21

TR is 'kinetic?'" Harry hadn't stopped muttering since they got into the coach. "What the hell does that mean?"

"Not sure, Harry. Hawkesworth definitely seems happy McKinley made it. Maybe he figures TR would have made good on all that talk about busting trusts. Bigger question is why he told us."

"Yeah, maybe. And all that applesauce about being fair to Isaak and Goldman. That's a load of crap, if you ask me. He's up to something. Maybe Mark Hanna too. I got the feeling he would have been happy if we found a way to pin this all on TR."

Walter drew a breath. "Why do you say that, Harry?"

Harry shrugged. "Shit, Walter, you got ears same as me. Hawkesworth hates TR. They're all kicking themselves that they stuck him on the ticket. Mark Hanna most of all."

"Why?"

"Jesus, Walter, for someone who reads all the time, you don't know shit. Hanna wants to be president. It's gonna be him or TR against Bryan or whatever other loser the Democrats put up in '04. That means it's gonna be him or TR in the White House."

"I didn't hear anything about Hanna running."

"Walter, you don't hear anything except what you want to."

"Yeah, maybe. Harry . . ."

"Yeah?"

"Do you think it could've been TR?"

Harry rocked his head from side to side. "Anything's possible I suppose. Gets him the job. But my money's still on Isaak and Goldman. They got her, you know. The coppers. Somebody climbed in a second floor window into a flat on Sheffield. She denied who she was, but Schleutter showed up . . . you know, the captain . . . and she owned to it. She's in City Hall."

"And?"

"She admitted meeting Czolgosz in July, but that was it. Then she said, and get this, 'I consider McKinley too insignificant a man for the purpose of assassination.' Woman's got backbone. Gotta admit that."

"And you waited to tell me all this?"

"Well, you were off checking something out. And I wanted you to meet Hawkesworth first."

"So, do we get to talk to her?"

"Not right away. Mayor Harrison and Chief O'Neill are personally conducting the interrogation. Nobody trusts Hannigan. We may get a shot tomorrow. Buffalo coppers want her too. Early word is, though, that she's got solid alibis to prove she didn't see the Polack again. Newspapers are already screaming that she was at the head of a conspiracy though."

"Newspapers will write anything."

"Usually." Harry chuckled. He didn't mind when newspapers wrote good things about him. "If she can prove she wasn't involved, it's going to make for some very disappointed coppers."

Walter nodded. "They can't just fake evidence with her. She's too smart."

"Too well known," Harry corrected. He knew Goldman was smart too, but wasn't going to admit it. "So what about now? Ready to tell me about your checking?"

"Not yet, Harry. I'll tell you tomorrow after we talk to Goldman."

Harry considered it. "Okay, Walter. But this better be worth it."

"Have I ever disappointed you, Harry?"

"We'll see." They both knew he wasn't talking about McKinley.

◆

Walter almost gave in and invited himself back to Harry's for dinner, but instead he ate alone. He'd never been a traitor to anything and he had no intention of beginning with Lucinda. After a passable slice of roast and undercooked spuds washed down with three beers at Henry's, Walter made for home.

As soon as he turned the corner of his street, Walter knew something wasn't right. Nothing specific—no sight or sound was obviously out of place—but somehow the air was wrong. In his younger days, Walter would simply have scoffed, dismissed the feeling as nerves, but after eight years in the saddle and six more in the division, he had learned that such instincts are to be heeded if one wanted to remain alive.

With his right forearm, he moved his jacket back, allowing him quick access to the Colt. Whoever was ahead of him was not announcing his intentions, meaning that those intentions were serious. This was not to frighten him or send a calling card. And he had not been followed since he returned from Cleveland. No one ducking into a carriage or disappearing around a corner. Perhaps this was why.

Some foot traffic would have helped him time his movements, but Walter was alone on the street. He moved toward the entrance to his building, a bit slower than his normal pace, but not so much so as to communicate wariness. Without moving his head, he shifted his eyes from side to side, studying the road ahead, looking for whatever had prodded his suspicions. No movement. Nothing. He continued on, waiting for whatever was waiting for him to show itself.

About ten yards from the entrance to his building he saw it. In the recess under the stairway that led to his front door. A flick of movement in the shadows. Walter shifted his body to allow him to grasp the Colt without being seen. He kept walking, prepared to draw his weapon and fire. A glint of metal from shadows or any sign of further movement that seemed threatening would have been all he needed. But whoever was there seemed content, at least for the moment, to wait and watch.

When Walter reached the stairway he walked heavily, he turned as if to go up, but instead darted past the stairs to the other side. The revolver was now in his hand. He jumped into the recess.

"Breathe and you're dead," he growled.

"No . . . don't."

"You?"

"I'm sorry," said Natasha Kolodkin, moving into the light. "I didn't mean to . . ."

Walter felt his eyes bug. "What are doing, hiding there like that? I almost shot you!"

"Don't yell at me."

"I'm not yelling!"

"I didn't want to wait for you where . . . someone might see me." She looked to his hand. "You might put that away."

Suddenly acutely embarrassed, Walter holstered the Colt. "Who were you afraid would see you? Your friends or mine?"

"Would it matter?"

"Then why did you come here? How did you know where I lived?"

In the half-light of the street, he saw her smile. "I came to deliver the drawings. I found out where you lived . . . well, that's my affair. You're not the only person in this city who can find things out, you know."

Walter heaved a huge sigh. He should have made her tell him, but he didn't. "All right. So where are the drawings?"

She reached down and picked them up. "I'm not going to show you anything down here. You'll have to invite me up."

"No," he said. Other than Harry and the anonymous woman who the landlord let in once a fortnight to clean, no one came into his room. He was as alone as a bear in a cave. "We'll go someplace."

"There isn't anyplace. If you want to find out what the men looked like, you'll have to ask me up."

"All right," he heard himself whisper. "But it's . . . messy."

Natasha giggled and Walter felt his throat go dry. "You can't shock me, Mr. George. I've seen the way single men live."

She moved out from the recess and marched up the stairs. "Well, you are coming?" she asked from the front door.

Walter followed, terror and longing mixing in an incendiary brew. But he was going to let her in. He was powerless to stop himself. At his door, he turned the key and stood aside. She glanced at him, smiled, and walked through. He followed and closed door. At least Swenson wasn't about.

"Oh, Mr. George, this isn't so bad. I've seen far worse."

Walter did not venture to ask where. Instead, he took stock of his rooms as if he had walked in for the first time. A sitting room and bedroom. A burner in one corner, a sink with hot and cold water nearby. Furniture that performed a function, but provided no esthetic enhancement. Gas lamps throughout. But Natasha saw something else.

"Very impressive," she said, walking to the bookcase. "Have you read all of these?"

"Most. A few I haven't gotten to yet."

"Darwin, St. Augustine, Francis Bacon, Emerson . . . even Marx. Did you like Marx, Mr. George?"

"Not especially. It's a lot easier to be profound about what's wrong in a society than it is to know how to fix it."

"Yes. That's true."

"You agree?"

"Do you think I walk in lock-step with Emma Goldman? Do you agree with everything your colleagues do?"

"No. Can I see your drawings now?"

"Of course."

Natasha looked around and, not seeing anyplace to open the portfolio, cleared the table of two dishes, which she deposited in the sink, then moved an empty vase to the window sill. Then she spread the portfolio and removed two drawings. Both were charcoal and each was a detailed depiction of one of the men who approached her sister. But they were more than that.

"These are excellent. As drawings I mean."

"Thank you, Mr. George."

Walter studied the portraits. They were in remarkable detail, with subtle shading along the cheeks and forehead and lines about the mouth and under the eyes. The men depicted appeared stolid and . . . dangerous.

"Do you really remember them well enough to draw these?"

"Oh yes. Once I began, details came back. The one on the left was a bit taller. He was the one who romanced Esther."

Walter studied the face, feeling a note of familiarity. Walter had seen it before. But where?

"You know him?" she asked.

"I've seen him. I'm certain. But I can't remember where. In a crowd, I think."

"Perhaps it will come back to you. These are for you to keep."

"Thank you, Miss Kol . . ."

"Natasha. And I should call you Walter."

"Of course. But . . ."

Before Walter could move to push her away, Natasha had taken his face in her hands and kissed him.

22

Wednesday, September 11, 1901

It was three in the morning. Walter had no clock near his bed but years in the saddle had taught him to tell time by instinct. He lay with his head propped up against a balled up pillow, Natasha nestled against him, her breathing deep and regular. Her body gave off a reassuring warmth, like spring sun. For one of the few moments in his life, Walter felt totally, utterly at peace. Was it because of the lovemaking, the presence of another person, or specifically Natasha? He couldn't be certain. Would he feel this way if it was Lucinda resting against him?

"You're awake?" Her whisper jarred him, left him feeling as if he'd been caught in a deception.

"Yes. I thought you were asleep."

"I was."

"Aren't you tired?"

"Aren't you?"

"I never sleep very much. And this is my favorite time of night. Peaceful. It's as if everything bad in the world has disappeared."

"Until morning."

"Yes."

"I've got to leave very early."

"I know. Will you come back?"

"Maybe. I'm not certain."

"Why not?"

"This was wonderful. You're a very nice man, Walter. But what is wonderful one time is often not so the next. It might be better to keep the memory of this night than risk ruining it by trying to replicate it."

"Are you this way with many men?"

"Not many. Some. There are few I have liked as much as you."

"Then why not see me again?"

"I didn't say I wouldn't. I'm simply not certain."

Walter had no answer. He had always been the one to cut relationships short, to avoid any chance that someone could get too close. Now, for the first time he could remember . . .

By seven, Natasha had slipped out the door.

All that remained of her, like the smile on the Cheshire cat, was the drawings. Walter blew out a breath. They would have to do. He made himself a cup of coffee and looked them over again.

One of the faces continued to be unfamiliar, but the other one definitely was not. He tried to give himself a context. Washington. That was where the telegrams went. But where in Washington? The division? No. He'd remember. A Pinkerton? They were crawling all over the town. Didn't register. Army maybe? He tried to envision the man in uniform. Easy to do. But still, Walter couldn't jog his memory into recognition.

Instead of place, Walter tried circumstance. In a crowd, as he first thought, but he was certain he hadn't heard the man speak. And it was a crowd in which an hombre like this would not have stood out. Other lawmen or just other men who looked fast with their fists. In a bar? No. Wasn't social.

Walter polished off two cups of coffee, never taking his eyes from the drawing. Natasha's rendition was so real, had so much depth, that the man himself, and not his charcoal likeness seemed to be looking back at him, staring him down. He almost expected the mouth to turn up in a smile, taunting his adversary for his impotence.

Wait. Talking. Walter remembered the man talking, against the wall at the far side of the room. To another man.

Then he had it.

23

Heard about Tomassini?"

When Walter had walked into the outer office, Finneran and Slocum, two of the other operatives—new, eager beavers—were perched behind desks. It took young guys a while to realize that Harry was oblivious both to flattery and any effort to impress. In fact, attempts to ingratiate themselves with the boss generally achieved precisely the opposite effect. Harry ignored them as he waved Walter into his office.

"The grinder? No. what?"

"He was killed yesterday. An accident. Supposedly run down by a carriage while crossing the street."

"Supposedly run down?"

"Sorry, Walter. I forgot 'to whom' I was talking. He was run down by a carriage. I meant that supposedly it was an accident."

"I take it no one saw this accident."

"Everyone saw the accident. They may be foreigners, but they aren't morons. Tomassini sees a shooting. Tomassini talks about the shooting.

Tomassini dies. That message is clear in any language." Harry eyed him for moment. "You look tired. Trouble sleeping?"

Did Harry know? But Harry changed the subject and let Walter off. "They operated on McKinley again. Cut the stitches. To drain the wound they said. Made it sound like nothin'."

"Did they get the bullet this time?" Czolgosz's second shot had proved too delicate for Mann, the gynecologist, to remove, so after fishing around a bit, he had concluded that the bullet had lodged in the president's back muscles and would not pose a threat to his life or his recovery. So Mann stitched just him up. When McBurney showed up, he decided to leaves things as they were. Up until now, it had seemed the correct call.

Harry shook his head.

"That's bad, Harry." As every soldier knew, nothing was worse than being gut shot.

"Yeah. But nobody else thinks so. Blood tests seemed normal. Hanna left town because he said McKinley's recovery is assured. Said everyone should throw up their hats and cheer. TR left too. McBurney is prancing around like McKinley just adopted him."

"TR? He's the only one in the whole crew who knows anything about bullet wounds."

"Don't forget the doctors, Walter. They know a little about bullet wounds too."

"I guess." Walter unrolled Natasha's drawing. That was enough about TR. "Ever see this guy?"

Harry studied the faces before him. "Nice. Who did them? Anyone we know?"

"Never mind who did them. Tell me where you saw this guy."

"I thought you asked *if* I ever saw him."

"Well you did, Harry. We both did."

"How many cups of coffee you had?"

"Two. So come on, Harry. Where?"

"Fuck, Walter, could we stop the riddles? Tell me where we saw this guy and what this has to do with the Goldman woman?"

"It has nothing to do with Emma Goldman. And we saw him in Buffalo."

"Buffalo?" Harry looked at the picture again, this time more closely, then shook his head. "This wasn't the guy we saw jumping into the carriage. I'm sure about that."

"Not there. When we went to see Hanna. At the Iroquois. He was in the lobby. I saw him again when I when to the Millburn mansion to talk to the president."

"He's a lawman? Okay. I believe you."

"He's also one of the two men who recruited Czolgosz and Esther Kolodkin."

Harry grabbed the picture from Walter's hand. "Lemme see that." He studied Natasha's drawing, eventually turning the sheet of paper slightly to the side as if that would help him identify the man in profile. Soon he gave a tiny nod. Then he looked up at Walter, his mouth tight and his eyes cold, but otherwise with a sudden exaggerated calm. Walter had only seen Harry this way once or twice before and in each case a man had died soon thereafter.

"He was at the far side of the lobby." Harry spoke in a dull monotone. "He was talking to another guy who had his back to us. Probably his partner. Smith . . . or Jones."

"That's how I remember it too."

Harry placed the drawing on his desk, running his hands along the sides to keep it flat. He looked down at the man again, as Walter had, as a flesh and bone adversary. "All right, Walter, you got your wish," he said softly. "It wasn't the Reds."

"Wasn't my wish, Harry."

Harry glanced to Walter for a moment as if he hadn't heard. But Walter knew he had. "Now what?" Harry asked simply, is if two words were all he could trust himself to say.

"We find out who they are and who put them up to it. Right now, they could be anyone."

"Not anyone. Not the Buffalo coppers. Likely not anyway. But we can check. Shit, Walter, I suppose I should be happy. At least it ain't nobody in the division."

"Can you be sure?"

"Almost. Not anyone I ever saw in Washington at any rate. Or in Chicago. New York maybe, but no one else in the lobby seemed to know them and the place was crawling."

"They were off by themselves at Milburn's place too."

"Okay. We got some idea who they weren't. The trick is to figure out who they were."

"Remember the telegraph office? The dead end in Washington? Maybe it wasn't such a dead end after all."

"We can't be sure they didn't phony that up. Even if they didn't, Washington's a big town."

"We can make it smaller. We already know a lot."

Harry nodded. "Okay. They had to be working for someone with a motive. Someone who would benefit from McKinley's death. Wasn't anything knee-jerk either. It's been in the works for more than six months, since before that librarian got persuaded to move to Buffalo. Lucinda was right . . . whoever was behind it knew the president would come to the fair sometime. And they had access to right kind of people. Whoever it was we saw, they had to able to get into a room full of lawmen without being questioned . . . meaning they probably had badges themselves, even if they were phonies. That what you mean, Walter?"

"Yeah. We can work forward and backwards. Try to find them through the badges and also by figuring out who they might be working for."

"That's a short list, Walter. Not too many people would have enough to gain to hatch a plot to kill the president . . ."

"But it had to be somebody."

Harry blew out a breath. "I don't much like where you're going with this, Walter."

"I don't much like it either."

"Could be all coincidence . . ." Harry couldn't come close to making that sound convincing.

"Maybe." Nor could Walter.

Suddenly, Harry looked up at Walter in a way Walter had never seen him do before. With fear. "But could he really do it? TR? The man's more American than an eagle. Kill the president to get the job?"

"Hawkesworth thinks he could." Walter decided to avoid using Abe Isaak to buttress his argument.

"TR. Shit."

"I like the man too, Harry."

"I guess I'm not really surprised. Who else would have the balls to try such a stunt? But why wouldn't he just wait until '04 and win the job on his own?"

"Impossible to ever know what's in someone's mind. Maybe he thinks Hanna's got a fix in to get the nomination. Maybe TR decided if he doesn't get the job first, he'll never get it. But let's not make the same mistake everyone made about Goldman. Before we start accusing the vice president of attempted murder, we best have a lot more to go on than a drawing from . . ." Walter bit off the name.

"From a concerned citizen?" Harry asked.

"Yeah. That's it."

"So you still want to go to City Hall."

"We've got to. We made such a stink about conducting our own interrogation, it would look pretty hokey if we cancelled. Besides, we've only got a theory. It's a little too soon to abandon all the others."

"And you want to meet Goldman."

"Yeah. Of course I do."

24

Walter despised Emma Goldman and all that she stood for, but still, how could he not be curious to meet "the high priestess of anarchy," as the newspapers had flamboyantly called her? The woman, no matter what her beliefs, held an undeniable fascination. She was smart, committed, and certainly every bit as tough as anyone Walter had ridden beside on the trail. As he and Harry were led through a labyrinthine passage at City Hall, Walter fought to suppress a disquieting need to impress her.

Two coppers stood outside an office down the hall from Mayor Harrison's. One of them opened the door and Harry and Walter walked through. The room was more parlor than office. Sitting on one side were Mayor Harrison and Chief of Police O'Neill. In another chair, back to the door, her manacled hands on her lap, was Emma Goldman. Standing off to one side, hands in his pockets, was Hannigan, a dumb smirk on his dumb face.

Goldman turned her head to see who was entering, but did so with the same insouciance as had Mark Hanna in the presidential suite in Buffalo. Here was a woman, Walter realized, who was accustomed to dominating every group of which she was a part, no matter if it was a roomful of enemies. Even the handcuffs, a ludicrous appurtenance with Mike Hannigan standing nearby, did not detract from the power of the woman's presence.

Walter had never seen anyone who could be at once so physically unattractive yet so commanding. Goldman's features were thick, without delicacy, a strong jaw and down-turned mouth, and small, watchful eyes behind the signature pince-nez perched on her nose, attached to a lanyard draped from one corner around her neck. She was wearing a white shirtwaist, blue cheviot skirt, and leather boots. In different clothing and with slightly shorter hair, she might easily have been mistaken for a man.

She squinted and blinked for a moment and Walter knew that Hannigan had used the lights on her. Even he would not have dared try anything more direct. Sucker punching Abe Isaak was one thing, striking Emma Goldman quite another.

Goldman turned back to Harrison and O'Neill. She behaved as if Hannigan was not in the room. "These are not your men, I take it." She spoke with an accent vaguely European, yet somehow totally American.

Neither man answered. Despite their even expressions, Walter could see that both were intimidated. It was all he could do not to smile. Walter was used to sizing a person up right away and, damn, he found himself liking Emma Goldman.

"As I suspected," she said softly. "In that case, I would prefer to speak to these gentlemen alone." She made just the briefest tilt of her head toward Mike Hannigan.

The mayor and police commissioner glanced at one another. Each knew that it was unconscionable to let a prisoner dictate terms—especially this prisoner—but each decided that they would be happy to leave the room. O'Neill cocked his head at Hannigan, giving only the tiniest bit more notice than had Goldman, and then the three walked out and closed the door behind them.

Harry and Walter pulled chairs to sit across from her. Walter thought about removing the manacles, but decided not to do so unless he was asked.

Goldman blew out a sigh, the sort of thing one does with misbehaving children. "I scarcely knew the man," she began. "He was leaving Rochester via Buffalo when he came up and had a few words with me. He said he had heard me lecture at some memorial hall in Cleveland last May and that he wanted to know me. I remember almost nothing about him save that his complexion was light. But he was zealous . . . much too zealous. As you know, Abe Isaak thought he was a police spy and even put a notice in his newspaper to that effect. I would have tended to agree."

Walter did not want to talk about Abe Isaak. "How did you feel when you found out he was the one who shot the president?"

Goldman shrugged. "I certainly realized he wasn't a police spy."

Walter waited. Harry was evidently going to let him run the show.

After a long pause, she said. "I thought, 'Oh, the fool.'"

"You have affection for President McKinley?"

"I have no more affection for him than for anyone else who gains power by exploiting the powerless. But I do not advocate violence."

"What about inciting Alexander Berkman to murder Henry Frick?"

"That was self-defense. Frick was systematically starving women and children. We work against the system, Mr . . ."

"George."

"Mr. George. Not to violence. Education is our watchword, not murder."

"Still, Czolgosz seems to think you inspired him."

"Am I to be accountable because some crack-brained person put a wrong construction on my words? Leon Czolgosz, I am convinced, planned the deed unaided and entirely alone. There is no anarchist ring that would help him. I think he was one of those downtrodden men who see all the misery the rich inflict upon the poor, who think of it, who brood over it, and then, in despair, resolve to strike a great blow, as they think, for the benefit of their fellow men. I understand what would motivate a person to violence . . . I simply think that it is an urge that must be suppressed."

Walter decided to change direction. "You will be charged with conspiracy to murder the president. I'm told that the Buffalo authorities are seeking to have you extradited. They claim to have sufficient evidence to prove you were involved."

Goldman offered a brief smile. "They can have no evidence unless they manufactured it themselves."

"But what about your recent meeting?"

"There was none. The young man came to Abe Isaak's house, asking to see me. I'm not certain how he even knew I was in Chicago, or why he came to be there. He seemed to believe that I would want to speak with him. I refused. Abe Isaak warned me that he was a police agent. When he came to see me on the train platform, I was civil with him, but nothing more."

Walter glanced to Harry who did not deign to break his silence. Not that it mattered. There was nothing more to get.

After they returned Goldman to her Chicago hosts, Walter and Harry excused themselves and left. Mike Hannigan looked oddly self-satisfied as they passed him on their way out.

"Well, Harry, what do you think?" Walter asked, once they were clear of the building.

"That's one hard woman."

"Pretty convincing too, wouldn't you say?"

Harry grunted.

"What say we try to run down the other lead instead of staying on this one?"

"Smith and Jones?" He thought for a moment. "Yeah. Let's do that. You think they're Chicago-based, don't you?"

"Makes sense. Unless somebody Chicago-based imported them."

But Smith and Jones did not prove easy to find, despite perfect descriptions. They were not coppers—both Harry and Walter checked their sources—nor were they local Pinkertons, or Pinkertons at all as far as anyone could tell. Harry even called on an old, retired saddle buddy who did a little checking with his army pals. No one had anything to go on.

"What a waste of a day," Harry groused into his beer.

Walter took another bite of his steak but didn't answer. They had splurged and gone to the State Street Chop House, sort of a concession to reaching a dead end.

"Doesn't make sense," he muttered.

"That's the worst thing you can say about anything," Harry grunted back. "At least you're off 'odd.' And it does make sense. To me anyway. The two guys weren't from here. Which leaves us exactly nowhere."

"Doesn't make sense," Walter repeated.

"Okay, Walter, I'll be an idiot and ask. What doesn't make sense?"

"That the trail would go cold. Doesn't make sense."

Harry was about to ask what the fuck that meant, when they spotted Tom Laverty striding across the room in their direction. Laverty was a Chicago dick, but one of the good guys.

"Hi Harry. Walter." Laverty was medium height, with rust-colored hair, and wiry like a boxer. He had a series of scars running across his face from when he went through a store window taking down some drunken Kraut who was chasing his wife with a butcher knife right on Michigan Avenue. He had clearly not come across Harry and Walter by chance.

"Tommy." Harry nodded. "How'd you know where to find us?"

Laverty shrugged. "I am a cop, Harry."

Harry decided to let that go.

"Those two guys you was asking about," Laverty went on. "We found 'em." He sighed. "Sorry, guys. They wasn't breathin'."

25

Thursday, September 12, 1901

I t was after midnight when Walter and Harry arrived at the sprawling Cook County Hospital on Harrison Street, site of the city morgue, and the current address of Smith and Jones.

They saw exactly what they expected to see. Each was dead from a single gunshot wound to the head, delivered from four to six feet away, with no signs of a struggle beforehand.

After that, they headed to police headquarters where they persuaded the night sergeant to let them see the report, persuasion aided by the two dollar bills Harry slid across the sergeant's desk.

Smith, whose real name turned out to be Gardner Beech, and Jones, whose name was actually Jones, Ezekiel Jones, had been found by their landlady in rooms they had rented only a half mile away, in Garfield Park. The door to Beech's room had been left open, and when the landlady happened by, he was quite visible, sitting in a chair with a bullet wound under his left eye. Jones had been found in a similar state in the room next door. Assuming the two were sufficiently professional not to just sit around when one of them was shot, it seemed apparent that at least two gunmen had been sent to dispatch them. Perhaps more.

"This make more sense to you now?" Harry asked Walter as they left the building and walked into a chilly, early fall drizzle.

"Yeah, Harry. Just like it makes sense to you."

"Closing the ring." Harry sucked in a breath. In each man's room had been found approximately $500 is crisp greenbacks. Beech had his stuffed in his socks, which needed mending, and Jones's fortune was in an envelope taped to the back of a drawer. Easy to find. Each man also had received a telegram three days earlier telling them to proceed as agreed.

The telegrams had been sent from Buffalo.

"Walter . . ."

"Yeah?"

"If whoever set this up is covering their tracks . . . you might want to see about that concerned citizen who did the drawings."

Walter nodded. "I was going there now."

"At three in the morning . . ."

"Just to check things out. I'll stop by later to make sure she's okay."

"Not too much later."

Walter nodded. "I'll be in time to catch the train." Walter threw Harry a surprised look. "I thought you'd be upset."

Harry shook his head and allowed a little grin. "She's seeing someone, Walter."

"Lucinda."

"Yes, Walter. Lucinda. I wasn't talking about the Kolodkin woman."

"Who is it?" Walter was extremely surprised to find himself . . . jealous.

"Guy works for Olds. The car maker. He handles accounts. She met him in church of all places. About a month ago. She wouldn't let on to me because she said I'd scare him off."

"You're a scary guy, Harry." He couldn't help but ask. "Have you met him? What's he like?"

Harry laughed. "I haven't met him, but evidently he's sort of round, and bald. Think she could find someone more opposite from you?"

"No. I guess not." But she'd said if he ever wanted her, she'd be there. Guess she finally decided he never would.

"Okay, Walter. Go do your errand. But be at the station by ten."

Harry spun on his heel and headed off to get a couple of hours sleep. Was he really not upset? Lucinda with a short, fat, bald accountant, instead of . . . him?

When he reached Natasha Kolodkin's street, he walked slowly, staying close to the buildings, looking for movement. Only one flickering gas lamp at the far corner provided light and the on-and-off drizzle would further obscure anyone lurking about. But Walter had been doing this long enough that he could sense movement and, except for a couple of pushcart vendors moving in the road to get an early start on their day, there was none.

But that didn't mean there wouldn't be any . . . or hadn't been already. Walter had no intention of leaving until he knew Natasha was safe and that he had warned her that she would have to be extremely vigilant in order to stay that way. He found himself a spot against a building that was completely in shadows and set himself to wait until he could knock on Mrs. Freundlich's door.

The sky began to lighten at about 5:30. Even with the drizzle, Walter could see now clearly up and down the street, but he could be seen as well. His hat brim had shielded his head and neck, but his vest, shirt, and pants had soaked through. He'd spent many days in the saddle like this, but had come to hate the damp. Still, can't very well pitch yourself a tent and sit smoking a cigar.

He heard a clatter and saw the milk wagon making its way up the street, the horse's head bobbing up and down as if it were keeping time. Milk delivery was a luxury so the mustachioed milkman, dressed in his white coveralls, made less than a dozen stops. One of them, however, was Mrs. Freundlich's. The man left one large and one small bottle—cream—before moving on. People fetched their dairy as soon as they awakened, so, as soon as the door opened, Walter would be able to move across the street.

While he waited, he once more tried to figure out what was going on. That Czolgosz had been baited into shooting McKinley there could be no doubt, nor that anarchists almost certainly had been no part of it, no matter what the newspapers were saying. Maybe Czolgosz would talk if he were confronted with Smith and Jones, but Walter didn't think so. The last thing he was going to admit was that he had been played for a fool.

Walter laughed softly. Or was it he that was being played for the fool?

The door to Mrs. Freundlich's cracked open. Walter made a move to start across the street but stopped when he saw that the head that emerged and looked up and down the street before snatching up the milk bottle and then the cream was not the German woman's. In fact, it was not a woman's at all.

The man was young, in his twenties, clean shaven, with sandy-colored hair and a furtive manner. Walter raced across the street and up the steps to the front. He listened for only an instant, and then, drawing his Colt, threw his shoulder against the wooden door. It creaked loudly, then popped open. Walter stepped through in a crouch holding the Colt leveled in front of him.

The next sound was not a shot but instead that of breaking glass as the milk bottle smashed on the wooden floor and Walter stood face to face with an utterly terrified Mrs. Freundlich. She was standing wide-eyed in her night dress, her right hand still held in front of her from where she had been holding the bottle. Walter looked at his feet and the puddle of white liquid that was slowly encircling the soles of his boots.

His mouth began to move, but nothing came out. He stared down at his own right hand and the Colt, and tried to return it to its holster, missing twice before he finally found the mark. The sandy-haired man suddenly appeared from the back and Walter realized that he had grabbed the bottle so stealthily because he was wearing only his underwear.

"Who . . ." was the only word Walter could manage.

"It's my nephew, Hans," Mrs. Freudlich whispered, the words coming out like they had been scratched with sandpaper.

"I'm sorry . . . I thought . . ." Walter looked down again. "Let me clean . . ."

Mrs. Freundlich shook her head. She started to say that she would do it, but the words wouldn't come. Hans disappeared into the back and returned a moment later with a bucket and a mop.

"She's not here," Mrs. Freundlich muttered. Her voice, still weak, held more wonder than anger as she stared at the remains of her milk delivery.

"I'll send someone to fix the door," Walter heard himself say, wondering why he didn't ask where she was.

"She left you a note." Mrs. Freundlich's slippers were soaked, but there was broken glass on the floor. She watched as Hans cleaned around her, picking up the shards as he mopped up the remains. Hans occasionally turned toward Walter with total contempt as he completed the chore. He had yet to utter a word. Walter wasn't even certain whether or not he spoke English.

When the boy had mopped up and cleared the glass, Mrs. Freundlich looked about, trying to decide whether or not to track milk across the floor in her sodden slippers or risk stepping on an errant piece of glass by walking barefoot. Her fastidiousness got the better of her and chose to tiptoe out the room barefoot. Her feet were thick and formless like small hams, but she was surprisingly delicate. After a few moments, she returned in a new pair of slippers, holding a small gray envelope.

"Dear Walter." The writing was flowing and letters perfectly formed. "If you are reading this, you have come by for one of two reasons. I hope it was to check to see if I had come to harm. If so, you have my thanks. I knew I was in extreme danger before you did, and have taken steps to ensure my safety. I will miss the children. They are our future and it pains me to leave them. But I have no choice.

"If, however, you have come for the second reason, please believe that I did truly have feelings for you and that nothing I said or did was in any way dishonest in that regard. I expect we will not see one another again, which would be better for both of us. I will always remember you with great fondness and can only hope you can feel something of the same for me."

It was signed, "With enduring affection, Natasha."

"Enduring affection?" Walter was stunned. He'd been jilted by two women in eight hours. Well, jilted wasn't exactly the right term, was it? But what was? And why did he feel as if he'd just been spat on?

And, just as important, even though it didn't feel that way . . . what was Natasha's second reason?

26

Emma Goldman wasn't going to be extradited to Buffalo after all. Nor was Abe Isaak or anyone else. In fact, one day after all but accusing her of masterminding a plot to assassinate the President of the United States, law enforcement officials in both New York and Illinois were forced to admit they had no evidence at all to tie her or any other anarchist to the crime. The Erie County District Attorney, Thomas Penney, insisted to reporters that Goldman hadn't been cleared, and that law enforcement officials were working tirelessly to find the link between her and Leon Czolgosz. He assured a nervous public that if she were released from jail, she would be kept under the closest surveillance.

The only two people going from Chicago to Buffalo turned out to be Walter George and Harry Swayne.

"What are we going to tell Wilkie?"

"That is the question, isn't it Harry." Walter thought. "I think we tell him about Smith and Jones and that the conspiracy notion is alive and well, but don't tell him that the two of them didn't seem like any anarchists we've ever seen."

"They could have been anarchists, right?"

"Sure."

Harry dropped his shoulders and made to look matter-of-fact. "What you gonna say about your friend?"

"Nothing." Walter waited but Harry didn't press. "I know she was involved in something, Harry. I'm not an idiot . . ."

"No? Coulda fooled me."

"Okay, I behaved like an idiot . . . but we don't know if she was part of this deal or some other . . . conspiracy. Let's just work from Smith and Jones and see where it takes us. If Natasha . . . Kolodkin . . . seems to be involved, I'll spill the whole thing to Wilkie myself. All of it."

Harry grunted, turned to rest the side of his head against the seat back and closed his eyes. Walter did the same, wondering if sleep would come. It did, within minutes.

27

Friday, September 13, 1901

Walter and Harry knew the second they stepped off the train. William McKinley was dying.

Just the day before, the president's blood tests once again showed "not a trace of blood poisoning," and his doctors proclaimed that, finally, less than one week after he'd been shot, he would be given food by mouth. He was running a low fever, 100.4, but his physicians were confident that his body was simply working overtime in its effort to heal his wounds.

Twenty-four hours later, everything had changed. They could see it on the faces of those milling about but, even more, could feel the sense of dread and doom that permeated the terminal. Walking across the open waiting room, snippets of overheard conversation filled in the story. President McKinley had indeed been given beef broth, some toast, and coffee the day before and had enjoyed it so much that he had asked for a cigar. The doctors had denied the request but were heartened at the president's robust enthusiasm. But a few hours later, McKinley had felt ill—the doctors said merely that the food had "disagreed with him."

His condition had deteriorated rapidly from there and by two in the morning, while Harry and Walter were bouncing around on the train, trying to get a couple of hours sleep, President McKinley was reported as being unconscious and near death. Now, just after eight, the president was hanging on to his life by the flimsiest of threads. The doctors had been reduced to praying for a miracle, but each of the three who had remained in Buffalo was reported to be dumbfounded at this turn of events. They had been certain the president was recovering. McBurney had returned to New York City and there was no mention of whether he would return. Both Harry and Walter would have given odds against it.

Fitting for the mood, thunderstorms had been pounding Buffalo for twelve hours, and another struck during the carriage ride to Milburn House. Neither Harry nor Walter talked of McKinley's impending death and the man who would move into the White House if it occurred. And another man, now sitting in the Buffalo jail, would most certainly die as well, taking whatever secrets he held as to the inspiration for his crime with him.

Rain continued to pelt down as the carriage pulled up to Milburn House, but neither Harry nor Walter quickened their pace to the front door. Wilkie was waiting for them just inside. The linen suit had been exchanged for one of dark gray wool. His expression was even and unflinching—he did not even seem to blink. When Wilkie saw Harry and Walter enter, he flicked his head ever so slightly left and turned to walk in that direction

The same conglomeration of operatives and Buffalo coppers were standing around as for their first visit—minus Smith and Jones—but this time they had been joined by a small army of nurses in white scurrying back and forth and up and the down the stairs, although Walter had not the slightest idea what they were doing. He had a feeling they did not either.

Wilkie went into a small anteroom off the hall and closed the door behind him when the other two had entered.

"Any hope?" Harry asked.

Wilkie shook his head, just once slowly to each side. "Officially, there's no change, but I don't think he'll last out the day."

"Shit."

"What's the matter, Swayne? I thought you wanted Roosevelt."

Harry took two steps toward Wilkie, his right hand balled in a fist, before Walter could intercept him. Wilkie hadn't backed up a step and never let his eyes go off Harry's. That made Wilkie either extremely brave or extremely dumb.

"Fuck you," was all the Harry could get out.

Wilkie nodded. "Okay, Swayne. I just needed to make sure."

"What the fuck is that supposed to mean?"

"We'll get to that. But first, tell me about the two guys."

"Beech and Jones?"

"Yes, Swayne. Who else? But you might as well stay with Smith and Jones. There's no record of anyone fitting that description named either Gardner Beech or Ezekiel Jones. Certainly not with anyone who could have gotten them in here."

"So they used aliases to cover up aliases," Walter mumbled.

"Aliases are pretty standard, wouldn't you say, Mr . . . George."

Walter just glared, wondering whether Wilkie tried to make himself detestable or it just came naturally.

"All right," Wilkie went on, "let's get this straight. We're going to have a new president and we're left trying to figure out what really happened to the old one. That's all I'm interested in. I know you two, and just about everyone else in the division, hopes they're going to get to work for someone else. Maybe you will and maybe you won't, but as long as I'm in charge of this investigation, I want it done right. Which means that if you or anyone else wants to cut corners, I'm the guy who'll hold the scissors. Either of you have any problem with that?"

Harry and Walter glanced at one another, but neither spoke.

"Good. So . . . Smith and Jones. We checked all the telegraph offices. No record of a telegram being sent to either of them."

Walter would have been surprised if there had been a record.

"So right now, they're just a couple of ghosts, right? Any way to give them a little meat?" Wilkie at least had begun to sound like a lawman.

"How about we show their pictures to the coppers around here?" Harry suggested. "We don't have to say why." That wasn't going to do any good, Walter knew but didn't say.

"Sure, Swayne, but it isn't going to take very long for even Buffalo coppers to figure out why you're asking. Question is whether they'll own to it if they recognize these guys. And what about the woman? Kolodkin isn't it?"

"We think she was killed by Smith and Jones to make sure she didn't talk."

"I meant the other one. Natasha. You knew her pretty well, didn't you, George?"

When Walter didn't reply, Wilkie barked out a laugh. "I'm from Chicago, George. I have a lot of friends there."

"She skipped." Walter told Wilkie about their meetings and the note, leaving out that she'd spent the night in his room. Didn't matter. Wilkie had already guessed.

"Okay," Wilkie said when Walter had finished. "So we know Czolgosz was put up to the job, and we know he thought he was part of an anarchist plot. So, likely, did the Kolodkin woman that was killed, and maybe her sister too. Smith and Jones were probably involved in the setup, but the Kolodkin woman ducking out puts the anarchists back in the picture . . . maybe. That about right?"

"Yeah."

"But you don't think it was the anarchists, do you George?"

Walter shook his head.

"You think it was the vice president."

"What?"

"Come on, George. Stop treating me like I'm a dunce. Maybe you want to ask him personally if he had anything to do with it. He'll be on his way here later today."

"I never said . . ." Walter turned to Harry who didn't turn back.

Wilkie put up his hand. "Forget it, George. But tell me . . . if this wasn't the president and vice president of the United States we're talking about, would you think that the number two was a suspect if the number one got shot?"

That, in fact, had been exactly what Walter had thought. "I'm not certain. You couldn't eliminate him . . ."

"No," Wilkie replied. "You couldn't." He removed his glasses, polished them, and returned them to the bridge of his nose. "Well, it's your investigation. You'd better find out one way or another. If it is Roosevelt, we can't have a murderer sitting in the White House, no matter what his pedigree."

And then you get to keep your job, Walter could not help thinking.

The second they were outside, Walter went at Harry. "Where did he get that from? We never said anything to anyone about it being TR." Walter took a beat. "At least I didn't."

"I don't think I like this, Walter. You think it was me?"

"No, Harry. But it wasn't me." Walter thought to Wilkie's crack to Harry about preferring Roosevelt and how Wilkie hadn't flinched when Harry came at him. Could it have been a setup? Harry?

28

Now that Leon Czolgosz was to be an assassin instead of a would-be one, security on his jail cell was increased and no one was allowed to speak to him, not even for interrogation. He would be assigned a lawyer in due course, brought to trial soon after, found guilty, and executed.

The means would likely be the electric chair, recently invented by, of all people, a Buffalo dentist. It was supposed to be more humane than hanging, but Walter had thought of it as literally frying a person to death.

Without being able to speak to the accused, and the telegraph office a dead end, there seemed little reason to hang around Buffalo.

But maybe there was a reason.

Harry was at the front desk of the Iroquois, looking at the train schedules, when Walter walked over. "Before we go, I want to check something out."

"What? There's nothing but cold leads here."

"Maybe not. I've got an idea."

"An idea, huh? Sounds a little smoky. We getting secretive again, Walter?"

Harry meant the question rhetorically . . . probably. But he was right all the same. "No, Harry," Walter replied patiently. "I'm not getting secretive. In fact, why don't you come along? I'm going make a visit to an art school."

Harry drew back. "Art school? What for? Want to learn to paint for after we're bounced out of the bureau?"

"Always good to have a trade." Walter spoke lightly, but all the while trying to see if Harry tipped anything. He didn't. But he wouldn't. "So, want to come along?"

Harry shook his head. "No, Walter. You go on ahead. I'll just go and visit the local whorehouse."

Assuming Harry meant that facetiously—not a certainty—Walter realized that his partner could be off for a reason as conspiratorial as his. Still, it was better that Harry didn't know what he was up to until he had some better information.

And possibly even then.

The desk clerk told Walter a woman who called herself Madame Romanova—same as the Russian tsar—had a "studio" four blocks away. She lived there as well, so it was likely she'd be home.

Five minutes later, Walter walked up a flight of stairs under a sign that read "Atelier Romanova," deep red script on a cream background, and entered a large room with north facing windows and skylights, its wide board floors speckled with every color of paint imaginable. Five easels were set up, positioned so that no student could peek at the work of another. Three of them were occupied, one by a scraggly man in his twenties, two by matrons wearing large smocks to keep the paint off their clothing. In the center of the room, on a stool was a large blue vase in which a single long stemmed white rose tilted against one side.

Each of the three students seemed immersed in rendering his or her unique interpretation of the objects.

Pacing behind the easels was a woman no more than five feet tall, dressed in a long skirt that featured as many colors as the floor, and a black long sleeved blouse that ballooned at the wrists. She appeared to be about eighty, but bounced around like a woman half that age. At Walter's entrance, she paused for a moment, glanced up, flicked her wrist at him to get out, and then resumed her pacing. She stared at each student's work but said nothing.

Walter watched the show for a few moments, trying to decide if he were witnessing a melodrama or a farce. When he made no move to leave, Madame Romanova stepped from behind the easels and strode in his direction, hands on hips.

"I asked you to leave, young man," she said, displaying an accent that was in no way Russian. "New students are interviewed by appointment only." The three students, obviously survivors of the interview process, stopped working to watch the confrontation.

"I'm not a prospective student, Madame Romanova. I came to you with a request I thought you might find interesting. Of course, I'm happy to make the same request of a different artist."

Madame Romanova crossed her arms in front of her and rocked sideways from one foot to the other, trying to decide if this bearded man in the bowler, at least twice her size, could possibly have an artistic request worth considering.

"Do you teach your students to paint traditionally . . . van Dyk, for example, or even Caravaggio . . . or more in the modern style? I very much like Cezanne's *Basket of Apples*."

Madame Romanova smiled despite herself. "Please, young man, don't take me for a fool, or try to impress me by throwing out a couple of names. What is the nature of your request?"

Walter smiled in return. "Fair enough. I won't take you for a fool if you will pay me the same courtesy. To answer your question, I'm with the United States Secret Service Division. I'd like you to recreate a face."

"Recreate? Secret Service Division? I've read about you people. Does this have something to do with that maniac?"

Walter nodded slowly. At least the political question was answered. "It might."

"I'll take that as a yes. Do you need this recreation done now?"

"If it wouldn't be too much trouble."

Madame Romanova spun on her heel, and aimed the same flick of the wrist with which she had favored Walter at the three students. "All right. Shoo. Leave everything as it is and come back tomorrow."

Madame Romanova must have been a sergeant in the army of whatever country she was actually from. The three put down their brushes, the women removed their smocks, and they were out of the room in forty-five seconds. The second the door was closed, she moved to a large drawing desk, cleared off some brushes and pencils, and placed a piece of drawing paper flat on the top.

"I saw," she said, her accent fading. "You guessed." She flashed him a small grin, and he realized she must have been quite pretty once. Actually, he realized to his surprise, she still was.

"Where are you really from?"

"Coventry," she replied, sounding like it. "But no one is going to take painting lessons from an Englishwoman. Russian isn't the best, but at least it's exotic. I just couldn't get the Italian accent right." She shrugged. "The Russian isn't that good either, but it's closer."

"I suppose. What shall I call you then?"

"Madame, of course. And what should I call you, young man? Officer something?"

"Walter will do nicely."

"All right, Walter." She patted his forearm, which for some reason made him blush. "Tell me what you have in mind?

Walter explained how Natasha had been able to draw lifelike portraits of Smith and Jones after meeting them only briefly, or at least so she had said. But perhaps Madame might be able to draw a similar portrait if

Walter supplied a description, making corrections to the details along the way. She replied with a wrist flick, indicating it would be no problem at all.

They set to work, Walter beginning with the shape of the face and moving on to details—eyes, nose, mouth, and ears. Madame worked quickly and expertly, drawing in lines lightly, and then erasing or altering them as Walter told her a feature should be longer, shorter, wider, narrower, or differently shaped. Within ten minutes, the face Walter wanted had begun to appear on the page, and he was able to move to more specific details, such as nostrils, eyebrows, and chin. Five minutes later, there it was, the face precisely as he had cemented it into his memory.

"And this person was involved?" Madame asked. "I've just drawn the face of a conspirator?"

"I'm not certain. Possibly."

Madame studied her handiwork. "This doesn't look like any of those bomb throwers I read about in the newspapers."

"I'm not certain of that either."

She patted his forearm again. "All right, Walter." She had reverted to her almost Russian accent. "But when you do know, will you come and tell me?"

"If I can, Madame."

Walter took his leave with the rolled portrait, bound by a length of ribbon, under his arm. He decided to make some basic inquiries before meeting up with Harry. If he got lucky, he might just be able to fit a name to the face before he had to tell Harry what he was doing. He didn't really expect anyone in Buffalo to recognize the face, however. This affair had begun in Chicago and was going to be unraveled there.

But Walter turned out to be wrong on two counts. Someone in Buffalo did recognize the face in the portrait and under circumstances he had not expected.

The question had been who to ask. If he went to the coppers or other operatives, he would tip that he was working on a new angle, which would be that much worse if someone *had* recognized the portrait. As he was convinced this was going to lead back to Chicago, he decided to try the Exchange Street Station, the one spot just about anyone coming from Chicago would have to pass through.

He would ask the gate agents, the redcaps, the vendors, the men in the ticket booths—there would be a return trip as well—and even the prostitutes. Thousands passed through the terminal every day, of course, most going to the Pan, but people who work in railway stations have little to do all day except watch the people come and go, and so most of them get to be extremely sophisticated observers.

He was at it for about twenty minutes before he struck gold. It was one of the gate agents, who looked the portrait over and initially handed it back. Then he reached back out. "Let me see that again." The agent cocked his head back and forth as if it would give him different lines of sight and then said, "Not Chicago, mister. New York."

"You certain?"

"Definitely. About two weeks ago. I remember because he came through the same time as that bunch of federal men."

"At the same time as or with?"

"I guess with. They was all like you, only I didn't see no badges. Made a lot of noise. They was pretty clear on why they was here though."

"For the president?"

The gate agent shook his head. "No. They said it was for Roosevelt."

Walter reached into his pocket and unfolded Natasha's drawings of Smith and Jones. "These guys there too?"

The agent nodded quickly and pointed to Smith. "Him definitely. He was doing most of the talking. Pretty sure about the other guy, but can't say I'm positive."

Walter nodded slowly and retrieved the three portraits. He was reasonably certain that the guy watching him and Harry, and the ones that took the shots at him were in the same group. To say nothing of the ones who eliminated Smith and Jones.

Before he rolled up Madame Romanova's drawing, he took another long look at the face on the paper. There was Tony Torrence, the salesman from the Stillman in Cleveland, staring back at him.

29

There was little choice now, whatever the risk. Walter had to let Harry in on what he'd found. Likely Wilkie as well. If one of them was rotten . . . hell, the way things were going, he wasn't going to live through this anyway.

Harry would be first, of course. When Walter returned to the Iroquois, Harry was sitting on a padded leather sofa in the lobby, glancing through a newspaper. He looked like the house detective.

"How was it?"

"How was what?"

"The whorehouse."

"Ha-ha. Funny man. How was the art school? Get to draw anything?"

Walter held up the rolled paper. "Not exactly. But I had something drawn for me." He unrolled the paper under Harry's nose. "Ever seen this guy before?"

"No. Should I have?"

"Not sure. I saw him in Cleveland. At the Stillman. Said he was a salesman. And a gate agent saw him arrive from New York with what he called 'federal men.' Smith and Jones were in the crowd too." Walter paused, but Harry was simply waiting to hear. "They came to see . . . TR."

"Shit." Harry ran his hand across his pomaded hair and tugged a few times on he ends of his mustache. "We gonna tell Wilkie?"

That was the question, wasn't it? "Dunno, Harry. What do you think?"

Harry sat pondering, while Walter tried to see if he could determine whether Wilkie knew already. But Harry, as always, didn't tip a thing.

After a couple of minutes, Harry blew out a big breath. "Might as well. If Wilkie's straight, we're gonna need his help, and if he isn't, there are likely a couple of slugs set aside already, reserved for us. Don't see how we're any worse off letting him in on it."

"I guess. Where do you think he fits in this?"

Harry shrugged. "No way to know. Hard to imagine he's rooting for TR to be president. He'll lose his job, and from everything I've seen, he likes it. His kid would be out too."

"Unless he's in on it. He did assign Foster and Ireland."

This time Harry didn't leap to defend the guys who were supposed to be guarding McKinley. "It's possible, no doubt. I just don't see it though. It would mean that TR or someone close to him would have had approached Wilkie, even though everybody knows Wilkie was McKinley's man. Maybe I'm wrong, but I don't see TR as being willing to take that big a risk. Also, if Wilkie had gotten a hint something was up, he'd be more likely to make sure nobody got near McKinley than to join up."

"What if TR promised him something?"

"Like what? He's already in the job he wants."

Walter nodded. "Yeah, that's how I see it too. I just wanted to make sure you and I were on the same road before we saw him."

"He's back here. Came back an hour ago. Asked me why we weren't on our way to Chicago. I told him you had to take an art lesson first."

"I'll bet."

"So should we go up?"

Walter laughed. "I'd rather go with you to the whorehouse."

"No kidding."

Wilkie had a suite one floor below where Mark Hanna had held the audience with them the week before. Still, it was opulent enough that as they walked in, Walter's doubts as to whether Wilkie would risk all this for vague promises of later riches were reinforced.

He was alone, so they set right to it, Walter doing most of the talking. Wilkie for the most part sat and listened, interrupting only a few times to ask a question. Detestable or not, Walter decided Wilkie was indeed no dunce, and, grudgingly, even began to respect him a bit. Maybe Hazen hadn't been the best man to run the outfit after all.

"All right," Wilkie said, after they were done, "you two better get on back to Chicago and see what more you can figure out."

"What about New York?" Harry asked, not hiding his resentment. "That's where this Torrence guy came from. Smith and Jones too."

"You two would be useless in New York," Wilkie snapped, matching Harry annoyance for annoyance. "You don't know anyone. What did you intend to do? Just show the picture around to the local police? Couple of operatives from Chicago that everyone and his brother know is working on the shooting. Wouldn't be ten minutes before the wind was up." He paused to see if Harry would protest further, but Harry kept his mouth shut. "Let me think about the New York angle. I'll find someone who can check around without making waves."

Neither Harry nor Walter spoke. Wilkie was right, but still . . .

"What's the matter, boys? Don't you trust me? I don't see that you have much choice at this stage. Consider this though. If I were in on this and you were getting too close, do you two think you're such brilliant operators that you wouldn't have a couple of holes in you each?" Wilkie paused to polish his spectacles. "Or is it that you're afraid of being cut out of the action? That the glory is going to go to someone else?"

Like you, thought Walter.

"First of all," Wilkie went on, reading Walter's mind, "if this was me, I'd want to be as far from it as I could be. To be honest, this is me now and I wish to God that it wasn't happening."

"Us too," grumbled Harry.

"But if you guys want credit when this is all wrapped up, I'll be happy to see that you get it. Like I said, you don't have to worry . . . no one, including me, is going to want his name on this."

"All right, Chief," Harry muttered without enthusiasm. "We'll go to Chicago."

"But, Chief," Walter added, putting a bit of extra emphasis on the second word, "you will keep us up to date, right?"

"Tell you what, George. I'll keep you up to date if you keep me up to date."

30

Saturday, September 14, 1901

President William McKinley was pronounced dead at 2:15 A.M. on Saturday, September 14, 1901. Harry and Walter heard about it an hour later, just outside of Cleveland, when a steward on the Limited awakened them with a telegram from Wilkie. The steward also told them that a special train carrying Mark Hanna had just passed them going in the opposite direction.

"Where is he?" Walter asked. He meant Theodore Roosevelt, now officially the designated President of the United States. He was, at the same time, being actively investigated for setting in motion the conspiracy that resulted in the death of his predecessor.

"No one knows," Harry replied. "He's somewhere in the Adirondacks. He left at six yesterday morning to go hunting in the woods. The lodge he's staying at is thirty-five miles from the nearest telegraph and ten from a telephone. Been raining like hell out there. They sent riders out to try to find him."

"He went hunting where no one can get in touch with him with McKinley still not even allowed out of bed yet? Doesn't that seem odd to you?"

"You mean like he was in mourning for a different reason than the rest of us? Because when he left Buffalo, it looked like McKinley was gonna be fine? Yeah. It's odd, all right."

"Harry, I didn't believe I'd ever say this, but it's starting to look like maybe . . ."

"Yeah. I know."

When they got to Chicago, the story filled in. TR had finally been tracked down on Mount Marcy, the highest peak in the Adirondacks. He had only been located after trackers had been sent into the wilderness, firing shotguns and yelling into megaphones. When TR and his hunting party finally heard them, they still had to trek back to the train station in the dead of night, through rain and mud. It wasn't until TR arrived at the special train to take him to Buffalo that he was informed that he was by then the nation's designated president. That would become official when he took the oath of office, later that day.

"That's a helluva way to find out you just got what you always wanted," Harry grunted.

"I'm certain after he heard, he didn't mind."

"Yeah." Harry cocked his head a bit. "Come on over. Lucinda can cook us up something. We're gonna have a long day trying find someone who knows your salesman pal. If he's even been here."

"I think he's been here. Just not sure he still is." Walter realized he wanted to see Lucinda. Why? Was he jealous? Did he want to compete with the bald cost accountant? For what? So he could avoid her again?

"Yeah," he said. "I'd like that."

Walter went home to wash up and change clothes—another concession—and got to Harry's by 10:30. He hadn't really slept, but he and Harry were used to functioning in that half-light consciousness that came from being barely awake.

From the minute he walked through the door, he tried to get a sense of her. Was she different now? Did she look happier? Did she shy away from him, even just a little? But Lucinda was just like Harry—she gave nothing away. She was just as friendly, just as efficient, just as funny, and just as welcoming as when he was last here for dinner.

Harry didn't talk about why they had come back, just that they'd be busy and wanted a good meal. Lucinda broiled a couple of steaks, and shredded some potatoes. Her coffee, as always, was dark, strong, and satisfying. When he'd finished, he felt as if he were operating on eight hours sleep.

Harry leaned back in his chair and patted his stomach. "How about a whiskey for good luck?" It was not yet noon.

Walter said that was just the sort of luck he wanted.

After Lucinda cleared the dishes and went to fetch the whiskey, Harry asked to once more see the guy they were going to spend the day hunting down. Walter spread out the portrait of Tony Torrence on the table. Harry tilted it right and left. "I know I've never seen this guy. I'd bet he's back in New York."

"I'm not sure, Harry. Whoever set this up . . ." He refused to mention Roosevelt's name. "Whoever set this up did it from here. Torrence was in Cleveland to keep an eye on me. I'm certain."

"Maybe. But TR's base . . ."

"If it is TR."

"If it is TR. His base is New York."

Lucinda emerged from the kitchen carrying a bottle of the good whiskey. Suddenly, she blanched, put down the bottle, and slapped Harry right across the face. It was something only about a dozen people, if that, could get away with. Harry's eyes went wide, but then he looked up at her meekly as if he were a little kid, even though he was a dozen years older.

"What was that for?" he bleated.

"The two of you," she growled. She turned to Walter. Her face was now bright red. "I should slap you too. Spying on me."

"What are you talking about?" Harry said. "We weren't spying on you."

"Then how did you get the picture of . . ." She stopped when she fully noticed the expression on their faces. She looked quickly from one to the other and back again, and she knew. "Who is he?"

"Tell us about him," Walter whispered. "Start with his name."

"Charley Taft. At least that's what he told me. Said he was from Moline. Went to University of Chicago because the president was a member of the clergy. He wanted to be a pastor. But then he changed his mind—didn't feel the call—but is still devout. He knows the Bible and always has intelligent things to say about the Sunday sermons. But he's bald. Why did you draw him with hair?"

"I only saw him with a hat on," Walter said softly.

"Is that all you talk about?" Harry asked, also gently, resisting the temptation to rub his cheek. "Does he ask about your . . . family . . . for instance?"

"Some, I suppose. Now that I think about it, yes, he always seems to maneuver the conversation around to my famous brother and his partner. The ones who broke the counterfeiting case. Seems awestruck about the exciting lives you lead."

"I'll bet. Does he ever ask what we're working on now?"

"No . . . well, yes. He never exactly asks, but the subject always manages to come up."

"One last thing," Walter whispered. "Whose idea was it for him not to meet us? His or yours?"

Suddenly, Lucinda let out a moan that sounded like a wounded animal, and slammed her palms on the table. Walter looked up and saw tears. He was stunned. Lucinda was every bit as tough as Harry. "God," she moaned. "I've been such a fool. I could be a character in one of those Mrs. Humphrey Ward stories. The blind, naïve spinster . . . or widow . . . who falls for whatever man talks sweetly to her. My God."

"That's not true, Lucinda . . ." Walter began.

"Shut up, Walter! Just shut up!" And with that, she ran from the room.

Walter started to get up, but Harry was out of his chair and blocking the way to the kitchen before he could move. "Leave her, Walter." He appeared to begin to say, "Haven't you done enough," but he bit it off. Instead, his shoulders dropped and he said, "I can't blame you. This is my fault."

It was Walter's turn to try be reassuring, but he couldn't. It was indeed, at least as far as he was concerned, Harry's fault. But hurting Lucinda was unforgivable and each of them had been part of it and each of them knew it.

"I'll get the whiskey," Harry muttered.

But before he could, Lucinda came back into the room. Her lips were pressed tightly together and her eyes were steady and unblinking, like a prizefighter's. "What can I do to help?" she asked.

31

Sunday, September 15, 1901

Harry wanted to go with Lucinda to church—he was her brother after all—but she and Walter persuaded him that nothing should alter her routine. Instead, Harry and Walter prevailed on a woman who lived across the street to let them sit in her parlor to watch the comings and goings. She was pleased to help two officers of the law and even more pleased to pocket the six bits Harry dropped into her hand. As agreed, she would wait in the kitchen in the back until the two men took their leave.

Lucinda arrived, as always, ten minutes before the 8:30 service was to begin. She went to the top step of the church and waited. Three minutes later, coming from the opposite direction, Tony Torrence/Charles Taft appeared. He wore a dark blue suit with a high starched collar, and was hatless, not at all like the checked-suited salesman with the topper who had yammered at Walter in Cleveland. He walked slowly, evenly, hands loosely at his sides, every bit the cost accountant that was his current identity.

Walter looked closely to see if Lucinda was doing anything at all to betray their conspiracy. But she was absolutely controlled—smiling, demure, and totally relaxed. She was, he realized yet again, quite remarkable. When Taft, as he decided to call him, extended his hand, she took it lightly and allowed him to escort her inside.

"I told you," Harry said softly, even no one could hear them.

"She was perfect," Walter agreed.

Harry could not help but glance over for just a second to see if Walter meant that in any way more than her skill at playacting. But Walter continued to stare across the street.

The service took about forty-five minutes, after which the parishioners walked out slowly, offering greetings to the pastor who had come to stand just outside the door. Lucinda and Taft emerged near the end, indicating they had sat near the front during the service. When you're going to play a role, Walter thought, might as well play it all the way.

After they had exchanged pleasantries with the pastor, the two moved down the steps and turned in the direction from which Taft had arrived. As they did every Sunday after services, they would be going to tea. Lucinda would then beg off any further activities, apologizing for some chores she could not do at any other time. In case he got suspicious and followed her, she would head to the mission where she had volunteered for the afternoon.

The tea shop was two blocks away and Walter and Harry made certain they were not seen. They had to wait more than thirty minutes, but then Lucinda and Charley Taft appeared. He took both of her hands in his and she leaned forward and placed a light kiss on his cheek. Walter could have sworn he saw the little rat almost blush. Then Lucinda, with a small wave, turned to leave. She never turned her head one degree in their direction. Taft waited a few moments until she had turned a corner, then put his hands in his pockets, and looking a lot more like Tony Torrence than Charley Taft, spun around and headed off.

Walter was too obvious to be the lead, so he let Harry, without his trademark skimmer, follow from across the street. Walter hung back, following Harry, out of eyeshot of Taft. He hoped their quarry would remain on foot. If he hopped into a carriage, Harry would have to get one alone, with Walter following along in another.

But Taft seemed to enjoy the sunny, brisk fall day, and bounced along quite happily. He was clearly a professional, though, for every once in a while, he paused to look in a shop window, positioning himself to able to see in the reflection if anyone was behind him. Once, he even snapped his fingers, turned around, and retraced his steps for half a block, before shrugging and turning back to go the way he had come.

But Harry was a professional too and wasn't spotted.

Taft walked for about forty-five minutes, mostly northwest, toward Oak Park. Taft's rooms were evidently in a quite decent neighborhood, streets lined with quiet, well-tended houses and no pushcart traffic to speak of. Just the sort of place a cost accountant for Olds Motor Works might live.

Taft played it cute the entire way. When he reached his destination, he circled the block once before returning to Berkshire Street. Even then, he tarried outside of one of the houses before moving three houses up. But then he walked up the front stairs and, after a last glance up and down the street, opened the door and went in.

Walter met Harry around the corner, where even someone sticking his head out of a front window could not see them.

"Now what?" Harry said. "How do we figure out which place is his before he figures out we're on to him? Can't ask the local coppers for help. And we can't exactly just march in the front door."

"You can. He's never seen you. Show the drawing to whoever is in charge of the place. Got to be someone in there. Then signal me and I'll go around back."

"And if he happens to come down while I'm flashing his picture around?"

"Then, Harry, you get to use your skills as a lawman."

Harry grabbed the picture and started up the street. He'd been in too many ambushes not to be reluctant to show himself, but there were only the two of them and they had no choice.

Walter checked the alley behind the house while Harry was on his way to the front door. The building was not that old and had one of the new fire scaffolds, which people referred to as the "iron z." It wouldn't be difficult for Walter reach the bottom of the drop ladder that was attached to the lowest platform and pull himself up.

He hustled back to the corner, standing as close to buildings as possible while still being able to see if Harry stuck his head out. Which Harry did a few minutes later. He held up two fingers, then waggled them backwards and to the right. After Walter nodded, Harry held up three fingers, meaning he would throw his shoulder against the front door in three minutes.

Walter went back to the alley. The window that corresponded to Harry's finger signal had a curtain across it on the inside, but was open about six inches. He hauled himself up on the fire scaffold and moved quietly up the iron stairs, He'd been counting to himself since Harry had held up the three fingers, and when he got to 180, he knelt at the window, listening, ready to throw the window open and barge in.

Walter heard a crash and he pulled up the window and ducked through. He was in the bedroom. The door was closed. He swung it open, taking care not to position himself in front, then ducked through, the Colt leveled.

"Don't move!"

Two heads turned. One was Charley Taft's, his revolver aimed at the front door, which Harry had thrown his weight against without the intention of breaking down.

The other head was Natasha Kolodkin's.

Taft lowered his revolver and placed it on the floor. He was too good not to be aware that he'd have been dead before he could have turned the gun in Walter's direction. Natasha had not moved. She stood like a tableau vivant, eyes wide and mouth agape.

Walter indicated with his head that Taft should open the front door. When he had, Harry stepped from the side, where he'd moved to avoid any bullets that might come through the oak door, and entered the room, his gun drawn as well. When he saw Natasha, he recognized her immediately, but restricted himself to a couple of blinks.

"All right," Walter said softly. "I think it's time we all had a little chat."

32

Walter took Natasha into the back room and closed the door. When he'd told Harry he wanted to question the two of them separately, Harry had agreed until Walter said just how he wanted to go about it. Still, it seemed clear that they should get her story first and someone had to stay with Taft. Given the choice of grilling Natasha Kolodkin in the back room or keeping a gun leveled at Charley Taft, Harry had agreed to the latter.

"All right," Walter said coldly when the door had closed. "Let's hear it."

"He said you were going to kill me," she said softly, looking down at the cheap rope rug on the floor. Then she raised her eyes to look into his. "Are you?"

"I don't think so," he replied, trying to see her only as a suspect in the murder of a president, but not quite succeeding. "But the hangman probably will."

Her lips pressed together, and Walter hated himself for his weakness in falling for it. "What do you mean, he said I was going to kill you?"

She blew out a huge sigh and sat on the edge of the bed. "He came to me at Saint Catherine's after you and I . . . after . . . and showed me a badge. It was just like yours . . ."

"Are you certain?"

"Yes, Walter, I'm certain." She'd gotten a little of her spirit back. "My powers of observation are undiminished. He said you were a rogue agent and part of the plot to kill the president."

"And you believed him?"

"Well, *someone* was. You said so yourself."

"Go on."

"He said that the shots through Mrs. Freundlich's window were a ruse to get me to trust you, so you could find out what I knew. And that afterward, you and your partner had killed Mr. Tomassini. He also told me that the two men who had approached Esther were in it with you, and that you and your partner had murdered them to keep them from talking. He showed me photographs of each of them, dead in a chair."

"Did he explain where he'd gotten these photographs?"

"He said he and other agents loyal to the president had tracked the men down, but by the time they found them, they were dead. These were official department photographs. They were even stamped, 'United States Secret Service Division. Official photographs.'"

"Were they now? And you believed him?" He had just her asked that same question. He told himself, almost audibly, that he couldn't let her get to him.

"I didn't want to, but . . ." She flashed him a brief smile. "Let me ask you something, Walter. If someone had told you that my . . . behavior . . . with you was just a ruse to get you trust me, and showed you some persuasive evidence to support it, would you have believed them?"

Walter started to say no, but they both knew the answer was yes. "What name did he give you?" he asked instead.

"Henry Tillman."

Probably as fake as the other two, but they all started with T. "Anything else?"

"He said you and your partner had killed Esther as well, and that I was the only loose end left. If I didn't leave with him right away, you were going kill me too. He had me write the note and leave it with Mrs. Freundlich to throw you off the scent."

"He said that? Off the scent?"

She nodded.

"So you left."

"Yes. He took me here. Said that the Secret Service Division had picked it and that you couldn't find out. I was to stay here until all of you had been rounded up and that it would be safe for me to leave." She thought for a moment. "How did you find out?"

"He was romancing Harry's sister. We followed him from church."

"Church?"

He nodded. "They made a stop at tea shop first, but, yeah, church." He sat in the chair against the wall. "You don't seem to think I'm going to kill you anymore. I could. Easily."

She smiled and shook her head. "Yes, you could. But I don't think you're going to."

"Do you think I believe you?"

She smiled. She really was beautiful. "Yes. I do. And you should. I'm telling you the truth."

Walter grunted. "You'd say that either way."

"Yes. But I am.

"All right. And did he tell you who was behind this plot that I was part of? Why I would want the president dead?"

She shook her head. "Just that you and the others had gone to a lot of trouble to make sure the killing was blamed on friends of . . . those who opposed the government. That's why it was so important to be rid of anyone who might know where it really got started. But it seemed clear that he thought some important people were involved."

"And did he say how he had come to be assigned to foil this dastardly plot?"

"He said he had been given the job by Vice President Roosevelt."

33

Walter told Natasha to stay where she was and went back to the front room. He was taking a risk, leaving her, but he didn't think she was foolish enough to duck through the window and try to scurry down the scaffold before he was on her. And besides, yeah, he believed her.

Harry and Torrence/Taft/Tillman were sitting in chairs opposite each other, about six feet apart, far enough that Tillman would be dead before he could leap across and close the distance. When Walter took him in this time, he realized that while their captive might have had a round face, he was anything but fat. He was, instead, thick, with a wide chest and shoulders, and arms that totally filled out his shirt. Walter couldn't help but respect the man's ability to pull off the charades he had.

"So what do we call you?" Walter asked.

"Whatever you like."

"Let's use Tillman. You being in the division and all. Don't suppose you'd like to show me the badge you flashed at her?"

Tillman grinned, but his eyes didn't move. They were taking in the room, sizing up any possibility of turning the tables. "She said I flashed a badge? She's mistaken."

"Harry's sister mistaken too? Care to quote me some biblical passages? Or maybe we should go back to Cleveland and share a meal at Emilio's?"

"I don't think you're gonna be seeing Cleveland any time soon, George. You either Swayne."

"Tough talk from someone on the wrong end of a Colt."

Tillman shrugged. "Ends can change."

"So you gonna tell us about what you're really doing?"

Tillman grinned. His teeth were uneven, which made it seem like a leer. "Protecting the president. Exactly what you boys thought you were doing."

"Which president?"

"We only got one, far as I can tell."

"Different than a couple of days ago though."

"No matter."

"Unless you had something to do with that."

"Ain't you guys read the papers? An anarchist killed McKinley. And every right-thinking American believes other anarchists were involved. The Goldman whore might have been let go, but other ones are being arrested. If you got a different theory, you're gonna need some proof."

"We've got you."

"Ha. I'm nobody. What are going to charge me with? Impersonating a salesman? Taking Lucinda Swayne to tea? By the way, Swayne, she's a terrific woman. Deserves better than you for a brother."

Harry was already halfway across the space before Walter stopped him. Harry sat back down, but the veins in his neck were throbbing so hard, Walter thought one of them might burst.

Tillman seemed unperturbed. "And now that you've got me, what do you intend to do with me? Can't very well just march me off to the coppers. I think you know I got friends in some pretty high places. About as high as you can get these days. And you ain't got shit."

He was right, of course. What could they do with him? In order to get anything done officially, they'd have to get word to Wilkie. And Wilkie wasn't totally above suspicion either.

"You're right, Tillman," Walter said, moving around behind him. "We can't just march you off." And with that, Walter brought down the butt end of his Colt against the side of Tillman's head, hard enough to put him out, but not hard enough to kill him.

"Let's truss him up," Walter said to Harry. "We can use the curtain sashes."

The curtains were in the back room. Would Natasha still be there?

She was. She watched as Walter and Harry used their knives to cut up the curtains and sashes into lengths of rope to bind Tillman's wrists and ankles to the chair and tie another strip around his waist.

Harry was already at the door. "Come on, Walter. We don't have much time. We've got to find a telegraph office and tell Wilkie." He smirked. "I'd rather have this mess in his lap than ours." He pointed at Natasha. "We do have to decide what to do with her."

But Walter put up his hand. "Not yet, Harry. There's something wrong."

Harry reached for the doorknob. "There's a lot wrong, Walter."

"No. Something else." He pointed at Natasha. "She's still alive."

Harry's hand dropped to his side. When Walter got like this, there was no moving him. Besides, that Natasha was still breathing after two days with Tillman had surprised him as well. "Okay, but can we make this fast?"

"Was everything you told us totally true?" Walter asked Natasha. "That Tillman made a point of telling you that Roosevelt sent him to protect McKinley from us? Did you leave anything out?"

Natasha shook her head.

"He was going to let her loose," Walter said, turning to Harry. "And tell her to warn her friends about us."

"Yes, that's right," Natasha said quickly. "He told me how Roosevelt was a fair man and even though he hated our politics didn't want anyone persecuted. But that you two and everyone you were working with were going to make sure we were blamed, dead or alive. He definitely implied dead was better."

"I don't get it, Walter," Harry muttered. "If the idea here is that TR arranged all of this to become president, what's the point of painting him as McKinley's savior? Trying to pin it on us I get."

Walter waved that off. "Trying to pin it on us wouldn't hold up for ten . . ."

Then he had it.

"Harry, we can't call Wilkie just yet." He gestured at Tillman. "And we're going to need a place to stash him for a couple of days. Can't be with the coppers or any of our people." He turned to Natasha. "How about it? Want to help solve the murder of a president you hated?"

34

Natasha was gone for about an hour before they heard a knock on the door. She had done exactly as she had promised. A heavy cart with a tarpaulin pulled by a large dray horse was waiting outside and two brutish huskies in overalls had driven it. They reminded Walter of Janos and Imre, the two Hungarians that Andrei Vytvytsky had been prepared to leave behind while he escaped with Walter and the phony greenbacks.

There had been some question of how to get the now conscious but still woozy Tillman down the stairs and into the back of the cart. Even with Walter and Harry present, no one trusted cutting him loose to make it appear to anyone passing on the street that he was just ill or maybe drunk. In the end, since none of the them would ever be coming back here, they decided to just carry him, chair and all, lay him on his side in the back, and throw the tarp over him.

The huskies did the carrying while Harry and Walter kept watch. Natasha said they'd be taking him to a warehouse where he could be kept safe and out of trouble until Walter had finished up whatever he had planned. He refused to tell anyone what that was, and wouldn't, he said, until he was certain.

When they got to the street, it seemed like they were in luck. Other than an old lady heading the other way, the road was deserted. Harry waved to Natasha's recruits to come on with Tillman. They each carried one side of the chair down the front steps with no more effort than if they were hefting a newspaper. In less than thirty seconds, Tillman and chair had been deposited in the back of the cart and covered with the tarp. He was in for a pretty bumpy ride, but neither Harry nor Walter had any desire make the journey more commodious.

They watched as horse and cart bumped over the cobblestones. Walter was about to turn and thank Natasha when suddenly, at the end of the street, a huge Winton automobile pulled into the intersection and stopped, blocking the cart. Two men leapt out on the near side and one on the far. Each was carrying a repeating rifle. Natasha's huskies reached inside their coats, but the hail of bullets arrived before they could draw their own guns. They slumped to the side, both surely dead.

Walter grabbed Natasha and ducked behind the stairs with Harry. Harry crouched and Walter stood higher, their Colts pointed down the street. Harry took aim and got one of the three gunmen in the leg as they were pulling Tillman and the chair off the cart. Once they had him down, the men from the Winton turned and began firing. Walter and Harry returned fire, Walter nailing another of them in the shoulder—the same man who had followed them in Buffalo. But there was no question of rushing in. They'd have been as dead as Natasha's huskies. Even wounded, the men dragged Tillman around to where the cart shielded them from fire, cut him loose, deposited him in the Winton, jumped in themselves, and drove off.

Walter made sure Harry and Natasha were okay and ran to the cart to make certain neither of the men was alive. There was no doubt. Then he ran back and gestured for them to move. "Come on. We've got to get out of here. Now."

"I can't leave them," Natasha snapped, as she started to move toward the cart.

Walter grabbed her wrist. She pulled, but there was no breaking free. She turned to glare at him. "I'm sorry, Natasha. There's no time. We've got to go."

"What's the rush, Walter?" Harry asked. "I don't think they're coming back when two of them already have holes in them."

"Not them," Walter replied, almost pushing them down the street. "Coppers."

"Coppers?"

"Unless I'm wrong, yeah. A lot of them. And they'll make sure none of us get out of here to talk to anyone."

They turned the corner, walking quickly at Walter's urging, but not running. They went one street up, then Walter made them turn again. When they were halfway down the street, they heard a clatter that got louder and louder. Walter directed the others down an alley. Just after they ducked behind piles of trash, two police wagons went by, each pulled by two strong horses and each with at least six coppers inside. As soon as the clatter began to recede, Walter pushed Harry and Natasha out and they resumed their flight, turning often and always listening for other wagons.

After about thirty minutes, they made it to a tavern just east of Garfield Park Conservatory. Walter motioned them inside and got them a table for three in the back room, where ladies were allowed, and slipped the proprietor a dollar to serve them beers, even though it was a Sunday.

"Okay, Walter," Harry demanded, after he'd taken a big swig of lager that had arrived in a coffee cup, "how did you know the coppers would be there? What's going on?"

"Yes, Walter," Natasha chimed in. "What is going on?"

Harry and Natasha glanced at one another, each of them equally surprised to now be allies, at least in this.

"I can't tell you yet. Not until I check some things out. But this is worse than any of us thought. Natasha, you need to go somewhere you'll be safe. Someplace low key. I'm certain you have friends . . ."

She nodded. "Yes, Walter. We wild-eyed revolutionaries can behave quite sanely when we're alone."

Harry grinned despite himself. "And me, Walter? Do I need to find someplace low key too?" Then he had a thought that turned him serious. "What about Lucinda?"

"Find her and see if she's got a friend she can stay with for a couple of days. But I think she'll be all right. She doesn't know anything that would threaten them. Besides, Harry, I don't think they're looking to make you mad."

"I'm already mad."

"Not as mad as you would be if someone bothered your sister."

"Sister?" asked Natasha, glancing between the two of them. "Who Tillman was romancing?"

"Is that how Walter put it?" Harry replied, shooting a glance at Walter. "Yeah, Lucinda is my sister. Walter knows her well."

"Thanks, Harry."

"You're welcome. And what will you be doing, if that's not too pushy a question?"

"Going to the library."

35

Monday, September 16, 1901

How to find something when you won't know what it is until you
see it? Walter had clues, maybe even too many, but there was
almost no way to know which of them were real and which not
relevant unless each was tracked through to conclusion, and he did
not have nearly enough time for that. To make matters even worse,
he might need to clarify or supplement information with one of the
players and none of them were now free of suspicion.

Walter got to the library on Michigan Avenue and Washington Street
just as it opened, at 9:30. He always loved coming here, this vast and
beautiful monument to knowledge, with its dome and hanging lamps
designed by the Tiffany Company. He always entered on Washington
Street, facing the wide grand staircase, and inscriptions of sixteenth-
century printers' marks and authors' quotations in praise of learning
lining the walls.

He went to the main desk and asked to see the newspapers. Two weeks' worth were always available for browsing, but the library kept stacks of the *Daily Tribune* going back six months, with older copies in the basement, which one could peruse on request. Six months would certainly be enough if what he sought was there. He set himself up at a desk in the reading room and fetched one month's worth at a time. He leafed through one edition after another, hoping some news item would give him the starting point he was hoping for. Even papers as recent as two weeks old had acquired that stiff, crinkly feeling that made them feel antique. By eleven o'clock, he had begun to give up hope.

After he'd gone through the entire six months of news, Walter placed his hand on top of the last stack and fought back frustration. He knew in his soul that he was right, but there seemed no way to even begin to prove it.

He stared at the stack. Maybe to get to the end, he'd have to change the beginning. He started through the stacks again, this time searching for a different entry point to the thicket. He'd gotten about halfway through when a familiar name jumped out in an article about another country, only a part of a country actually, which under normal circumstances, no one would care very much about. But the article seemed to indicate that circumstances might be anything but normal. One hundred million dollars' worth of anything.

He checked further to see if there was anything that might provide a clear link to the McKinley assassination. There was nothing direct. But Walter had the same feeling when he finished as he had when he knew an ambush lay around a bend in the trail. He spent another hour trying to fill in some blanks, some of the material supplied by a helpful young librarian who favored him with a becoming smile with every query. When he was done, he had his hypothesis. There were a bunch of gaps and a good deal of smoke, but he felt certain he knew what lay behind Leon Czolgosz's visit to the Pan and the murder of a president.

Walter had arranged to meet Harry at Claude's, a tavern they both knew on North State Street. Claude himself was an old trail hand who had been smart with his money and bought a run-down bar for peanuts, fixed it up, and acquired a clientele as loyal to him as he was to them. He had no use for coppers and only palled up with Walter and Harry because they had spent some time together riding in the Dakotas. Claude had rooms in the back, with an exit that provided cover to any of his less savory customers who might require it.

It was about a fifteen-minute walk from the library, one that required serious vigilance. Unlike Tillman, Walter cut a figure that couldn't be disguised by a change of clothes and phony bonhomie. There was no question now that he was marked, especially in Chicago. Still, the word wouldn't be out to beat coppers, just to select few on the force, of whom Hannigan was certainly one.

When Walter arrived at Claude's, he looked up and down the street, but didn't see anyone. That meant that Harry had taken his advice and not gone home, where there were certainly observers stationed at both ends of the block. Lucinda was probably safe as well.

Walter pushed in the front door and checked out Claude behind the bar. He was at least sixty, but could have been forty, tall and lean, with skin as browned and dry as if it had been made of old leather. He had light blue eyes, which always seemed to be peering from behind slits. Gunfighter's eyes. Claude never talked about his past and Walter had always wondered.

If Claude acknowledged him—a tiny nod was all you'd ever get—the coast was clear; if not, Walter would turn and leave. But the nod was there, and Claude's blue lights flicked just a bit toward the back room, so Walter knew Harry was waiting for him.

So was Lucinda.

Walter wanted to ask what she was doing there, but one look at Lucinda knocked the words right back in his throat. For just a second, he had the terrible thought that Harry had invited Natasha as well.

Lucinda read his mind. "I thought I might be useful . . . seeing how you were looking for clues at the library."

Walter nodded and mumbled an almost unintelligible thank you.

"Did you find any?" Harry asked. Walter was still looking at Lucinda. "Clues, Walter. Did you find any?"

"Yeah. I did." That came out a little better.

"Well?"

Walter turned toward the door to the front, and called out for Claude to bring him a beer. When it arrived, he asked Claude to close the door behind him. Claude would take no offense—riding trail together engendered doing what was asked without a lot of questions.

After he took a pull on the lager, Walter began. "Okay. Let me tell you a story . . ."

When he was done, Lucinda spoke first. "What's next?"

"We need to know where the money went. Who got paid and for what. Some of it will be impossible to trace, but some of it has got to be findable if we had someone who knew how to look. Too bad Tillman wasn't really a cost accountant."

"What's going to happen to him?" she asked.

"He's probably already out of the city. The others we saw too. And unless I've got this very wrong, there'll be a whole new crew in their place, but this time they won't be just keeping watch on us."

"What about Wilkie?" Harry asked.

"Yeah," Walter replied. "That is the question. If we can trust him . . ."

"And if we can't, we're not going to be around to complain about it."

Walter had to ask. "Harry, when we were in Buffalo . . ."

"And you thought I might have sold you out?"

Walter rocked back, as if were avoiding a punch. "How did you know?"

"Shit, Walter. I don't know how many times you need to hear it, but you get yourself in trouble when you think everyone in the room is a dumbass but you."

"I don't think that . . . at least not all the time."

Lucinda chuckled. "Most of the time though."

What could he say? "Maybe."

"Like you don't know that I know all about you and the anarchist woman, and not because anyone told me. I know you're drawn to her in a way you're not drawn to me."

"That's not . . . I'm not certain, Lucinda. And that's the truth. I'm not certain how I feel about anyone . . . that way." How did they end up talking about this?

"All right, Walter. At some point though, you should try to figure it out. Facing a life spent alone isn't pleasant."

Walter felt his mouth moving, but nothing was coming out. Harry, yet again, came to his rescue. "But what about Wilkie? Who, by the by, I have no deal, arrangement, or share secret messages with."

"Sorry, Harry. Truly."

"Forget it. In fact, you were right to be suspicious. I also got the feeling that someone had been feeding him information . . ." Harry grinned. "Although I didn't think it was you." Harry waited, but Walter had nothing to say. "So do we contact him or not?"

"He'd be able to find someone to trace the money," Lucinda said.

Walter turned to look at her and she smiled back at him. Why couldn't he? What was wrong with him?

"It's all right, Walter," she said, patting his hand. "At this point, we probably know each other too well."

"I'd never let anything happen to you," he said.

"I know."

"This is all very sweet," Harry interjected, "but can we get back to Wilkie? Are we going to tell him or not?"

"Not yet," Walter replied. "We need a little more information first. And I'm pretty sure I know where to get it."

"About the money?" Lucinda asked.

"Some of it."

After Walter told them what he had it mind, Harry was livid. "I thought you said you wouldn't let anything happen to my sister?"

"And we won't, Harry."

212

36

A little luck never hurts.

If Mike Hannigan had decided to go home, as he should have after a long day of shakedowns and sweating suspects, he would have been difficult to corner. But he didn't. Five minutes after his pert young secretary bounced out of City Hall and headed for the streetcar on Clark Street, there was Hannigan, bouncing right after her. And just behind him was Lucinda Swayne.

There was no way either Harry or Walter could have kept vigil near the building and not be spotted by somebody, but no one there knew Lucinda. She proved remarkably adept at observation, never getting close enough to draw Hannigan's attention, but always close enough to be able to go where he went, which in this case was the northbound streetcar that came along minutes after the one boarded by his secretary. Even luckier, it allowed Walter and Harry to engage a hansom after the streetcar had left and keep it in sight as it headed to Fullerton, where both Hannigan and Lucinda debarked. Lucinda made a point of letting Hannigan get off first and then let three people go before she stepped off herself. Hannigan glanced around and, seeing nothing untoward, walked west on Fullerton.

Harry and Walter waited a few minutes before paying the hansom driver and getting out. Lucinda was already almost out of eyeshot, walking west on Fullerton, past the new St. Vincent's College. Harry and Walter split up, each of them walking on a different side of the street, and tailed Harry's sister. When she saw where Hannigan was headed, she would retrace her steps until she found them, although she was likely unaware of how little distance she would have to cover.

When she reached Racine, Lucinda slowed down, so Walter and Harry did as well. When she turned south on North Wayne Avenue, they made their way to corner but did not follow. The street was only three blocks long, and unless Hannigan was taking a circuitous route, which was unlikely, they would be near their final destination.

After a few minutes, Lucinda was back, and when she turned the corner, gave a start when she ran into her brother. Walter crossed the street to join them.

"I've got it," she said, not hiding the triumph in her voice. "It's a row house, only two families. Doesn't have a lock on the outside door. He went up the stairs and into the door on the second floor. He took off his hat and threw it inside the second the door opened. Then he just about dived in, with a big grin on his face."

"How did . . ." Harry began.

Lucinda shrugged him off. She had a blush in her cheeks and was positively ebullient. "Because I'm good at this, dear brother. Maybe even better than you."

"Definitely," Walter piped up.

"Shut up, Walter. Anything else?"

"Yes. I'm certain that if you go there now, he won't be wearing his gun. Or anything else."

"Well, let's not waste time then," Walter chortled.

Lucinda suddenly barked out a laugh and threw her arms around him. At first, his skin prickled, but he realized he liked it. Like it a lot.

"Oh, this was great fun. Thank you for letting me help you."

"Sure," Walter replied, feeling a smile spread across his face.

37

Lucinda wanted to stay, but Harry and Walter said no. At first, she refused to leave, but they told her they would not move against Hannigan unless she did. Muttering how men have all the fun, she sulked her way toward the streetcar. They waited until she was out of eyeshot before deciding on a plan of attack. Hannigan was no genius, certainly, but nor was he going to be taken in by a second rate-ploy, like knocking on the door and saying it was a neighbor.

Hannigan's hideaway was an older building with no fire scaffold, which meant they couldn't use the same move as they had with Tillman. It also meant that no one could slip out the back. That left frontal assault. They'd have to break down the door before Hannigan could retrieve his pistol and greet them with lead. They hoped Lucinda was right, and Hannigan's pants were somewhere other than on him.

They made their way quietly up the stairs, Colts drawn, and examined the door to the flat. It was wood, four pane, but appeared to be pine and not oak. The door was fastened with a Yale Cylinder Lock, but one of the simpler designs, with only a flimsy strike plate over the cylinder.

They had done this before. Harry would ram his foot against the spot where the tongue of the lock met the doorjamb, just as Walter threw his shoulder against door itself. Unless the lock was stronger than it appeared, the door would pop open and allow them to rush in. If not, they would have to shoot out the lock and take their chances.

They looked to each and counted silently . . . one, two, three. Harry's foot crashed against the jamb at the precise moment Walter threw his left shoulder against the door. It popped open as if on a spring and they were through into the front room. They dashed through, past Hannigan's hat and shirt, which sat on a chair, and into the bedroom.

Mike Hannigan might be a bully and a grafter, but you don't get to be a police captain in a rough and tumble city like Chicago without being tough, and Hannigan was as tough as they come. He leapt from the bed, naked, holding a club—where he got it, they could only guess—and swung it right at Harry's head. But Harry was quick too and slipped the blow, taking it on his upper back.

It must have hurt like hell, but Harry only grunted and moved forward. Their guns were useless, since Hannigan was fully aware neither Harry nor Walter was going to shoot him. Hannigan's secretary was in the bed, her knees drawn up, sheet pulled around her, her eyes like pie plates.

Just as Hannigan drew back the club to launch another shot at Harry, Walter lunged across the bed, leading with his right. It caught Hannigan flush on the jaw and, tough or no, even a granite jaw would crack under Walter's right. Hannigan's knees buckled, but he didn't fall. He turned to face Walter, but before he could swing his club, Harry had planted one on the other side of his jaw and Hannigan went down.

He never lost consciousness, something of a miracle, but couldn't put up much resistance when Harry and Walter shoved him into the front room. He looked like a bear, with as much hair on his body as on his head. He was broad, thick, and fleshy without being fat, and even with bruises on both sides of his jaw, looked more like someone who would win a fight than someone who had lost one.

Walter told Hannigan's still unnamed paramour to stay in the bedroom and keep her mouth shut. She nodded so quickly, her breasts jiggled under the sheet. Harry would have pulled the sheet away, just for sport, but Walter let her be.

When he turned back, Hannigan was in a chair facing off with Harry.

"Tough break, Mike. Bet you thought you were going to get to us first."

"Fuck you, Swayne" Hannigan spat. "You mind if I get my pants on?"

"Of course not, Mike," Harry grinned. "I can see why you'd want to cover up."

"Fuck you," Hannigan repeated. But after Walter retrieved them from the bedroom, he pulled them on fast and then grabbed his shirt.

"You already said that," Harry replied, enjoying himself immensely. "But before you fuck us, how's about you answer a couple of questions?"

"I ain't saying shit to you two. Not that it's gonna matter, seeing you both'll be dead soon."

"Don't be so sure about that, Mike," Walter put in.

"I'm sure. Where you gonna hide? In a freak show?"

"Maybe we won't need to hide, Mike. Maybe it'll be you. Ever think of that?"

Hannigan sneered, but there was the tiniest pause before he did. He wanted to ask why he would have to hide, but refused to give them the satisfaction.

"Yeah, Mike. Think about it for a second." Harry was speaking with mock patience, as if he were addressing a five-year-old. "What if you picked the wrong side?"

"You mean against you guys? Don't make me laugh."

"No, Mike." It was Walter again. "Not us. I mean *really* the wrong side. I mean what if you picked against the president?"

Hannigan eyes flashed from one of them to the other. "McKinley's dead."

"He's not the president anymore."

"Roosevelt?" They now had Hannigan's full attention.

"Yeah, Mike. That's who's president now. What if you picked against Roosevelt? He wouldn't be too happy about that."

"But I didn't." Then he recovered. "Fuck you. What does Roosevelt have to do with this?"

"Everything. And if you picked the wrong side, TR can be one mean bastard."

Hannigan took a beat to consider. He was such an experienced grafter that he knew better than almost anyone that loyalty was ephemeral when it butted up against self-preservation. But he also knew not to switch loyalty too quickly.

"How do I know that you're not feeding me a load of cow shit?"

"You don't," Walter said. "But didn't you wonder when all of a sudden, out of nowhere, someone told you that it wasn't the anarchists after all, but instead a plot that we were involved in? When nobody, not even you, thought we were anything but a couple glory-hunting pains in the ass? And that for the good of the country, we had to be stopped—permanently— before anyone found out? That's how it happened, right?"

Hannigan nodded slowly. Processing alternatives was not his strong suit. "Yeah."

"But they were never really clear on what the plot was or who cooked it up or who would benefit? Except, of course, TR, who got to move into the White House?"

Hannigan didn't answer.

"And you did wonder, didn't you, but you were so happy to have the opportunity to bump us off that you didn't wonder for very long."

Hannigan again looked from Walter to Harry.

"The only problem is, what if we are actually the good guys and if the people who were putting you up to get rid of us were the ones who wanted McKinley dead? If that's the case, Mike, you're going to be in some very serious trouble and, if you're lucky, all you'll lose is your job and this little nest you've feathered for your . . ." Walter looked toward the locked door. "Your birdie."

"But no one put me up to it. The word came right from O'Neill."

"And who told him?"

"He never said."

"And I'm sure he paid you for going beyond the call of duty to undertake such a difficult job. Did he tell you where the money came from?"

Hannigan shook his head.

"But I'll bet it was enough to make you stop any wondering you might still have left."

Hannigan didn't need to reply.

"So, what's it going to be? You going to fill us in a little, or do we mark you down as one of the guys on the other side?"

This was the moment, Hannigan knew, when he had to make a choice. "What do you want know?" His voice had grown scratchy.

"Exactly what O'Neill told you. How he put it. That'll give some idea of how it was put to him."

"You think he's in on it?"

Walter shrugged. "Dunno. Maybe, maybe not. But if we can figure out who started the story . . . they're in on it."

Hannigan heaved a sigh. Chief O'Neill had come to him three days ago with a startling revelation. Despite all appearances to the contrary, O'Neill had just learned that Emma Goldman and other anarchist leaders had not been involved in the attempted assassination of President McKinley. Czolgosz had been a dupe, as they thought, but he had been deceived into shooting McKinley by Americans, not foreigners. The conspirators, whom O'Neill did not name but implied were highly placed within the government, had recruited some rogue Secret Service Division operatives to ensure the success of the plan. And, as amazing as it seemed, it was Swayne and George. There may have been others but Swayne and George were the only ones so far identified. Those at the highest levels, although O'Neill once more did not identify who they were, had decided the threat to the country, to a democratic America, was too great if the secret got out, so they had issued an order that Swayne and George were to be killed on sight, before their betrayal could become known.

"And you believed it?" Harry asked incredulously. "I know you're not the brightest guy in the world, Mike, but didn't that sound a little weird, even to you?"

"How much did O'Neill give you?" Walter asked.

"Five hundred." Hannigan had the decency to look at least a bit embarrassed. "Said it was from a grateful nation."

"I'll bet. And he gave you any idea who these big wheels were?"

"No. Just that they would be in a good spot with McKinley out of the way."

"Well, turns out O'Neill was right about that."

"What do you mean?" Harry asked.

"Never mind. What did you take him to mean, Mike?"

"Well, I wasn't sure. But I sort of thought he meant Roosevelt."

"And now?"

"Not so sure."

"Mike, I misjudged you," Harry grunted. "Always thought you were dumber than a jackass, but I see you're actually just as smart."

"What about you, Swayne? I ain't the one on the run."

"Not yet."

"So who did you figure clued O'Neill in to this plot?" Walter cut in. "If you believed him, you obviously didn't think he made it up himself."

"Didn't think about it much, but I figured it had to be someone federal. Maybe your boss."

"Maybe."

"And O'Neill?" Hannigan asked.

"No way to know."

"So what happens now?"

"Well, Mike, we can't hold you here," Harry replied, his face stern, "so I guess we've either got to let you go or kill you."

"You'd like that, wouldn't you, Swayne?"

"Oh yeah. Wouldn't bother me a bit."

"But we'd rather let you go," Walter added hastily. "I think you know where you want to end up when all this is sorted out. If you help us, Harry here won't have to kill you."

Hannigan thought it over. Even he realized he'd have to pick a side. There was simply no reliable way to play both ends, at least for the moment, because he had no idea who knew what.

"Okay, Swayne. I'll help you. What do you want me to do?"

"Mostly keep your ears open," Walter said. "Hear anyone say anything about Roosevelt, let us know. Or about . . ." Walter stopped. "Never mind. Just Roosevelt. Or anything else you think might help. Might want to stay away from O'Neill until we figure out where he fits on this."

"Sure. Easy enough."

"So how many men do you have in on this?" Harry asked.

"Only about two dozen. O'Neill said to keep it quiet. Everyone else just knows to look out for you."

"Where are your two dozen?"

"Most at the train stations. Some on each of your houses and some just looking around the city. Want me to pull them off?"

"No. We're not going home, and we're not fool enough to travel by train anyway. Got an Olds stashed at the north end of Lincoln Park. Besides, we don't want you to do anything out of the ordinary."

"Yeah, Mike, just act natural," Harry chimed in. "Maybe you can beat up a witness."

"Fuck you, Swayne."

"Kill it, Harry," Walter growled. "We're on the same team now. Right, Mike?"

"Yeah. Now." But the way he looked at Harry, one of them wouldn't be around for his pension.

"What about her?" Harry jerked his head in the direction of the closed door.

"She'll be fine. Does what she's told." Hannigan could not help but smile. "That's why I hired her."

Walter flashed a look at Harry, telling him to keep his mouth shut. "Anyone else on the list?"

Hannigan sneered. "You mean the anarchist whore you fucked?" He continued before Walter could slug him. "Yeah, she's there."

"Anyone looking for her?"

"Not really. She don't know enough and even if she did, she's not gonna be broadcasting it. Wouldn't sit well on her side of the fence or ours. Figured we might have found her with you guys. Then we could get rid of the whole crew at once."

"Tough break, Mike. Now you can't get rid of any of us. Play this right, and you might end up chief of police."

"Fuck you." Despite Hannigan's limited vocabulary, it was clear that he'd thought the same thing himself.

Walter told Hannigan to finish dressing, make sure his secretary really did keep her mouth shut and take off. They hated to let him go, but there really was no other choice but killing him.

Walter and Harry closed the apartment door as best they could and followed Hannigan out. He was halfway up the street and there was Lucinda, tailing him from across the street. Harry started to call out, but Walter grabbed his wrist. "Let her go, Harry. Mike will never be looking for a tail now and maybe she'll actually find out something."

"Are you sure she'll be all right?"

Walter chuckled. "Yeah. Actually, I am."

They waited until the newest member of their team was out of sight. Then Harry asked, "You don't really trust him, do you?"

"I trust him totally."

"What?"

"Harry, there are two kinds of trust. You can trust someone to be honorable or trust them to be predictable. Mike is the second in spades. He runs on two motives. Greed and fear. We just trumped the first with the second, but that's going to change back fast. Maybe it has already. We'll know when we hear from Lucinda." Walter suddenly felt ashamed. "Harry, I . . ."

"Forget it, Walter. I don't like it when anyone tries to run my life. I shouldn't have tried to run yours."

"You weren't. I wish I was smart enough to listen to you."

"Me too. But what were you going to ask Mike to listen for back there? When you changed your mind?"

"Panama."

◆

They had arranged to meet Lucinda where she was staying, in a guest bedroom at her pastor's house. Lucinda had asked that she be able to stay for a few days with no questions, and he had asked none. They arrived at nine o'clock to find her still breathless and blushed from thrill of the hunt. The pastor and his wife left them in the parlor and closed the door behind them.

"He didn't go home," she began, speaking so quickly that Harry and Walter had to strain to follow her. "I thought he might and then it would be over, but he didn't. He went back to City Hall. I followed him inside, but not up the stairs. It was busy so no one paid any attention to me. I went to the table where they keep the forms—you know, for permits and things—and made to fill to one out while I waited. I wasn't sure how long I could just stand there, but I didn't have to. I almost missed him because he came down from a different staircase. He was with someone that luckily I recognized from the papers."

She waited with a broad grin on her face.

"Okay, sis," Harry said finally. "Who was it?"

"Chief O'Neill."

Neither of them was surprised that Hannigan had sold them out—they just didn't expect it to happen so soon. But they were surprised at what came next.

"They got into a hansom. I took the next one. Here's where they went." She unfolded a piece of paper and handed it to Walter. He recognized the address.

"Okay, Harry," he said. "It's time to lay our cards on the table. I only hope we pick the right table."

38

Tuesday, September 17, 1901

Walter told Harry he had an errand to run before they caught the late train to New York from the La Salle Street Station, but refused to give any hint of what it was. Five minutes before the Metropolitan was due to depart, Harry was trying to decide whether he should get off or go on alone, when Walter suddenly appeared on the platform and hopped on the train. He refused to say where he had been, but told Harry it was nothing he should worry about. They hoped the train would be on time, because they only had twenty minutes to catch their connection to Washington.

Walter had been right about Hannigan. He had pulled his men out of the train stations to fan them out at the north end of Lincoln Park, waiting for Walter and Harry to appear in the Olds with its distinctive "curved dash." They would be waiting a long time.

The body of William McKinley had been transported from Buffalo by special train and had arrived in Washington the night before. The president's casket was taken to the White House, where it lay on twin pedestals and draped with a flag and flowers in the East Room. Later that morning, just before Harry and Walter were due to arrive at Union Station, after their connection in New York, McKinley would be transported to the Capitol, where a state funeral would be conducted in the Rotunda. From there, the martyred president would begin his final journey to Canton, for burial.

As William McKinley's finale was being played out, Leon Czolgosz, now refusing to speak to anyone, even his court-appointed lawyer, was indicted for first degree murder in Buffalo. The only question was how long he would be allowed to remain alive before two thousand volts were sent through his body. Word was the betting line said thirty days.

President Roosevelt, of course, was now also in the nation's capital, the reins of power now firmly in his powerful hands. As a sign of respect to his martyred predecessor, he was not staying in the White House, but rather at the home of a friend, where he was also conducting the business of state. The head of the Secret Service Division, John Elbert Wilkie, was, as his job dictated, at the new president's right hand.

Harry had a telegram sent ahead informing Wilkie of their arrival. The hansom ride from Union Station to the Treasury Building took only fifteen minutes. Harry and Walter didn't say much on the way. This was the moment, they both knew, when the risk to themselves and to the government would become most acute. They were about to officially report that the murder of an American president had been an inside job, possibly masterminded by his vice president, to a person who may well have been a part of the plot. If they were wrong, either in what had happened or who was involved, the odds were strong that they had seen their last sunrise.

The Treasury Building was a vast, sprawling affair, five stories high, set on five acres, just east of the White House. It was the first building specifically devoted to a department of government, begun during Andrew Jackson's presidency. There had been persistent rumors that Jackson, who detested many of those in Congress, had ordered the building placed where it would block his view of the Capitol. Harry and Walter entered from the north, up the wide set of stairs, leading to the great hall with its fireproof, brick vaulted ceilings. They were surprised to see Wilkie waiting for them.

Wilkie nodded to acknowledge their presence and then gestured for them to follow him as he walked off to the left. Down two narrow halls, he led them into a small office and, once they were inside, closed the door.

"All right," he said without any pleasantries. "Let's hear what you've got."

Wilkie sat behind the desk and Walter and Harry sat in chairs opposite. They spoke for about fifteen minutes. Wilkie interrupted once or twice with questions, but otherwise let them tell the tale exactly as it had played out. When they were done, he stood and paced about for a few seconds. Then he told them to wait, that he'd be back soon.

When he opened the door, however, instead of leaving, he let three men Walter and Harry had never seen before in. Each was holding a drawn pistol.

"I'm afraid I'm going to need your weapons," he said to Harry and Walter.

They glanced at one another, each silently querying the other as to the prospects of making a fight of it, but the three men had separated—they were quite clearly professionals—and they knew it would be suicide, at least for one of them, probably both.

The man in the middle gestured for them to pull back their coats and remove their weapons with thumb and forefinger only. One of the other two took the weapons out of their hands, never obstructing the line of fire from the others.

After he'd retreated, Wilkie said, "The knives too. And your Derringer, Swayne, if it wouldn't be too much trouble."

Harry frowned. Wilkie was better informed than he thought.

When all the weapons had been safely stowed, Wilkie gestured to the door. "We're going to my office. There are two more men outside to help escort you. I hope you won't think of causing a scene in the hallways. I think you'd agree that Washington has had enough drama in the past week."

As he was being marched through the halls, scores of unsuspecting federal workers scurrying about on all sides, Walter tried to decide if he had blundered. If Wilkie had tipped his hand earlier and he had missed it. It was a silly exercise, he knew, but still could not resist, even now, trying solve the problem.

But no, he decided in the end, there had been no choice. It wasn't as if he had trusted Wilkie and been stunned at his betrayal. Wilkie had always been a risk, but there was simply no way to have dealt with what he had uncovered without the aid of someone in power and Wilkie was the best choice. Even Mark Hanna, McKinley's closest ally, was a lesser choice after what Walter had learned. No, he had taken a risk with his eyes open, and it simply hadn't worked out.

It came down to one inescapable fact. Sometimes you can play a hand just right and still lose.

39

They were deposited in a large, airy office, lined with floor to ceiling wood paneling, and with an unobstructed third-floor view of the White House. It was about the most opulent holding cell for an execution either Walter or Harry could imagine. A lot more luxurious than Leon Czolgosz was going to get, although the end result would be the same.

Wilkie had left as soon as they were inside and locked the door behind him. Neither Walter nor Harry sat, but nor did they pace. And they waited in silence. They had been together too long for speeches or apologies. It was only a question now of how Wilkie planned to get rid of them without making too much noise.

Thirty minutes went by before they heard the click of the key in the lock. The door swung open and Wilkie walked through.

Directly behind him was President Theodore Roosevelt.

Once Roosevelt was inside, the door closed behind him. There would be no one else in the meeting.

The new president was five weeks short of his forty-third birthday, the youngest man ever to hold the office. Despite his age, he looked the part, nothing like the caricatures that tabloid cartoonists were so fond of drawing. He was tall, almost six feet, and powerfully built without looking the least bit fat; he moved smoothly, and was light on his feet; his eyes were not beady, and his mustache not enormous, but rather his features were regular, even handsome. But mostly, Theodore Roosevelt was a man who wore privilege like his perfectly cut suit. He exuded breeding and self-assurance, and appeared more comfortable holding the reins of power than even Mark Hanna, and certainly more than William McKinley. He seemed every inch a man for whom no mountain was too steep, no challenge too great.

"Good afternoon, gentlemen," he began, adding a curt nod. His voice, while slightly high-pitched, was in no way tinny, and every syllable was enunciated with precision, the product of study with the finest tutors and then Harvard University. His eyes never wavered. "I believe we have some matters to discuss." He gestured to the leather sofa and chairs grouped around a table at the far end of the room.

When they were seated, Roosevelt spoke first. "Let's set the scene, shall we. That way we can get to the salient issues without wasting time." Roosevelt paused, but it was not to let anyone speak. "After President McKinley was shot, the two of you were called on by Mr. Wilkie here to lead the investigation, in theory because the plot, which at the time, was assumed to have been hatched by anarchists, seemed to have originated in Chicago. As your investigations proceeded, there were any number of incidents, some of them surprisingly improbable, which led you to believe that this Czolgosz fellow had been duped not by his own people but, after you investigated a bit, by members of the government. Most probably me. But other than giving some impressions to Mr. Wilkie, you kept your theories to yourselves. Am I correct so far?"

Walter and Harry both nodded.

"But then you, Mr. George, in the wake of another series of improbable incidents—and a bit of research—concluded that the conspiracy was even deeper and more pernicious than you had first thought. At that point you decided to risk all and inform Mr. Wilkie of your suspicions, uncertain as to whether he—or I—was involved. After you were locked in here, I assume you decided you had made a grievous error and would never leave this room."

Roosevelt waited, this time for a response.

"Yes, Mr. President," Walter replied, surprised at the uncertainty in his voice, "that's the situation."

"And Mr. Swayne," Roosevelt asked. "Do you believe this outlandish tale?"

"I didn't at first, Mr. President."

"But you do now?"

"Yes. I do. There is no other way to explain what happened."

"Including my own involvement?"

"No, Mr. President," Walter said quickly. "In fact, I think the facts point very much against your involvement."

"Don't be so certain, Mr. George."

Walter drew back.

For the first time, Roosevelt smiled, that famed crocodilian grin. In person, however, it wasn't at all grotesque. Still, neither Walter nor Harry felt like smiling back.

"I didn't say I was involved, Mr. George, simply that the facts, as you will learn, do not bear against it. If it will make you feel any better, I was not nor would ever be in any way involved in any action that would threaten the integrity of our nation."

"Thank you, Mr. President. That definitely does make me feel better."

"All right then . . . to cases. Let's hear what you know about Panama. Start at the beginning. You won't bore me." Before Walter could speak, Roosevelt held up his hand and turned to Wilkie, who seemed to have disappeared into the paneling. "But first, let's get these men a drink. I suspect they could use one."

Wilkie went to a sideboard and opened a door to reveal a very impressive array of alcoholic beverages. No wonder he didn't want to give up the job. He poured some whiskey from a cut glass carafe into two matching glasses, brought them over and set them on the table. Harry downed his instantly, but Walter hesitated.

"Go ahead, Mr. George," Roosevelt said in way that made a request into a command. "I can assure you it's neither poisoned nor drugged. I'm a Roosevelt, not a Borgia."

Walter could not help but smile. He could see how people were so drawn to the man. Suddenly, he wanted very much to remain in the division and work for this president.

He threw down the whiskey, which was of a better quality than anything he'd had in . . . maybe ever . . . and set to tell his tale. The president had asked him to begin at the beginning, so that is what he did. In truth, he was more than a little pleased to show off, to try to impress the president with both his intelligence and his imagination.

Walter explained how, when looking for a motive that someone in power would have to do away with McKinley—even at that point, he told Roosevelt, he had become convinced that he was not involved—he had come across the two competing plans to build a canal across Central America to link the Atlantic Ocean to the Pacific. Everyone in government agreed that a canal that eliminated the long and arduous voyage around Cape Horn was vital to the nation's economic growth as well America's status as a world naval power. As Navy Secretary, Walter noted to Roosevelt, he had been perhaps the nation's foremost proponent of sea power.

Roosevelt favored him with a grin, and Walter's pride soared.

The issue, Walter went on, speaking faster now, was where to dig. In the 1870s, the French had made an aborted attempted to locate the canal across the Isthmus of Panama. They raised $400,000,000 from speculators who expected to make a fortune, since Ferdinand de Lesseps had been named to head the project. But Lesseps discovered that Central America was far less hospitable than Suez. Thousands died of disease, costs exploded, and eventually the project had to be abandoned. Less than half of the canal had been completed and a good deal of heavy equipment was left behind. And there things stood until 1894, when the French created a new company to either finish the canal or sell off the assets and the rights to continue digging where they had stopped. It was clear from the first that the French would never resume construction, that they had just formed the company to avoid losing rights to dig and to get the equipment, much of which had rusted, in shape to be sold. It then became only a matter of how much a half completed canal and a good deal of heavy equipment was worth. The current asking price was $105,000,000, with the United States assumed to be the most willing buyer.

"But I'm assuming the French would take a good deal less," Walter said.

"Quite a good deal less," Roosevelt agreed. "But in addition to negotiating cost with the French, there is also the question of the United States obtaining favorable terms with Colombia. Panama is a part of their country, after all, and the French concession is not currently transferrable."

"Yes, Mr. President, that is part of what led me to my conclusions."

"Very well," Roosevelt nodded. "Go on." He was leaning ever so slightly forward, which pleased Walter immensely.

"As you know, Mr. President, to decide which option would be best for the United States, President McKinley convened the Walker Commission. At the time, everyone assumed that the Panama option would be chosen because so much work had already been done and much of the necessary equipment was already at the site. No one really took the one-hundred-million number seriously, so it seemed merely a question of whittling down the price. But the commission surprised everyone by choosing Nicaragua instead, and President McKinley then announced he favored that route as well. As did you, Mr. President."

"But I don't favor the Nicaraguan option any longer, Mr. George. I've changed my mind. Panama seems by far the better choice. That's what I meant when I said the facts would not support the conclusion that I was not involved."

"Have you made those feelings public?"

"Not public, no. But there are a few who are aware of my intentions. I intend to instruct Secretary of State Hay, one of those few, to begin negotiations immediately with both the French and Colombians."

"And Secretary Hay has been on record as favoring the Panama route from the beginning. As was Mark Hanna."

"They were."

"Then assuming that those outside of government were unaware that you now favor Panama, anyone who had speculated with large sums of money on the Panama route would have believed that either man in the top two positions of government was about to cost them a good deal of money."

Roosevelt leaned forward further and Walter felt as if a physical force was pushing him backward. "And who might that be?" he asked.

"First, Mr. President, think of what is at stake. There would likely be bond sales to fund both the purchase and construction, and the need for whatever authority was set up to run the operation to procure a good deal more equipment. Land around the site would skyrocket in value, so if speculators could obtain the right to purchase it from the Colombian government, they would make millions on that alone. That, of course, would mean that money would need to be spread around in Bogota, long in advance of any official announcement. All that would be lost if President McKinley . . . or you . . . pulled the plug. And they couldn't afford to wait as the House of Representatives is already at work on a bill authorizing a canal in Nicaragua."

"All right," Roosevelt nodded, pulling himself back. "This is a very tidy theory. What you are saying is that if President McKinley is murdered and I am blamed for it, we're both out of the game, and Secretary Hay, who is unequivocally for Panama, becomes president. And the beauty of it is that Secretary Hay can be totally ignorant of the conspiracy to make him president . . . as I am certain he is."

Roosevelt waited and so Walter had to say it out loud. "Yes, Mr. President. That's how it seems to me."

"But you need more than theory, Mr. George," Roosevelt went on. "Do you have it?"

"I think I do. A prominent financier has made three trips to Colombia in the past two years, and has met repeatedly with President Marroquin and senior members of the government and the military. The visits were reported in the newspapers and a presidential reception was given in his honor. Just after he left the last time, which was five months ago, there seem to have been some significant purchases of land in Panama, by an American, described as 'committed to the country's development.' The article didn't give what this American paid for the land, but I believe he got a very good deal. I recognized the name, because he summoned Harry and me to his home last week and demanded progress reports on our investigation. Said he was speaking for Senator Hanna, but we didn't believe it. He also implied that you would not be displeased if President McKinley died."

"Do I get a name, Mr. George?"

"Anthony Hawkesworth."

40

Wednesday, September 18, 1901

Walter and Harry did not die in Wilkie's office after all. Instead, they were to return to Chicago and close out what had the potential to be the worst scandal in American history. For this, they had been assigned personally by the president, with the understanding that no one else was to be aware of their assignment. Wilkie would remain in Washington, trying to determine who, if anyone, in the government was involved.

"We're spending a lot of time on trains these days, Walter. At least this one is first class."

"Just be happy we're sitting up and not riding in boxes in the baggage car."

"I am. You think TR was serious? And if he was, will he back us up?"

"He was serious all right. He wants this closed out without it leaking to the newspapers or anyone else. If he wasn't, he wouldn't have said it in front of Wilkie. And yeah, I think he'll back us up. To a point, anyway."

"What's that supposed to mean?"

"He's not going to risk his position. He'll support us as long as we're invisible."

"Yeah. I suppose. Has it occurred to you that we probably saved Wilkie's job?" Harry snorted at the irony.

"I think it even occurred to him. He couldn't wait to tell TR that we were shining examples of the high quality of his operatives. He stopped just short of saying we were his sons."

"If he thought that much of us, what was the point of taking our guns and locking us in a room?"

Walter laughed. "He only adopted us after TR did. If TR thought the story was horseshit, we'd still be in there."

"You told TR you didn't think Hanna was in on it. Sounds to me like you just didn't want to say what you really thought."

"No way to know. He definitely prefers Panama and probably has some money in it, but he and McKinley were pretty close."

"But Hawkesworth said he was speaking for Hanna. You think he was lying?"

"Dunno, Harry. He certainly wasn't telling the truth about why he was interested."

Harry grunted. "Think we're gonna be able to bag him on our own?"

"We'd better. There won't be any reinforcements. At least Wilkie made sure the Chicago coppers won't be after us."

"What about O'Neill?" Harry felt no need to mention Hannigan.

"The wild card," Walter agreed. "If he's in on it, we're probably screwed. Even if he's not . . ."

"He's gonna know something was up with Hawkesworth. Of course, he might realize that the best thing is a sudden lapse of memory. He's not stupid. Wilkie was right. No one is going to want to be within ten miles of this when it's all over."

"Including us."

"Gonna be kind of hard to outrun it."

"Well, Harry, we're just gonna have to be inconspicuous."

"Yeah, Walter. We're so good at that."

When they arrived at La Salle Street, Walter had a strange request.

"Are you sure?" Harry was stunned.

"Yeah, Harry. We can't do much until tomorrow anyway."

"Okay, Walter. I guess."

41

Walter felt like a circus clown and was certain he looked like one as well. He probably should have just showed up in his usual clothes, grimy and worn as they were. Instead, the dress pants and shirt had been worn so seldom, they felt stiff and scratchy against his skin.

He stood before the door for a full minute before working up the courage to knock. In the few seconds before it swung open, he had to force himself not to turn and run. What could have possessed him to do something so incredibly stupid?

"Why Walter George, don't you look handsome."

Lucinda stood before him, looking like an angel. She was dressed in a dark green frock that made her skin look luminescent.

"It's Pforzmann. Walter George Pforzmann."

Lucinda giggled. It sounded like bells. "Can I still call you Walter?"

Walter started to answer, but nothing came out.

"But please come in, no matter what your name is. I cannot risk leaving such a fine looking man at my door lest you're spotted by others."

"You're making fun of me."

Lucinda blushed. It shot up from her neck. "No, Walter. I would never do that. I mean it. You look wonderful. And you should never, ever grow back that beard."

Walter mumbled a thank you, although without the beard, he felt as if he stepped out from behind cover while men were shooting at him. Lucinda stepped aside and, finally, Walter walked into the flat.

Lucinda was still staying in the spare rooms of the rectory until Harry could be certain she was not in danger. Part of the bargain they had made with Wilkie after TR had left the room was that, when it was all over, Lucinda would be protected. Wilkie had readily agreed and he would have no reason not to keep his word. They had no real choice anyway.

The table was set for two, with two long candles burning in the center. Walter looked at the tablecloth, linen napkins, and china place settings and wondered if he could really live this way for the rest of his life.

Why not?

Lucinda gestured to a decanter. "Reverend Jennison ordinarily only keeps wine in here, but I persuaded him to let me borrow some of his whiskey. He only agreed because I told him you were good at keeping secrets."

"Thank you, Lucinda. I'd love one."

"You certainly look like you could use it. Am I that scary?"

"No. Well, sort of. Not your fault. I . . ."

He was still mumbling when she handed him a hefty glassful, which he downed in one gulp. Quite decent rye.

"Lucinda," he began, "I don't know how you feel about me, but . . ."

"Walter George . . . Pforzmann, that is simply not true. You know precisely how I feel about you. I have been in love with you since we met. Are your really saying you didn't know?"

"I suspected, but . . . can I have another drink, please."

241

She shook her head. "Not a chance. Not until we've talked a bit."

Despite himself, Walter almost laughed. "Are you making rules for me already?"

"Someone has to."

"All right. I suppose I prefer it be you. I'd like to tell you why I came tonight."

Walter didn't go on. "All right, Walter. Why?"

"I wanted you to know who I am."

"I know who you are, Walter. At least in the ways that matter. But please. Go ahead."

Walter took a deep breath and spit it out. "You know I was raised in an orphanage. Run by the sisters. In New York. I was left there just after I was born, with a slip of paper that had my name but nothing else. I'm not even certain what my birthday is, only that I'm thirty-five years old.

"The sisters were all right, I suppose. Or could have been. They tried to show that they cared for us, but they seemed more interested in making sure we were going to be good Catholics. One of them, she was young, took a liking to me because I learned to read early and liked books. I owe her a lot, I suppose, but I can't remember her name."

"You can't remember someone who helped you?"

Walter scowled. "I don't remember any of them."

"All right, Walter. Go on."

"I was always big for my age, so I sort of protected other boys when the older ones got after them. But no one could protect them from Father Timothy." He stopped and breathed heavily. "Lucinda, please, just one more drink."

She nodded and refilled his glass. Walter downed it.

"They all knew, of course. All the sisters, all the boys. He'd pick his favorites and call them into his rooms at night. We all knew the next morning what had happened. But no one could do anything. The boys were afraid of being thrown out on the streets, and the sisters knew the bishop would always take a priest's side over a nun's. Each of us waited, knowing eventually it would be our turn."

Walter looked down and spoke to the table. "Then it happened to me. One night, when I was twelve, he came into the room where we slept and told me to come with him. I knew what it meant, but I went. When I was walking, my legs felt stiff, as if my knees wouldn't bend. When we got to his room, he closed the door, and then stood with his back to it. Then . . . right away . . . he started to . . . was going to . . ." Walter looked up. Lucinda drew back when she saw the fury on his face. "There was a bottle of wine on the table he was going to make me drink. But I grabbed it and swung it him. I was so tall that I was able to hit him square across the cheek. He didn't fall, but his eyes went wide, like he couldn't believe what was happening. But suddenly, I felt free. The bottle hadn't broken, so I hit him again. Wine had poured out and was all over my clothes. When I hit him a third time, the bottle broke and glass was everywhere. Finally, he went down . . . like he was shot . . . and didn't move.

"I stared at him for a couple of seconds . . . lying there. It was like I'd just woken up after a dream. I ran back to where we slept and grabbed my hat . . . funny, I didn't want to leave without my hat. Dumb hat too. I didn't take anything else, but there was really nothing else to take. I came out again and ran down the hall. The sisters had come out and were standing there, watching me. They didn't know what to say . . . they could hardly discipline me, since they knew what Father Timothy was up to. The doors were locked, so I screamed for someone to open them up. I must have looked like a wild animal. The Mother Superior's hands were shaking . . . she was terrified. But she managed to unlock a side door and I ran out. To this day, I don't know if that priest lived or died."

Lucinda had not moved, but managed to say, "Oh Walter, I'm so sorry."

He nodded, but then went on. It was all going to come out now. Finally. "So then, I was just another orphan living on the streets. But I was big, strong, and mean. I got into a lot of fights at first, but the other kids learned not to tussle with me. One time, one of them tried to rob me while I sleeping. We were in an alley. I woke up and grabbed him around the throat, but he stabbed me with a penknife. For some reason, it didn't hurt. I held him with one hand and hit him with the other until he stopped moving. I was bleeding, but the wound wasn't very deep, so I was able to keep pressure on it until morning. A local pharmacist . . . a nice old man . . . stitched me up. After that, word got around that you couldn't kill Walter, even with a knife.

"I missed reading, so one day, I wandered into a library. Started pulling things from the shelves to read. A lot of history and science. Started coming back every day. One of the librarians noticed me and gave me other things to read. Wonderful books. A lot of philosophy, men I had never even heard of before. After a few months, she offered to let me stay with her, but I couldn't. I didn't trust anybody that much and by then I couldn't bear to sleep inside. I always wanted a way to escape from wherever I was.

"Then, when I was fifteen . . . but I looked a lot older . . . I joined the army. Volunteered to go west. Where I met Harry. He was a sergeant. Helped me learn to ride a horse. Never had to in the streets. We were sent to the Dakotas. I had a flair for soldiering and soon I was a sergeant myself, always a stripe short of Harry though.

"You know the rest. I was there for eight years. I loved and hated the army. I loved the . . . well, I guess you could call it family. I hated what we were doing though. Every year, we squeezed more and more land out of the Indians. We made treaties and broke them, killed people who wanted nothing more than to stay on the land they'd been promised. Harry felt the same way. It was little more than theft and murder. Harry heard about this division of the Treasury Department that officially went after counterfeiters, but also helped investigate bank robberies and a bunch of other crimes. It seemed like a better way to live, so we joined up."

Walter slumped in his chair. He was more exhausted than if he'd been awake for two days on the plains. He was soaked in sweat and felt dizzy. He grasped the sides of the table because he thought he might fall off the chair.

After a few seconds, Lucinda put her hand on his arm. "You've never told anyone before, have you? Not even Harry."

Walter managed to shake his head.

"Thank you then, Walter, for your trust." She leaned over and kissed him lightly on the forehead.

He looked up. "I've never been able to . . . trust . . . anyone . . . to . . ."

She smiled and he was filled with . . . what?

Peace.

"You can trust me."

"I know."

They spent another two hours together. Walter managed to eat a slice of perfectly cooked roast, and had only one more shot of rye. They talked some, but not too much. Mostly they were just *with* each other, two souls adrift, each of whom had found an island in the other. When Walter left, she kissed him lightly on the cheek and they knew, if he came through this, they would be together.

42

Thursday, September 19, 1901

M y God, what have you done to yourself. You look like a kid."
Then he realized. "You did it for L . . . my sister."
"Yes, Harry. Brilliant deduction."

"Are you . . ."

"Yes, Harry. Now how's about we figure out how we're going to get Hawkesworth and stay alive."

Wilkie hadn't sent them in totally blind. Hawkesworth, according to Wilkie's sources, was living in his country estate in Lake Forest, although his reasons for leaving his more palatial Prairie Avenue home were unclear. Wilkie had also obtained an architect's plan of the house and grounds, although how he had done it was equally unclear.

The question, of course, was how many men Hawkesworth would have guarding the house. Even if he believed no one was on to him, he would certainly have some. However many it was, they would need to be neutralized before Walter and Harry could get to Hawkesworth himself. Wilkie had reported that Hawkesworth's wife was visiting relatives in Minnesota, a convenient state of affairs that made it more likely he was on his guard.

Or that it was a trap.

In any case, they would have to go in at night, between two and four in the morning. That was the window when those left on guard would be most bored and drowsy. Any earlier and they might still be alert; any later, they'd have perked up, waiting for their shift to be over.

In order to make this work, Walter and Harry would need to devise a plan that anticipated what Hawkesworth's guards would do. There were two scenarios—if it was a trap or if it wasn't. In the first case, they'd probably leave a lure, either a guard easily visible backed up by one that wasn't, or an open ground floor window or a door that was ajar. If it were not, security would be less visible but no less present.

Looking at the map of the grounds, the obvious avenue of approach was the back of the house, to come in off the lakefront. Although there was a two-hundred-foot expanse of lawn, there were hedges and a good deal of tree cover to shield them from view. The front had a high wall, but once inside, there was an equal distance of lawn to be negotiated with only a few large trees for cover.

Which was why they decided to climb the wall and approach from the front. The back might seem safer, but it was actually much more dangerous. Everything that might provide cover for them could also provide cover to their enemies.

The front provided them distinct advantages. It was mid-month, so only a sliver of moon would be visible, and they chose a day where the sky would have broken clouds. Harry and Walter, big as they were, knew how to move and use shadows to approach undetected at night across open terrain. And they were also expert at detecting movement and so what little light there was would allow them to pick up on anyone trying to gain position on them.

They decided to scale the wall at the north corner, where a large hemlock would the block view from the house of anyone coming over the wall. From there, the ground was open until, about halfway to the house, a sprawling elm tree provided cover. But if they kept the elm between them and the building, no one would see them from the front porch.

They were satisfied with the plan, but what did that mean? No saying was more idiotic than "going according to plan." Nothing ever did.

Lake Forest was not exactly a place where you could ride a horse, or even worse, take a motor car, arrive after midnight outside an estate, and not expect to draw attention. So Harry and Walter rented a carriage that they tied up in the woods at the south end of town just after ten o'clock. From there, they walked, keeping out of sight until they arrived in another woods—Lake Forest was not called that for nothing—about a quarter mile from Anthony Hawkesworth's country getaway. And there they waited.

There is a feeling before going into battle, a unique combination of quiet and frenzy, where the senses seem to report everything as if through a thick filter of water. Nothing from the outside really penetrates as the seconds tick away. The first time this happens, the person waiting is convinced he will be incapable of movement when the moment arrives, frozen in place, and when motion is possible, it will be so stiff and ponderous that it will result in quick and certain death.

For Walter and Harry, who had been through this more times than they could count, waiting for an assault to begin was simply time that needed to pass. They both knew how unlikely they were to succeed at what they'd been asked to do, and wondered what TR and Wilkie would do to get Hawkesworth if they failed. Or if they would do anything at all.

Finally, it was time. Within minutes, Harry and Walter were at the foot of the seven-foot-high brick wall. Walter cupped his hands and boosted Harry up so that Harry could get a good handhold on the top. As thick as Harry was, that was how strong. He pulled himself up almost effortlessly, swung over the top, and dropped to the other side. Seconds later, the rope that had been wrapped around his waist came sailing over. Walter pulled on it to make certain Harry was bracing it on the other side, then used it to get high enough to pull himself up. When he dropped over, not fifteen seconds had passed and there had not been a sound.

The hemlock was as sprawling as the plans showed and the elm halfway up the lawn even wider. They checked for movement along the wall and then toward the house. There was none, nor did it seem as if a guard had been stationed outside the front door.

They made it to the elm easily, always keeping the huge tree between them and the house, and then checked around, more carefully this time. If it were a trap, this was the time someone would be slipping in behind them, but no birds flew, and no rabbits or squirrels scurried. Nothing but crickets.

The front of the house appeared normal for a rich man's estate in the middle of the night. One light was on in the middle of the porch—it appeared to be electric—and it cast shadows of the furniture on the veranda. Although dim, there was sufficient light to make movement across the lawn visible to anyone stationed at a window. There was a soft glow from inside the house, indicating lights in the hallways, and what seemed to be a light on back porch.

Their object was a small, ground-level window on their side of the house that led into the storage area of the basement. From the plans, it seemed that Harry would fit easily and it was just large enough for Walter to squeeze through. If they could get there and then inside undetected, they would have made it through the first great peril of their attack.

The only way to minimize the chance of being seen was to hug the ground and creep up slowly, never rising up enough to cast a telltale shadow on the grass. The last time they'd done that was in the Dakotas, sneaking up on a renegade Sioux encampment. Renegades—that's what the officers called them, at least.

But however honed, the skill was invaluable. He and Harry went wide to avoid the light at the front door, and moved slowly, never enough to flick an image to someone's peripheral vision, but sufficient to get them to the house in the least possible time. The window was just where it was supposed to be and they were relieved to find that it was locked. An unlocked window was almost a guarantee that there would be a welcoming committee inside. It was still possible, of course, but less so.

The next problem was getting the four-pane window open without making noise, and for that Walter had brought a wheeled glass cutter. Ordinarily, the blade would squeak when it scored the surface of the glass, but applying a thin film of oil would muffle the sound. The window was hinged and would open in. Walter traced a hole large enough for his hand to go through a pane near where the lock would be on the inside, then placed a suction cup over the hole.

Then came the tricky part. He had to pop the piece through but hold on to the rod on the suction cup so that the glass wouldn't make any noise. He'd done this once or twice in Chicago, getting into houses that were dangerous to enter in the normal way. But it demanded a deft touch, and even a couple of practice sessions didn't make it a sure thing.

Walter nodded to Harry, who used a balled up glove to pop at the glass lightly, just under where the suction cup was attached. The cut piece broke free at the instant Walter pulled at it, and it made just the barest click on the way out. They waited for a few seconds, but there was no sound other than the crickets.

Walter reached through the hole, pulled the handle on the lock, and opened the window. He and Harry slithered through and dropped to the floor of the storeroom. Walter closed and latched the window behind them. Someone looking at the window from either inside or out would have to be very close to see the hole in the glass in the dark.

The room was quiet enough to hear breathing and it was only theirs. Almost no room is totally dark, although this one was close. They waited until their eyes got used to what minimal light there was, then made their way across the floor, feeling with their hands and feet for boxes, stored furniture, and whatever else lay in their path to the door opposite the window.

Harry got to the door first and tried the handle. If it was locked, they would have to risk some noise jimmying the bolt, but it wasn't, at least not from the inside. The full-time servants—two maids and a cook—slept in rooms at the top, so there was no one who should be down here at this hour. Even a guard was unlikely. Still, Harry pulled the handle down very slowly, and then opened the door the tiniest crack to peek through. The basement hall was dimly lit and there was no one about. For the first time, Harry and Walter began to feel just a bit of confidence that TR and Wilkie had played straight with them.

But now was when the battle would be joined. They had to hope that any of Hawkesworth's minions who had drawn the night shift were stationed separately. They would need to be taken out one at a time, in a way that did not draw the attention of the others. Once that was done, whoever was asleep in the house would need to be dealt with. The servants could be locked in, but the more dangerous employees would demand special attention.

Harry and Walter made their way down the hall, two big men making no more noise than falling snow. There was a dim light about ten yards ahead, thrown from a staircase that led to the first floor. They climbed the stairs, but paused at the top before peeking out. Whenever they were out on an operation like this, Harry carried a tiny mirror attached at a forty-five degree angle to a small rod. At floor level, Harry poked the mirror out, turning it one way and then the next. He turned back to Walter and nodded that all was clear.

When they made their way down the first floor, suddenly they heard the murmur of voices, coming from somewhere toward the rear of the house. At a turn, they saw a small shaft of light through a set of what appeared to be double swinging doors. Men, talking in the kitchen. They listened for a few minutes. Two voices only.

No matter how well trained a man is, tedium can do him in. Night after night of sitting up, doing nothing but watching and waiting, listening for sounds when there were no sounds, looking for movement when there was no movement. These two were apparently the night watch, taking a break to grab some food or make themselves coffee. What's a few minutes off during an interminable night? While there might be a third man awake, sitting alone elsewhere in the house, it was unlikely. He wouldn't be able to resist the temptation. It also meant that Wilkie and Roosevelt had played straight with them after all.

So how to take them?

They would come out either one at a time or, more likely, both at once. In either case, they must be silenced before they could raise an alarm. There was a recess under the stairs just outside the doors big enough for Harry to crouch in the shadows. Walter would wait at the bend of the hall.

The murmuring continued for another few minutes, and then, "Okay, back to work," could be heard distinctly. The doors swung open and two men appeared. One had his arm in a sling, a souvenir of the bullet from Harry's Colt. The two men were walking abreast. When they reached a point about halfway between Harry and Walter, Harry sprung out from the recess and Walter leapt from around the corner.

They were on the two guards before they could make a sound and a second later each of them was sinking to the ground, a knife wound between his ribs, and a hand over his mouth until he could no longer call out.

That had been their deal with Wilkie. No one who had been involved in the plot to murder President McKinley and blame it on the vice president could remain alive. The story could not be allowed to get out.

Harry and Walter dragged the two bodies to the recess that had hidden Harry and deposited them. Blood had soaked the dead men's clothes, but the wounds had been too clean and they had been moved too fast for blood to have made it to the floor. By day, of course, the bodies would be plainly visible, but no one walking through the house before dawn would notice them.

There would be others in the house to be dealt with—or at least one. The house had eight bedrooms on the second floor, and he would be in one of them. Both Harry and Walter were willing to wager that it was the one across the hall from Hawkesworth. And it would not be locked, just in case the master needed him, as Hawkesworth's would not be locked in case he was needed.

But first, the other bedrooms would need to be checked, just in case. They made their way up the stairs, then listened carefully at the door of each one, before peeking inside. Nothing. They returned to the bedroom across the hall from Hawkesworth's. With a glance, they turned the handle silently and slipped inside. There he was.

Perhaps it was training or just a tiny draft from the door moving, but Tillman, or whatever his real name was, was awake as soon as it opened. Had Walter and Harry been an instant slower, they would have been nailed by the pistol that Tillman withdrew from under the covers. But they weren't slower and Tillman saw he had no chance. He lowered his weapon. Walter, without crossing in front of Harry, quickly moved to retrieve it. Then he turned on the room light and quietly closed the door so nothing could be heard across the hall.

"Well, well," Tillman said with a sneer. "Snookered by a four-flusher and two ghosts."

"You're gonna be the ghost," Harry growled.

Walter touched Harry on the forearm. "What do you mean? Who's the four-flusher?"

"I gotta draw you a picture? It's Wilkie."

"Because he let word out that we were dead."

"Yeah, George. Why do you think there's only two other men here? You took care of them, I take it."

Walter didn't answer.

"Dead, huh? Well that figures. So I'm next?" Tillman shrugged. He was still under the covers but his hands were visible. "Nobody lives forever."

"Care to answer a couple of questions?" Walter asked.

"Gonna make a difference?"

Walter couldn't help but smile a little. Hard not to respect a man so tough. And Tillman was that. He was tough and he was good. Hawkesworth had chosen well.

"Not to you."

"Didn't think so. Whaddaya wanna know?"

"What's your real name?"

"Can't help you there."

"Where did you learn . . . everything?"

"Not here."

"How many of you know the real story of what happened?"

"After me? Nobody." Tillman gestured with his head to across the hall. "Except him, of course. Gonna kill him too or is he too rich?"

Walter didn't answer. Instead, he asked. "Why did you do it?"

Tillman barked out a single laugh. "Why do you think? For the money. Couldn't interest you two in a similar arrangement, could I? He's got buckets full."

Neither Walter nor Harry budged.

"Didn't think so. Two patriots. What a joke." Tillman got serious. "All right. Get it over with."

So they did.

43

That left Hawkesworth.

After Harry wedged in the servants' doors, they stood outside the master bedroom, waiting for a moment, and then Walter turned the handle and they walked in. The room was wired for electricity and there was a switch on the wall. When Harry turned it, the immense room, at least eight hundred square feet, glowed to life as the bulbs in the chandelier built up a charge.

Hawkesworth was alone in a massive four-poster bed, covered with a canopy. Walter thought with some amusement how the bed resembled pictures he'd seen of the sleeping arrangements of kings. Hawkesworth blinked awake and when he saw Walter and Harry standing inside the door, he reached instinctively for the pull rope next to the bed, but Harry pulled his Colt and shook his head.

"Don't bother. They're all dead."

Hawkesworth looked one way and then the other as he tried to wake up. He seemed small, gray, and insignificant in the giant four-poster, but within a few seconds, he had regained his bearing and, even in night-clothes, once again appeared to be every bit the killer he was.

"I assume you gentlemen wish to chat before you kill me. Would you mind if I got out of bed and put on a bathrobe?"

"Not at all, Mr. Hawkesworth," Harry replied. "But if you're thinking of grabbing a gun you have stashed somewhere, I'd advise against it."

"Never crossed my mind." Hawkesworth was smiling. He did not appear even the least bit afraid.

"And we're not here to kill you," Walter added. "Although we were instructed to get a signed statement."

Hawkesworth kept his eyes on Walter as he pushed his way out of bed—he had to reach with his feet to get the floor—and padded across the room to grab the robe tossed across the back of an overstuffed armchair. He was light on his feet with no sign of the shambling walk common to men in their sixties. There were a pair of leather slippers on the floor, which he slid his feet into. He then settled into the chair, leaning full against the back to maintain excellent posture.

"A statement? Which will be used how? I would rather die here than on the gallows, and death is certainly preferable to prison." He directed his conversation to Walter.

"I don't know how it will be used, Mr. Hawkesworth," Walter replied, "but I have a hard time believing anyone is going to want to see you stand trial. Our orders are simply to get a signed statement."

"And your orders about the others?"

"We followed them," Harry said.

"So then, gentlemen, you are asking me to take your word that you have no orders to similarly dispatch me once you have what you want."

"I think that's a risk you should take, Mr. Hawkesworth," Walter offered. "If I were in your position, I'd think it more likely that we would . . . dispatch you . . . if you refused to cooperate." That, in fact, had been their instructions.

Hawkesworth considered his options. "If I come through this, Mr. George, I wonder if you'd consider working for me."

Walter shook his head.

"I thought not. Pity." Then he smiled. "I am the man responsible for you being here, you know. You too, Mr. Swayne, although only by association."

"I'm not certain I feel indebted to you for that, Mr. Hawkesworth." Harry was seething at being made out to be some sort of servant, but knew enough not to interrupt.

"Be that as it may. I checked very carefully to find someone clever enough and persevering enough to follow an obscure trail . . . manufactured though it may have been. Manufactured with great care, I might add. Every detail had to be precisely as it would have been if it were true, with just enough crumbs to keep you moving in the right direction. And you did not disappoint me, Mr. George . . . until now, of course. It turns out I underestimated you. I don't make mistakes of that sort very often."

"Nobody's perfect," grunted Harry.

"Don't be sensitive, Mr. Swayne. You were quite good too. It's just that Mr. George has that rare combination of high intelligence and unwillingness to give up on a question until he has the answer."

"You mean he's pig-headed," Harry replied. "You had him right there."

Hawkesworth leaned forward and let his hands drop between his legs. "All right, gentlemen, here it is. This is my offer. I will give each of you one million dollars in whatever manner you wish if you agree to end this right here and now. And I don't mean by pulling those triggers."

One million dollars. Neither Harry nor Walter was willing to speak without looking at the other.

"Sorry, Mr. Hawkesworth," Walter said. "We wouldn't know how to spend it."

"You'd learn. It's quite easy." Hawkesworth sighed. "But very well. The signed statement it shall be." He gestured to a desk against the far wall. "May I?"

"Would you be willing to answers some questions first?"

"For you, Mr. George? Of course. What would you like to know?

There was a lot Walter wanted to know, more about the man than the crime. "Why did you do it? You've already got more than enough money."

Hawkesworth chuckled. "That's how I got it, Mr. George. And how I keep it. My father was born wealthy. He inherited a thriving lumber business from my grandfather. He wasn't a bad businessman, exactly, but he was weak. Thought the business would run itself. It did not. By the time I was old enough to begin working, it had lost well over half its value. That is the price of weakness, Mr. George. Loss of what one holds dear. That fool McKinley was going undertake a disastrous misadventure in Nicaragua. It would have failed miserably. I would have lost a good deal of money, it is true, but the nation would have suffered grievously as well. There would have been no Central American route from the Atlantic to the Pacific, and the wasted expenditures could easily have set off another stock market panic. We have barely recovered from '93 and '96."

"So you consider yourself a patriot?"

Hawkesworth looked surprised. "Oh yes. Most definitely. The nation needed to be saved from McKinley and I did it."

"For which you will be richly rewarded."

"Of course. Doesn't one always deserve to be compensated for services rendered? Don't you two expect to be rewarded for undertaking this thankless task?"

"We hadn't thought about that."

Hawkesworth smiled. "You should have."

Walter decided to move on to specifics. "Was Mark Hanna involved in any of this? He favored the Panama route as well."

"Oh no. Senator Hanna would never have betrayed his friend and I would never have suggested such a thing to him. But there was also no need to enlist his support. Nor Secretary Hay's. As you know, both of them favored Panama. With McKinley no longer involved, and Vice President Roosevelt also removed, the option would have sailed through. There was the matter of dealing with the Colombians, if they become difficult, but there are always . . . alternatives."

"Such as?"

"There are many in Panama who wish to be independent of Colombia. Who knows but that those freedom fighters might find a reservoir of support they did not know they had?"

"You would foment a revolution."

"Not at all. Sometimes things just happen on their own."

"Yes. You often seem to be the beneficiary of coincidence, Mr. Hawkesworth, although not with our new president."

"Mr. Roosevelt? Don't be naïve, Mr. George. Mr. Roosevelt wanted very much to be president and wishes to remain so. All this talk about trust busting . . . there is only so much he will do to alienate the people who make the real decisions in this country. Those like me will be just fine. And Panama . . . he will be a welcome ally now that he has seen the situation properly. No, no. Things may not have worked out quite according to plan, but they did work out."

"And you?"

Hawkesworth turned his hands palms up. "That remains to be seen."

"You don't seem concerned."

"When you reach my age, Mr. George, you accept events as they come."

Walter blew out a breath. Harry looked a bit deflated as well. Hawkesworth had succeeded in robbing them of any sense of triumph, any feeling that they might have done something important by bringing a presidential assassin to justice. If they had indeed brought him to justice. That was far from clear.

"Just one more question, Mr. Hawkesworth. Where did you find your . . . employees?"

"Ah yes. You had a great deal of difficulty there, if I am not mistaken. Identifying them, I mean. I had equal difficulty in locating men who were . . . suitable. Who would not be squeamish about the task at hand. Europe seemed a better alternative than the United States. I thought men who had already left the country . . . and were possessed of the appropriate skills . . . were a better alternative than those still here. I found these men . . . soldiers of fortune, I believe they are called . . . in St. Petersburg, working as the personal guard of a grand duke. I persuaded them to take on this assignment. Thanks to you, they won't get to enjoy the source of that persuasion."

"Too bad," Harry said.

"I am still willing to offer you gentlemen similar persuasion."

"No deal." This time Harry didn't wait for Walter to agree.

"Very well, then. If you have no further questions, I should get to my statement. I would like to finish in time for breakfast . . . unless, of course, you gentlemen were not telling the truth about your assignment."

"We were," Walter replied. "Go ahead and write."

With a nod and a smile, Anthony Hawkesworth rose from the chair, walked to the desk, and calmly set to writing the tale of how he set in motion a plot to murder the President of the United States.

44

awkesworth wrote for almost ninety minutes. Harry and Walter moved to the far side of room and sat in two ornate armchairs, waiting for him to be finished. If the document said what it was supposed to say, they were to place a telephone call to Washington, where Wilkie would be waiting. If it did not, they were to . . . dispatch . . . Hawkesworth.

But Anthony Hawkesworth was no fool and did precisely what he had been asked to do. When he was done, Walter inspected the five-page letter and, seeing it contained all the information Wilkie or Roosevelt could ask for, allowed Hawkesworth to place it in a sealed envelope on which he wrote his name. Harry placed that envelope inside a larger envelope, and wrote, "To be opened only by Director, Secret Service Division." Wilkie apparently did not want his name on it.

Hawkesworth had installed a telephone line in his downstairs parlor. Harry left Walter to sit with the banker and went to place the call. It took almost five minutes for all the trunk lines to be connected, but when Harry heard Wilkie's voice—or some garbled version of Wilkie's voice—on the other end, he simply said, "It's done. We have what you wanted."

He heard Wilkie thank him and say that he and Walter would soon be relieved by a special detail sent to take Hawkesworth into custody. And then, after a "Well done," the call was ended.

When Harry returned to Hawkesworth's bedroom, he expected to see him and Walter chatting—they seemed to get along so well—but each man was sitting on a different side of the room, not even looking at one another.

"Do you mind I get dressed?" Hawkesworth directed the question to Harry.

"No. Go right ahead."

"Can I do so in private? I give you my word that I will neither pick up a weapon nor kill myself."

"Don't think we can . . ." Harry began.

"Let him!" Walter snapped, and got up and moved for the door.

Harry wasn't certain how to take that, but after looking from one man to the other, nodded. "We'll be just outside the door."

When they were in the hall with the door closed behind them, Harry asked Walter why he'd agreed to break a cardinal rule. You never left a suspect alone to do anything.

"I'd be just as happy if he killed himself," Walter replied, "and if he tries shoot anybody, I'll be happy to kill him."

"I don't get it. What went on in there?"

"He tried to give me money again."

"Come on, Walter. I know I don't have your 'high intelligence' but I'm not a moron. Had to be more than that."

"He told me I might as well hook up with him, because nothing was going to happen to him anyway, and that I should be working for someone who appreciated my talents."

"Don't see how you could turn that down. You've been looking for someone to appreciate your talents for years."

"Fuck you, Harry."

"I take it my talents weren't part of the deal."

"I was supposed to cut you out. That was the only thing that made the offer appealing."

"Well, at least you've got your sense of humor back. Do you believe him? That nothing will happen to him?"

"Who knows? This affair is so smelly, nothing is impossible."

"So what he's saying is that the statement he had to sign is going in someone's drawer and as long as he does what he's told, it'll stay there."

"That's how I read it. He's just got so much money, he's better in somebody's pocket than in prison or dead."

"Maybe we should kill him then. I'm getting a taste for this." Harry said it with a grin, but Walter saw that he meant it.

"You going to pull the trigger?"

"I thought you would. You're the one with the burr."

"One thing to do it because the president thinks it needs to be done, another to do it on our own."

Neither man spoke. Was it possible that they had done all this for nothing? Tracked down the perpetrator of one of the worst crimes in American history, only to see him slither out of responsibility?

"Wait a minute, Walter."

"What?"

"How does Hawkesworth know what's gonna happen? He's just guessing . . . or hoping. Unless you think Wilkie or Roosevelt knew about this before and spoke to him."

"No. I don't think that. But why the statement then?"

"Shit, Walter. It's a confession. Don't we always try to get one of those?"

Walter considered it. "Maybe."

"More than maybe. It's at least as possible as his story. That it's gonna sit in a drawer . . . that I believe. No one wants to see this in the newspapers. Blaming the anarchists suits everyone a lot more . . . except the anarchists. But I don't see that because Wilkie, or even TR wants a record of the truth it means that Hawkesworth's gonna get off. I figure they're gonna take him off to some quiet place and shoot him. Then they can just say he disappeared. Harder to get away with that if he was killed here."

Walter thought about it. Harry was right. It made just as much sense as Hawkesworth's version. Maybe more.

"Okay, Harry. But let's just hand the son of a bitch off and get out of here."

"You bet."

Walter knocked on the bedroom door just a second before it opened. Hawkesworth stood in the doorway, dressed in the same suit as he would have worn had he been heading for his office in the bank. And he looked as unconcerned. Could he really be so calm? But Walter realized that demeanor was as much of a source of power to people like Anthony Hawkesworth as brains or ruthlessness. A demeanor that inspired fear and uncertainty in his enemies. If there were a firing squad on his front lawn, Hawkesworth would still appear exactly as he did.

"We'll wait downstairs," Walter said evenly. "Your escort should be here any time now."

"Very well."

Once in the lobby, Hawkesworth settled into a chair and sat waiting. He made no further attempt to engage Walter or Harry in conversation, and Harry and Walter did not speak to one another. Fifteen minutes later, through a window, they saw a carriage pull up outside the front door.

Four men got out, none of them known to Harry or Walter. All of them had the obvious bearing of lawmen. Harry opened the door to let them in.

"You Swayne?" one of the men asked, apparently the man in charge. Harry nodded.

The man withdrew an envelope from his coat and handed it to Harry. Inside was a telegram. It read, "These men come on my order. Please deliver your prisoner to them. This will conclude the arrangements made in my office. Please accept the thanks of a grateful nation. I will see you when you return to Washington." It was signed only with a "W."

"Okay," Harry said. "He's yours." One of the others immediately escorted Hawkesworth out the door.

"There are servants locked in upstairs and some cleanup," Harry said. "Mind if we get out of here?"

The man shook his head. "Nope. We'll take it from here."

As Walter and Harry got their hats, and started for the door, suddenly they were facing three drawn pistols.

"Sorry fellas," said the first man, and all three opened fire.

EPILOGUE

Tuesday, October 15, 1901

T here's someone to see you."

Lucinda looked up. She enjoyed Charlotte. The other volunteers at the orphanage shied away from her because of the burns . . . she was difficult to look at, it was true . . . but Lucinda saw the bright and talented little girl underneath. In the two weeks that she had been working here, Mrs. Morgan saw that Lucinda Swayne would work with children that most of the others would not. Because of her brother, no doubt. She wore scars on the inside every bit as livid as Charlotte's on the outside.

"Who?" Lucinda hadn't told anyone that she was working here. And she didn't intend to. Nor did she intend to tell anyone where she lived, now that she had given up the rooms she had shared with Harry. She intended to live out her life in isolation and swore that she would never again attend a funeral. Let others bury the dead. She had done more than her share.

"A woman," Mrs. Morgan replied, not moving in from the doorway. "She says she was a friend of Mr. Swayne and Mr. George."

"Tell her to go away."

"I did, dear. I told her you didn't wish to see anyone, but she insisted. She said she has something for you . . . from Mr. George."

Lucinda turned quickly and looked up. Mrs. Morgan, as always, was perplexed, unable to decide if she was looking at an old-looking young woman, or a young-looking old one. Lucinda patted Charlotte on the hand, feeling the parchment-like flesh against her fingers, and then stood.

"Where is she?"

"In the front parlor," Mrs. Morgan replied. And then, feeling embarrassed but unable to determine why, she added, "She's a nun."

"Why didn't you say that before?" Lucinda asked. It was probably someone from St. Catherine's, although how she had gotten something from . . . Walter . . . was a mystery.

But when Lucinda reached the front parlor, the woman sitting primly in the straight back chair was not from St. Catherine's, nor was it anyone she had ever seen before.

"You have something for me?"

The sister looked up at Mrs. Morgan, who had trailed Lucinda into the parlor. She looked slightly out of place in her habit. She was too . . . not beautiful, exactly, nor glamorous, but there were hints of both.

Lucinda turned to Mrs. Morgan and asked her to leave them. Mrs. Morgan stifled a frown, but did as she was asked.

"My name is Natasha Kolodkin," the woman said softly.

"I know who you are," Lucinda answered. Except to the children, she had taken to speaking in a monotone.

Natasha waited, but Lucinda did not say anything else.

"Walter asked me to give you something . . . if anything happened."

Lucinda still did not speak. Natasha reached into the folds of her habit and withdrew an envelope. When Lucinda didn't move, Natasha reached across and offered it to her. Lucinda stared at the envelope, a look of fear crossing her face.

"I lost my sister too. The same people murdered her as your brother and Walter."

Lucinda suddenly looked up, fury passing across her face. Natasha jumped. But the look passed and Lucinda reached out her hand for the envelope. "Let me see it," she said, a sharpness returning to her voice.

Natasha handed the envelope over. Lucinda's name was written on the front, and the seal was unbroken on the back. It was thick, not just a note, and Lucinda turned it over in her hands a few times, but did not open it. Instead, she looked to Natasha.

"This, I take it, is a disguise and does not reflect a sudden conversion."

"There are many who want me dead. I wouldn't survive a week dressed normally. But no one looks closely at a nun."

"Were you and Walter lovers?"

"No. He was in love with you. It could not have been more clear . . . to everyone but him."

Lucinda nodded. She was not going to cry. In fact, she had made a vow never to cry again. "Thank you for lying. But I know you were."

"Only once. And it was at my initiation, not his. And I was not lying about him being in love with you."

Lucinda held up the envelope. "When did he give you this?"

"The night before he left for Washington."

"Do you know what's in it?"

Natasha nodded. "He said that if anything happened, he wanted you to decide what to do with it."

Lucinda opened the seal and withdrew the contents. There were four pages, written on front and back. On the top of the first page was written, "A true and honest account of the murder of William McKinley."

Lucinda read through Walter's testament, trying to feel him where he had handled the paper. She knew most of what he had written, but not the end. Walter hadn't told her. Anthony Hawkesworth. The banker.

He had been in the news. Hawkesworth had suddenly announced his retirement, sale of his holdings, and his intention to move to Europe. But then he and his wife seemed to have disappeared. They were not on the passenger lists of any of the trans-Atlantic steamships, and no one had a record of them traveling to the east coast. Columnists on the society pages had concluded that the Hawkesworths, for reasons unknown, had decided to become rich recluses. But now, Lucinda was fairly certain they had disappeared permanently.

Leon Czolgosz would soon join them. The poor, naïve dupe had been brought to trial less than two weeks after McKinley's death. The trial had lasted eight hours and it took less than an hour after that to find him guilty.

That would close the door. All of the conspirators were certainly dead as well. And Walter and Harry . . . they were in Arlington, buried in private ceremonies. No one in authority had shown up, although Wilkie had sent her a note that said they had died heroes in the service of a grateful nation, but their duties had been so vital, so secret, that only those closest to them could know the truth.

Lucinda hadn't believed a word. Harry and Walter were far too accomplished to be killed by people they had been tracking. One of them perhaps, trying to save the other. But not both. Unless they had been betrayed.

When Lucinda had completed the reading, she refolded the papers and put them back in the envelope. She didn't hate Natasha any more. They had too much loss in common. Too much betrayal.

"What will you do?" she asked.

Natasha shrugged. She looked more and more incongruous in the nun's habit. "Keep trying," I suppose. "Working for justice. Fighting the people who get rich off the misery of others. Just as you're doing here, in your own way."

"Is that what I'm doing?" Lucinda thought it over. "Perhaps. Do you think it will make a difference?"

"To some people it will."

"Is that enough? For you, I mean?"

Natasha smiled. "It will have to be, won't it?"

Lucinda nodded. "Yes. I suppose it will."

Natasha got up and Lucinda followed. Lucinda put out her hand. Natasha took it, held it for a moment, and then turned and walked out the door.

AUTHOR'S NOTE

This is a work a fiction. Although, as will be noted below, most of the people, events, and locations are historically accurate, there is no evidence of that any of the skullduggery depicted in the previous pages comports to the actual history. In other words, no reader should come away from this story thinking that I endorse my version of events as true. Of course, if I've done my job, readers will not find any definitive cause to consider these events false.

Walter George, Harry Swayne, Lucinda Swayne, Natasha Kolodkin, and Anthony Hawkesworth are fictional, as are the minor players involved in the conspiracy. Mike Hannigan is also fictional because there is no evidence the real chief of detectives in Chicago on whom Hannigan is based indulged in any of the shenanigans attributed to him.

All the other major characters—Wilkie, Czolgosz, Abe Isaak, Emma Goldman, Big Jim Parker, Foster and Ireland, Mark Hanna, and, of course, William McKinley and Theodore Roosevelt—are real and drawn

273

as closely as possible to real life. Wilkie did remain on as head of the Secret Service Division, which after President McKinley's death, was given official responsibility for protecting the president. Leon Czolgosz, who had indeed said that he "done his duty," was executed in the electric chair at Auburn State Prison on October 29, 1901.

The shooting of President McKinley, his convalescence at Millburn House, and subsequent death are as they happened, drawn from newspaper accounts of the time. The same is true of the roundup, questioning, and eventual freeing of the anarchists in the wake of shooting. Foster and Ireland never could adequately explain their failure to notice the oversized bandage on Czolgosz's hand, although at one point they said their line of sight was blocked.

The debate over whether to place the Atlantic-Pacific canal in Panama or Nicaragua took place precisely as is depicted. McKinley favored Nicaragua, as did Roosevelt initially, while Secretary of State Hay, third in line for the presidency, always favored the Panama option. The United States ultimately paid $40,000,000 for the French rights and equipment, and did foment a revolution in Panama that resulted in its independence from Colombia.

ABOUT THE AUTHOR

I was born in Brooklyn, and had one of those idyllic city childhoods—stickball in the streets, riding my 400 pound Schwinn two-wheeler down the steep hill abutting the cemetery, and playing cops and robbers with the children of real cops and robbers.

I grew up with an extremely critical eye for history. I eventually got a PhD from the New School for Social Research, writing my dissertation on the underemphasized role of slave economics at the Constitutional Convention of 1787. Thirty years later, I turned it into a book, *Dark Bargain*.

At various times, I've been a lecturer, senior member of a Wall Street trading firm, taxi driver, actor, quiz show contestant, and policy analyst at the Hudson Institute. My first real writing gig was a $10 op-ed column for a local weekly in the Berkshires, which was invaluable as both an outlet and learning experience.

By now, I've written well over a dozen books of both fiction and non-fiction, six of which were co-authored with my wife Nancy. In either discipline, I think it's the writer's responsibility to engage the reader, to tell a compelling story, not the reader's responsibility to try to figure out what's going on. I've had articles, reviews, and opinion pieces that have appeared in, among other publications, the *Boston Globe*, *Los Angeles Times*, *Wall Street Journal*, *Chicago Tribune*, *Miami Herald*, *Hartford Courant*, *New Republic*, and *Berkshire Eagle*. I've also written for a number of magazines that have gone bust, although I deny any cause and effect.